SEASON OF LOVE

Once again it seems the season of love is upon us. As the days get colder and the magic of the holidays fills the air, take a break from shopping and spending time with those you love to snuggle up with stories by three of your favorite Arabesque authors that are sure to put you in the spirit of the season.

BOOK YOUR PLACE ON OUR WEBSITE AND MAKE THE ARABESQUE ROMANCE CONNECTION!

We've created a customized website just for our very special Arabesque readers, where you can get the inside scoop on everything that's going on with Arabesque romance novels.

When you come online, you'll have the exciting opportunity to:

- View covers of upcoming books

- Learn about our future publishing schedule (listed by publication month and author)

- Find out when your favorite authors will be visiting a city near you

- Search for and order backlist books

- Check out author bios and background information

- Send e-mail to your favorite authors

- Join us in weekly chats with authors, readers and other guests

- Get writing guidelines

- AND MUCH MORE!

Visit our website at
http://www.arabesquebooks.com

SEASON OF LOVE

Angela Winters
Niqui Stanhope
Kim Louise

ARABESQUE

BET BOOKS

BET Publications, LLC
http://www.bet.com
http://www.arabesquebooks.com

ARABESQUE BOOKS are published by

BET Publications, LLC
c/o BET BOOKS
One BET Plaza
1900 W Place NE
Washington, DC 20018-1211

All Kensington Titles, Imprints, and Distributed Lines are available at special quantity discounts for bulk purchases for sales promotions, premiums, fund-raising, and educational or institutional use. Special book excerpts or customized printings can also be created to fit specific needs. For details, write or phone the office of the Kensington special sales manager: Kensington Publishing Corp., 850 Third Avenue, New York, NY 10022, attn: Special Sales Department, Phone: 1-800-221-2647.

First Printing: October 2002
10 9 8 7 6 5 4 3 2 1

Printed in the United States of America

CONTENTS

HOME FOR CHRISTMAS   7
by Angela Winters

THE GIFT   111
by Niqui Stanhope

IMPROMPTU   203
by Kim Louise

HOME FOR CHRISTMAS

Angela Winters

DAY ONE—SATURDAY

Nia Randolph was feeling that ever so wonderful mixture of joy and nausea as she walked down the steps of the home she had grown up in. Joy because she was back home in Evanston, the small suburb of Chicago that held all the fond memories of family, church, and friends that made her who she was. Joy because she loved her parents and her sister and was looking forward to seeing them again.

So what about the nausea? That would come the second after good-mornings were exchanged.

"Morning, Nia." Gene Randolph sat against the atrium windows at the breakfast table as he always did in the Randolphs' modest kitchen. His trim figure was dressed appropriately for brutal Chicago winters in a turtleneck, sweatshirt, and pants. His raisin-brown skin was smooth, not showing a wrinkle that might be expected after sixty-two years and a lifetime of delivering and sorting mail. He winked at his oldest daughter as she approached the table, quickly returning to his copy of the Chicago Sun-Times.

"Morning, Daddy." Nia sat down. "Morning, Mama."

Sharon Randolph, still in her thick, wool housecoat, turned from the stove toward the table, placing a plate of food in front of Nia. She was a healthy, full-figured woman who held her weight well. She had caramel skin, fine features, and blazing green eyes. Just like Nia. Nia looked exactly like her mother, and she wasn't so sure how she felt about that sometimes.

"Good morning, baby," Sharon said. "Did you sleep well? Your flight got in so late last night. I thought we were going to have to get a room at the O'Hare Hilton."

"Mama, I told you I would rent a car and just drive home." Nia picked at the food. She was never a breakfast person, but she got such a headache for it when she was home that she pretended to be. "You really didn't have to wait."

Sharon waved her hand at her daughter. "It was no trouble. Besides, you don't need to be driving with all the stress you're under right now."

Here we go, Nia thought. *Like clockwork.*

"Have you spoken to Joseph?" she asked, taking a seat at the table. Sharon looked at her daughter with her brows drawn. She appeared so tenderly concerned.

"Mama, I really don't want to talk about Joe." Nia knew such a statement was a waste of her time. *Whatever.* Joe had dumped her for another woman. He'd broken her heart and left her in an abyss. It wasn't the first time this had happened to Nia. But it would be the last. She knew that much.

"You need to talk about it, Nia." Sharon snickered at her husband, who gestured for her to be quiet. "Gene, you should be concerned about this as much as me. Nia, you have to face up to your responsibility in all of this."

"Where exactly is my responsibility, mother?" Nia squeezed the fork in her hand tightly to keep back any tears that threatened to come. It had been only a month and it was still very painful. "Oh, yes, I see. I had the nerve to turn thirty. If I had stayed younger, maybe Joe would have never wanted a twenty-two-year-old model."

"That's not what I'm talking about. He didn't want that girl because she was twenty-two. He wanted her because she wanted him."

"You don't know the story at all, Mama." Nia bit back the sting her mother's words caused. "I wanted him. I loved him. I gave Joe everything I had."

"We both know that's not true. You've never given any man all you had. You've always put that career of yours first."

"That career?" Nia shook her head. "What is 'that' career? You mean *my* career? How I make a living doing something that I'm good at and that brings me joy? How I pay my bills?"

"Public relations." Sharon rolled her eyes. "You write press releases and launch parties. Is that worth losing a man?"

"My career did not break up my relationship with Joe!" Nia had told herself on the way home from Virginia that she wouldn't do this. She wasn't going to let her feelings, or anyone else's for that matter, get to her. "He said he wanted space; he wanted to be single again. Doesn't fit with him needing more of me."

"Because he already tried it, and it didn't work." Sharon sighed. "Just like with Donavan and Phillip."

"Now, Sharon," Gene said, "Let's not bring up the past. That doesn't help the situation."

"I think it brings something to light," Sharon said, looking pretty perturbed that her husband wasn't on her side. "They both broke up with Nia because she was too focused on her career."

"Mother, please." Nia didn't want to go through this.

Angela Winters

Partly because it was true. But she couldn't live through it again. She wasn't as strong as she made herself out to be. "That's not fair."

"I love you, Nia. I don't have to be fair. You have to look at the pattern."

"I am looking at the pattern," Nia said. "I have bad taste in men."

"You don't have bad taste in men. Joe was wonderful. We all loved him. A successful lawyer, well behaved."

"Not well behaved enough, Mama. He cheated on me and left me for another woman."

"What led him to that?" she asked.

Nia leaned back in her chair in a gesture of surrender. "Well, that was a lovely quote from the 1950s. Thanks, Mama."

"Look at your sister." Sharon got up in response to the teapot's whistling. "Ellen is only twenty-five years old and just got engaged to a doctor. A doctor. You know how that happened?"

"Sold her soul to the devil?"

"Nia," Gene admonished her with one of his textbook looks. He paid attention sometimes.

"She put finding a man and starting a family first on her to-do list," Sharon answered. "Her career was a distant second. It's just a paycheck, Nia. You could learn from your sister."

Actually, Nia felt more like her sister could learn from her. They were not the closest of sisters; the last time she had spoken to Ellen, a nurse at Northwestern Hospital, was probably three months ago. At the time she had just met a young doctor, Jamie Vincent. She liked him, thought he was cute. They were about to go on a third date then. Three months later, while planning her trip home for the annual Christmas flogging, Nia had been told to book her flight a few days earlier. Ellen had gotten engaged and was getting married in four months, and the engagement party was happening now.

She was pregnant. That was the obvious explanation. But no, Ellen swore on a Bible that she was in no such predicament. She was in love, and they didn't want to wait any second longer than they had to. They had come close to eloping, but Jamie's parents were apparently high society people and would have fallen down dead without the chance for a reception.

Nia knew she should have just been happy for her sister. She loved Ellen with all of her heart. Then a tinge of jealousy set in. Why was everyone else able to find that perfect someone, and not her? She was so certain Joe had been that someone for her. Boy, had she been wrong. And it was that experience, which her heart was still reeling from, that urged her to come home and talk some sense into her sister. Three months was in no way, shape, or form enough time.

"What do we know about this Jamie person anyway?" Nia asked.

"He's perfect, perfect, perfect. That's what we know."

As bubbly as ever, and cuter than a kitten and a rosebud put together, Ellen Randolph entered the kitchen. She brought her genuine smile that seemed to spread across her entire face, including the large brown eyes that made her look closer to seventeen than twenty-five. She was a petite beauty, with milk chocolate-colored skin, a perfect figure, an ever-optimistic attitude, and an annoyingly perky personality.

"Morning, baby." Sharon planted a kiss on her baby as she passed by. "Sit down. I'll get you some breakfast."

Ellen sat next to Nia. "Morning, Daddy."

Gene grunted something like a good-morning, too engrossed in the sports section to care.

"Nobody is perfect," Nia said.

"Nice to have you home, too." Ellen stuck her tongue out at her sister.

"Don't take it the wrong way, baby sister."

"I won't. Sorry I couldn't be at the airport last night. I was at Jamie's. I can't wait until you meet him, Nia. He's the best. He's absolutely gorgeous."

"Gorgeous isn't why you marry someone." Nia knew what she sounded like, but she wanted to spare her sister what she was feeling right now.

"Nia, stop it." Sharon gave Ellen her plate. "Be happy for your sister."

"Of course, he's more than that," Ellen said. "You'll see when you meet him later tonight at the engagement party. Mama, Jamie's mother, Jonelle, wants me to tell you thanks for planning this engagement party with a week's notice."

"I hope it meets her standards." Sharon rolled her eyes again.

"What is that about?" Nia asked.

Ellen shrugged. "Mama thinks the Vincents are snobs. They're a wealthy family, but that doesn't mean they're snobs. Jamie's father is a judge. His mother is a lawyer. Used to be, at least. She's kind of a socialite now. I guess that's what you'd call her. His brother is a hotshot investment banker in Denver. But they're all good people."

"I'm sure they are, Ellen." Nia scooted her chair closer to her. "But three months? Come on, sister. If you aren't pregnant—"

"Nia." Gene lowered his paper. "I don't want to hear dirty talk at this table."

Nia ignored him. "Either way, you can't know him well enough to want to marry him. Why can't you wait?"

"We don't need to. Haven't you ever heard of love at first sight?"

"No such thing," Nia said. From experience, she knew.

She thought Joe was the beginning and end the first night she met him.

"You're just in pain," Ellen said, gently touching her sister's arm. "I'm sorry about what happened between you and Joe, Nia. But I've found forever in this man, and in four months we're going to be married. And in forty years we'll still be married. He's just right."

"If it's right, then what does it hurt to wait?"

"Nia." Sharon approached the table, hands on hips. "Stop it. This is all sudden to everyone, but Ellen is happy and she's getting married. We're going to support that. All of us. Besides, it's Christmas. Let's just be happy."

Easier said than done, Nia thought to herself. She would give up for now. The peripheral audience was hindering her ability to communicate. She needed to get Ellen alone. Maybe after the engagement party tonight, after their parents had gone to bed. Whatever the case, she loved her sister enough that she didn't care if she appeared to be the jealous spinster. If it meant she was saving Ellen from the pain that she had been going through, it would be worth it.

First class isn't what it used to be. Michael Vincent stared straight at the two-year-old with snot running down his nose in the seat in front of him. He remembered the days when all the whining, annoying kids were in coach, and he could fly in peace. Denver to Chicago wasn't a short trip. It was long enough to get on one's nerves. All the help a first-class seat could provide was appreciated. It was different now. Everything about flying was different now. That was why he didn't come home as often as he used to.

Who was he kidding? He wasn't coming home as often as he used to because each time he didn't, his family made it harder and harder on him. If he were honest with himself, they weren't completely to blame. He would admit that he had really dropped the ball the last three Christmases. The first two, he'd shown up on Christmas Eve and left early the day after Christmas. He had a lot of work to get back to. Besides, Chicago was so doggone cold! Yeah, Denver had more snow, but Chicago had it beat by a mile when it came to actual temperature.

Then there was last Christmas. A temporary case of insanity was all he could say to excuse it. Yes, he had done it. He had passed up Christmas at home with his family to spend it at an Aspen lodge with a supermodel. It was one of those torrid-affair things: started quick, ended even quicker. Hot sex and ulcer-causing arguments. It lasted six months, and ended badly. But at the time, spending a week trapped in a condo with a six-foot-tall bombshell from Somalia seemed like a better choice than freezing his butt off while being told that at thirty-five, he needed to start settling down.

Besides, he got at least four new clients out of the relationship. It was worth it.

"You're an ass, Michael Vincent," he whispered to himself.

"Excuse me, sir?" The flight attendant leaned over the sleeping passenger next to Michael. She had been noticeably more attentive to Michael than to any of the other passengers. "Did you ask for something?"

"No, thanks." He smiled with a charming nod, turning his attention to the window. They would be in Chicago in less than an hour.

But this trip wasn't about him. Yes, he had agreed to come home a week early this time to make up for the last three years, but he wasn't coming to share quality time with his family. He was coming to get to the bottom of this so-called engagement. Jamie had known the girl for what, three months? They were getting married in what, four months? Ridiculous. He had to put a stop to this.

He had warned Jamie several times before about the women who made it their sole purpose in life to snag a doctor. Getting pregnant was still the snare of choice, but other methods could be used. Especially with someone like Jamie, who lacked that hard edge that a man needed to deal with conniving women. So if this little nurse wasn't pregnant, what was it?

A hot bed hastened many a man to the altar.

Regardless, it was all too soon.

Jamie wouldn't speak up. He hated to disappoint their parents. After all, that was Michael's job. He would get to the bottom of this, however. And if his assumptions were right, this wedding would be called off, or at least put on hold, by the time he hopped the plane back to Denver.

"Who would have thought?" Robin Johnston had her hands on the hips of her fur coat as she stood in the doorway to the back room at Ben Pao's, the Thai restaurant in downtown Chicago that had been chosen as the place for the engagement party. It was Ellen's favorite restaurant.

"Who would have thought what, Robin?" Nia tried to force a smile for the woman who was a so-called friend of hers. She had grown up with Robin. Their parents were friends, and they had been thrust together their entire lives, but never really got along.

"That your little sister would get married before you." She squeezed at her coat as if to make sure everyone was aware of how comfortable it was.

"Still into dead animals, I see." Nia's smile disappeared as she stared the woman down. *Don't mess with me, girl*, her look said. That usually worked with Robin. She was more bark than bite.

Nia had had enough talks of joyous love and marriage that day. She had gotten it endlessly from her mother and all the friends she was forced to call up and give her happy holidays and "I'm in town in case you're interested." If it wasn't a pity-laced message on how the heart mends from worthless men, it was a message on how marriage was the foundation of everything good. "It'll happen for you one day," they all said.

She left everyone behind to get some fresh air, driving along Lake Shore Drive in Ellen's car. She tried desperately not to reflect on the scene of Joe's telling her it was over, telling her he had found someone else. Of course, it was after she had found unfamiliar jewelry under his bedroom pillow. It was hard. It seemed etched in her mind, unwilling to go away. Her tears, disbelief, anger, and feelings of worthlessness were still so fresh.

What had those years been? She wished she could figure it out. A waste? All of it? Had she really driven him into that girl's arms? What if . . . No, no, no. She didn't deserve this.

Joe was a dog! Most men were, and Nia had just had to keep that in mind.

After a quick cry, she made her way over to the restaurant to help out where she could for the party. She met Jamie, who she thought was a great guy despite her desire to make him otherwise. His parents were attractive people who oozed style and class. A little on the snobbish side, but in general kind folks as well. Jamie's brother hadn't made it in yet, but she would meet him later. Everyone just seemed entirely too happy and okay with this for her taste.

An escape to the back room, where the planning was taking place, had now resulted in a visit from Robin, which was enough to send her in search of another space. She just needed a few moments more, and she would be all smiles for Ellen. For everyone.

The coat check area seemed empty at the time, except for an attractive man on his cell phone. He was tall, with pecan-

brown skin and a trim, muscular build. Even in casual khaki
pants and a blue button-down, something about him looked
conservative and professional. Whatever the case, he wasn't
bothering her, so Nia took a seat in the phone booth next
to him. She grabbed the phone, just in case someone walked
by and she could pretend to be making a call.

She took the scrunchie wrapped around her right wrist
and used it to put her long, wavy auburn hair up in a ponytail.
As it usually did at some point every day, it was starting to
get on her nerves. She was going to get it cut as soon as
possible. She had let it grow for Joe. He said he liked long
hair.

So you see, Mama, I had tried to please him somewhat.

"I'm sorry, Matt." Michael took a deep breath, returning
to his cell phone. "I don't mean to be short with you. I just
want to make sure everything is okay. I know you've handled
the office plenty of times when I've been away, but it's the
holidays. Things tend to fall through the cracks a lot. I'm
under a lot of stress."

"How's it going in Chi-town?" asked Matt Becker, the
only other senior partner with Shanahan and Smith Invest-
ments besides Michael.

"Not good. I showed up late, so I didn't get a chance to
pull my brother aside. I don't know who these Randolphs
are, but I'm pretty certain they're a bunch of working-class
social climbers. They're probably all in on this."

Nia's eyes widened. Had she heard that right? She peeked
around the barrier of the phone booths.

"They're probably the ones who convinced her to latch
on to my brother so they can get somewhere. I wouldn't
put it past them. I've been through this before. Jamie doesn't
know what he's gotten himself into."

Nia bit her lower lip to keep from saying something. Her

stomach tightened, and she felt her usually reserved temper begin to heat up.

"A family of gold diggers," Matt said with a laugh. "You're being pretty presumptuous."

"I don't think so," Michael answered. "This whole thing smells. Some nurse out of nowhere all of a sudden shows up. I still don't believe she isn't pregnant. She could be blackmailing him. She's nothing like the caliber of women Jamie usually dates. What other reason could there be?"

Nia couldn't take it anymore.

She leaped from her seat and right into Michael's face. He backed up, surprised by the sudden presence of a beautiful young woman. Those electrifying green eyes stood out to him. And man, were they angry.

"Maybe he loves her!" she shouted. "Have you ever thought of that?"

"Who are you?" He backed up, but she only moved forward.

"I'm part of that whole family that smells to you. I know who you are, Michael Vincent. You're an elitist asshole who happens to think so little of women that you can read them like a book before you even meet them."

"I . . . I . . . I . . ." Michael realized what had just happened. Man, had he stepped in it now. He had to do damage control.

"I . . . I . . . I . . ." she mocked him, taking pleasure in the flicker of anger that showed in his black eyes in response. "I'll have you know Ellen Randolph is about the best thing that could ever happen to any man, including your brother. No, she doesn't come from money, but that never mattered to her. Never, as in it still doesn't. And she's still a ton of steps above any debutante you and or your brother may have assumed was good enough for you. I question whether or not your brother is good enough for Ellen. I mean, if he's anything like you, I'll grab my sister and head for the hills."

"Look." Michael tried to control his temper, but it was hard. No matter how attractive she was in this black, fitted sweater dress, nobody talked to him like this.

"No, you look," she corrected, looking him up and down. "Men like you . . . men like you who think you know what every woman is after, what every woman is worth, are the reasons why relationships fail. You don't know anything. You don't know my sister or the rest of my family. And you certainly don't know me. So, Michael Vincent, I suggest you stick with what you do know, and keep your mouth shut about the rest."

She was gone before he could get another word out, but the damage had been done. No one got away with telling him off! Who did she think she was?

"Michael! Michael!"

Michael lifted the cell phone back to his ear. "Hey, Matt. I'm sorry about that. Had a little problem there."

"Sounded like someone was ripping you a new one."

"Something like that. Look, I have to go. I'll call you later."

Hanging up, Michael was still shocked enough to be frozen in his steps. This was great. Just great. The situation was bad enough. Now she was going to go off and tell everyone what she'd heard him say, and he would be the bad guy, his usual label within his own family. She had taken his remarks out of context.

And who was she to tell him who he was? No matter how attractive she may have been, Michael didn't take lip from any woman. She had quickly presented herself as an obstacle, but she didn't know whom she was up against. Michael had made a living crushing his obstacles and running right over them.

* * *

As the engaged couple each gave their own speeches on how true love triumphed over all, Nia had to clench her hands into fists for the strength to keep from throwing up. Between their saccharine-laced words of fantasy, and Michael Vincent sending her disapproving stares, she thought she would go insane. He wouldn't stop looking at her. But she was smarter than he gave her credit for. He was trying to break her down, to make her feel bad for putting him in his place.

That wasn't going to happen. He deserved every bit of the tongue-lashing he'd gotten. At least. And she somehow felt rejuvenated and refreshed after their encounter. The only reason she'd held back on him was because in her heart she didn't want this wedding to go off either. It was just that his snobbish reasons were inexcusable. And he stood there so smug in his spotless clothes, with that this-is-all-beneath-me look on his face. He was a handsome man; she'd give him that. Strong nose, thick eyebrows, and full lips. His jet-black hair was cut neatly to his head. Everything so neat, almost sterile. One thing Nia knew was that good looks on certain men were a curse. Like with Joe.

"Enough with the sappy talk," Jamie yelled out, his glass of wine raised high in the air. "Let's d..nce!"

On cue, the prerecorded CD came on, and the sounds of Janet Jackson lured a small crowd to the center section of the private room.

Michael knew where he wanted to go immediately, but as he headed for her, he felt his arm being gripped by a soft, yet strong hand. He turned to face his beautiful mother, Jonelle.

"Yes, Mom, I know. I was late. I've already apologized for that."

"That's not what I want to talk to you about." Jonelle Vincent gracefully wiped a strand of hair from her face. She was a dark woman with flawless skin. Everything about her spoke of her lifestyle: not ostentatious at all, but elegant and classic. She was a well-taken-care-of woman, and she obviously took a lot of pride in that.

"You know what this week is about, right?" She pulled him closer, looking sternly into his eyes. "It's about the family. Both families. We're spending the week with the Randolphs. So this is not about you catching up with your boys or checking in on the many women you ran around with when you lived here."

"Maybe a couple," he said with a pleading squint of his eyes. "Rachel, Mom. You remember Rachel Carter. I can't pass up—"

"Stop being cute." She slapped him on the arm. "Besides, Rachel Carter got married last Christmas. If you had been here, you would know that."

"Damn." He hadn't remembered that at all. Rachel? Was everyone getting married? "Fine, Mother. I know. I know. I'll be nice and I'll stay home. I'll follow you everywhere all week long. You can count on me."

"That would be something new," she answered with a quick nod of her head.

"Thank you." He smirked. "I'm dying from all the love. Can you release the leash for a few minutes? I would like to dance."

"Don't you leave here with some girl," she said before letting him go. She was serious.

Finally free, Michael headed for Nia Randolph. Her back was to him, which made it all the better when he came up from behind, tapping her on the shoulder. He stood close enough so that she almost bumped into him when she turned around. Catching her off guard, he grabbed her by the waist and led her to the dance floor.

Nia hadn't even had a chance to protest. When she adjusted to the shock of his grabbing her and pulling her to the dance floor, she was already pressed against him and being led in some type of fast/slow mixture. She felt blood rush to her head as the smell of his cologne touched her nose. It smelled great, which for some reason made her angry.

"What are you doing?" She thought to push away, but the dance floor wasn't full enough. Everyone would notice. The last thing she wanted was more attention.

What was this? Michael asked himself. A little ping in his groin? That was okay. An instinctual reaction. She was an attractive woman. *No matter. Just concentrate.* "I wanted to talk to you."

"If you expect me to apologize," Nia said, a little unnerved by his hand at the small of her back, too low, "just forget it. Hey, can you loosen up a bit?"

"Do I make you nervous?" he asked. So what if she smelled incredible? That wasn't the point.

"More like nauseous," she answered. Actually he was making her nervous. She was a little too aware of the feeling of his stomach muscles against hers. He loosened up a bit, but Nia wasn't satisfied. She still felt a little dizzy. "What do you want?"

"First, I want to apologize for before. I was stressed out. You know, long flights, surprise engagements."

"Get on with it." Nia felt it best to stay away from their earlier encounter. She was feeling a little warm. "Can we get off this dance floor?"

"Actually, when I'm up to no good, I like to create an illusion of normalcy. I'd like to stay."

"I get the impression that you're always up to no good." Nia made an attempt to create a greater gap between them, but he was too strong. She couldn't move.

"Pretty much." He couldn't turn away from her face, even though she was doing everything to avoid looking at him. "You're quite beautiful, you know."

She looked at him, taken off guard by his words. He was good-looking, the jerk. "Yes, I do know."

He smiled, showing perfect white teeth. So she had an attitude too. "Okay, Nia. I deserve the smart-ass comeback. Can we call a truce now? I think you want to hear what I have to say."

"Get on with it."

"I was watching you earlier."

"I know. A little creepy, I'd say."

He ignored her snipe. "And I noticed something interesting. First of all, you bite your nails like no one I've ever seen. That's a bad habit, sugar."

"Is this your incredible piece of news for me, Michael? Flash for you: it's old hat. I picked it up from my mother when I was eight."

"So I'm thirty years late in telling you, then, huh?"

Nia's eyes widened in horror as she froze in place. The smile on his face was so smug. She wanted to slap him. "Very funny, jerk."

"Just trying to lighten the mood, honey. You don't look a day over thirty-seven."

Nia pressed her lips together for a moment to quell the smile that wanted to form independently of her will. "Why don't you check the 'sugar' and 'honey' crap at the door and tell me what you have to tell me."

"I'm a pretty good judge of character, Nia."

"That is interesting," she said, batting her eyes. "Considering you have no character yourself."

"Enough." His brows narrowed at her. Man, was she attractive. "What I noticed was that you're not happy about this wedding at all. Now, it could be the bitter older sister pissed off because—"

"That's it." Nia struggled free, but he only pulled her tighter. She was hot all over. "Let me go. I don't need this crap."

"Or . . ." he said, holding tight. She was very light, with a thin frame. It was nothing for him to keep hold of her. "Or, it could be that you, like me, don't think this wedding is a good idea. It's too soon."

Nia stopped, not certain how to react. "I don't know what you're talking about."

"I think you do. And I think you and I have something in common."

"I disagree, Michael."

"Call me Mike."

"No, thanks."

He groaned, letting a little frustration get through. "I know what I saw, Nia."

"You don't know jack," she answered, taking advantage of his sudden displeasure in the rap song that came up. It seemed to mess with his concentration. "Let me go now."

Michael did as he was told, aware of the letdown he felt at her release. He watched as she turned and walked away, liking very much what he saw. He didn't care what she said. He knew what he'd seen earlier, and he was going to make her admit to it. He just had to figure out a way around that supreme attitude problem she had.

So maybe the week wasn't going to be as unbearable as he'd once thought.

Nia finally found her way outside the restaurant. The nightlife around her was on and jumping. The amazing thing about Chicagoans was that even in unreasonable weather, they knew how to get their party on. She had missed this town. There was always something to do, sleet or snow.

"Miss." The doorman to the restaurant approached her with a curious look on his face. "You're going to freeze without a coat. Do you need me to get your coat?"

"No, thanks. I'll just be out here for a minute. I need some air."

The reality was, Nia was burning up. She wanted to convince herself it was anger at Michael for being so presumptuous as to grab her and tell her how she felt about all of this. The fact that he was right made her angrier. But what really got her was the way she was feeling in the pit of her stomach.

Maybe she was so messed up inside that she didn't even know what she was feeling. Because after all, there was no way she was attracted to this man. She had called a moratorium on all men. At least until she figured out what her problem was. Especially men like Michael. Men who reminded her of Joe—so sure of themselves, so centered on themselves.

"Nia, what are you doing out here?" Ellen, with Jamie practically wrapped around her, approached her sister. "Are you okay?"

"Just needed some air," she said with a nod. "Don't you think it's a little warm in there?"

"Not at all," she answered with a careless shrug. "Jamie and I just wanted a break from everyone. We get the feeling that we won't have a lot of opportunities to be alone over the next week, so we might as well take them where we can get them."

"Do you want me to get you a coat?" Jamie asked.

To Nia, Jamie was completely perfect: so nice, so cute, so smart, so successful. Everything. He dressed like a Gap model, and had the glasses to match. Unlike his brother, he was more of a café-au-lait complexion. He looked like his father, only thinner. *Good genes in that family,* she thought.

Personally, Nia preferred a little more of a challenge, but maybe that had been her problem. Maybe what she really needed was a man like Jamie for herself. *No, stop it! You don't need any type of man right now.*

"No, I'm fine. Thanks, Jamie. That's nice of you."

"He's always nice," Ellen said, as if she were trying to convince someone. "Everything is so perfect, Nia. You should go back inside and enjoy it. Just think: this time next year we'll probably be having my baby shower here."

"Baby?" Nia's eyes widened.

"No," Jamie said, holding his hands up. "Nothing like that. Just wishful thinking. We want to start a family right away."

"We both agreed," Ellen said. "Three kids, all two years apart. Just perfect."

"What about your career, Ellen?" Nia was a little shaken by the choice. Three kids. That was what she had wanted.

"I'm going to take care of Ellen while we have our children," Jamie said. "I want her to come back to work in her own time. Whatever she wants is fine with me."

"That's great," Nia said, forcing a smile. "I think I'll go back inside now."

Inside the restaurant, Nia relived the words in her mind and her heart. Joe had wanted three kids: two boys and a girl. They had talked about it a couple of times, not a lot. How would she work three kids into her career so close like that? *However you want to. Nia,* he had said. *I'll let you decide that. I'll take care of you regardless.* Promises made, promises not kept.

Her mind was made up. Nia searched and found Michael in the coatroom on his cell phone again. She took a deep breath before making herself known to him. *Just listen, Nia. It can't hurt to listen.*

Michael smiled, knowing exactly why she was back. He knew he was right. She was a stubborn one. She wouldn't for one second let her face give it away. She wanted to hear what he had to say. He quickly ended his phone call.

"What nonsense are you talking about?" she asked, hands folded across her chest.

"I don't know, Nia." He shook his head, making a smacking sound with his lips. "You've been a little sharp with me. I'm not sure I want to talk to you any—"

"Cut the bull, Michael. You deserved everything I gave you and more. Let's hear it."

"Can I get some wine first?"

Nia rolled her eyes. This guy was a piece of work.

They found a private corner near the restaurant bar. Nia's temperature was boiling again. He had taken his own sweet time getting a drink, stopping to say hello to everyone he knew. He took one step every two minutes. It was all just to goad her. He liked to rub it in.

"Neither of us wants this wedding to happen four months from now," he finally said, feeling satisfied that he had her full attention.

"I know your reasons," Nia said. "What do you figure mine are? I mean, you know so much, so you can tell me."

"First of all, you don't completely know my reasons. Honestly, I don't know what your sister's intentions are. I just want my brother to err on the side of caution. And you . . . maybe you want the same for your sister."

"I just want her to make sure she's making the right choice. That takes time. You can fall for a guy real quick, think he's the world, and you fall flat on your face. I don't want that to happen to her when she's married and pregnant."

Michael saw the glint of pain rush through her eyes. "Somebody has a broken heart."

"This is not about me, Michael." She eyed him with a stony stare, angry at herself for giving her feelings away. "You stay out of my life. This is about Jamie and Ellen. Go on."

Touchy subject. Okay. It probably wasn't a good time to say that she'd probably still have the man if she weren't such a witch. "Whatever the cause, we think they should both take more time to get to know each other before getting married. So, what do we do about it?''

"I'm having a long talk with Ellen tonight. I'm going to tell her—"

"No, you're not."

Nia gritted her teeth. "Do not interrupt me, thank you very much. I am going to—"

"No, you're not. I'm staying with my brother, and I know for a fact that he and Ellen are ditching this party and staying out all night. He gave me a set of keys to get in tonight, since he wasn't going to be with me. Do you plan on tagging along?''

She waved her hand away. "Fine, then tomorrow."

"What are you going to say?"

"Why am I answering all the questions? What are your plans?''

"I don't know yet."

"That's very helpful." Nia slapped her hand on the counter of the bar, then made her way past him. He grabbed her by the arm, pulling her back. "Hey!"

"Look." Michael wasn't sure why he was suddenly so upset. He didn't like it when people walked away from him, but she made him particularly angry. "With everything that I've got going on, the last thing I need is to partner up with a self-righteous, bitter woman, but—"

"How dare you?" Nia didn't know what she was doing, but she got right in his face, hers only a few inches from his. "I swear, Michael Vincent, if you call me one more name, I'll . . ."

Neither of them spoke. They both realized it at the same time: something about this, about all of this, was turning them on, and they had no control over it.

Nia quickly backed away, unable to think about being so close to him. What was that? She had gotten in his face, and all of a sudden the hair on her arms stood up, her belly swirled, and she felt a tingle run through her. It made no sense.

Michael couldn't remember a woman catching him off guard with his feelings. He was usually in control of this type of thing. But suddenly she was so close to him, and he wanted to grab her and kiss her, and at the same time he wanted to yell at her. He needed to think. Focus.

"Nia, I think we've had enough of each other for tonight. You're coming over tomorrow with your family to plan the week, right?"

Nia nodded, wondering how she could get out of tomorrow's festivities. Something told her she didn't need to be around this man.

"Fine." He placed his glass on the table, having taken only a sip or two. "We can talk then. We'll put our heads together and come up with a plan to push this wedding back."

"So what," she said, "we're like partners in this thing?"

He nodded. "And no one else knows about it. I think both of our parents would kill us if they knew. And my brother and your sister would never understand we were doing this for their own good."

"Agreed."

He held out his hand to her, wanting to touch her, and not wanting to at the same time. When she accepted it, he quickly shook her hand and pulled away. Still, in such a short time, he had felt something: a little jolt that warned him of hits to come. How many glasses had he had?

Nia got away from Michael as soon as she could, and made a point to stay away from him for the rest of the night. She convinced herself that the feelings she was having were just a by-product of her emotional homecoming, memories of Joe, and overall confusion about her heart and her emotions. That was it.

She just needed a good night's sleep that she hadn't gotten last night. Tomorrow would be totally different.

DAY TWO—SUNDAY

Nia's stomach was a mess as she stepped inside the Vincents' enormous home in Hyde Park, a southern suburb of Chicago. It wasn't the old stone exterior with the dark oak trimmings, although that in itself gave the house an old-money, intimidating nature.

It was him. As much as she tried to brush last night's various encounters with Michael off, she couldn't. He was going to be a thorn in her side this whole week. It was bad enough that every waking moment was spent with her mother and Ellen talking about the wedding. Her father, as usual, was no help, since he barely spoke a word. Ever.

"Welcome to our home." Jonelle Vincent opened her arms wide to greet the Randolph family as they entered the tastefully decorated great room. The house was full of classical styles and colors, and decorated with bold antiques. One could tell that a lot of time had been put into every nook and cranny of this house time and time again.

Jonelle gestured for the maid—a young Caribbean

woman, from the accent she had when she greeted them—
to leave them alone.

Jamie and Michael were standing near the elaborate fireplace, seeming deep in conversation. To her dismay, Nia's
first thought was how incredible Michael looked in a fitted
cream turtleneck and coffee-colored slacks. Her second
thought was what he might be talking to Jamie about. Hope-
fully, out of this wedding thing.

"What's the matter with you?" Sharon asked Nia as they
sat on the plush white sofa.

"What?" Nia hugged the edge of the sofa, wondering
why it upset her so much that Michael hadn't acknowledged
her presence yet.

"I can hear you gritting your teeth," Sharon said. "It's
very unflattering."

Nia rolled her eyes. She watched as Ellen wrapped her
arms around Jamie's waist, stealing his attention away from
his brother. Finally Michael turned to the rest of them, to
her.

This is weird, Nia thought. She felt her stomach take a
little leap as his eyes connected with hers. It was as if . . .
as if his attention made her happy.

"This is ridiculous," Nia mumbled under her breath,
turning away.

"What is that, Nia?" Jonelle asked as she leaned forward,
offering her a glass of wine.

Nia refused the wine. "Nothing. Sorry."

Sharon's eyes set on her daughter as if she had never seen
the woman before in her life. Nia shrugged an apology.

"You ladies look wonderful," Michael said as he joined
them on the sofas. He sat directly across from Nia. He
enjoyed having her in full view.

He had been eagerly awaiting seeing Nia again. He was
starting to like that annoyed look she had on her face all
the time. Plus she looked hot in her black jeans and lavender

cashmere sweater. *Good quality, nice choice.* He was wondering when he would get to smell her again. She smelled incredibly clean.

Reaching over, he shook Gene Randolph's hand, finding some amusement in the fact that the man obviously didn't want to be there. *At least he came,* Michael thought, knowing his own father, Edward, hadn't bothered to show up.

"You're looking for my father, Mr. Randolph."

"Call me Gene. And yes, I thought this was a family event we all *had* to come to."

"Don't get me started on that," Jonelle said, her expression showing her utter disappointment.

Stop staring at me, Nia was screaming inside. Michael had his eyes set on her with that smile that she was beginning to hate—hate with a passion. Here came the heat! Was it one hundred degrees in this castle or what?

The conversation began working Nia's nerves immediately. The families were at odds right away. Every topic related to planning a quick wedding fell on two separate sides: the Vincent way or the Randolph way.

What's the best date? A Sunday or a Saturday?

Where should we have the reception? A hotel or a museum?

How far should we ask people to drive? Downtown Chicago or in the suburbs?

If the suburbs, Evanston or Hyde Park?

How many people should we invite? Under a hundred or over two hundred?

Beef or chicken? No veal, of course.

Nia found it shameless that Sharon and Jonelle did all of the arguing when it was Ellen and Jamie's wedding. They barely let Ellen get a word in. Whatever the Vincents wanted was too ostentatious. Whatever the Randolphs wanted didn't make enough of a statement. Gene Randolph shifted in his seat, not saying a word.

Nia put a word in where she could, but Michael said nothing. He just stared. He stared at her. She could tell he knew he was making her angry, furious. And he loved it.

"Look!" Nia surprised herself with her tone. It was harsh enough to get everyone's attention. "What are we doing here? We've been sitting here for almost an hour, unable to agree on anything, so we just pass on it and go to another topic we can't agree on. We're wasting time and getting nowhere."

Silence fell upon the room as everyone stared at her. Nia felt herself breathing hard. Suddenly she wanted to cry, and she knew she couldn't stop it. She had to get out of there.

Michael saw the tense lines form on her forehead. He didn't get what this was about, but he knew she was about to explode.

"Nia," Ellen said, apparently concerned. "What's wrong?"

"Nothing." She squeezed her hands into fists to get control of herself. "I'm just getting a little stir crazy. Church was so long, then that long drive out here, and—"

"You just need to stretch your legs, honey." Jonelle nodded nervously. "Why don't you go pick up the spread I had Noss's put together for us to eat?"

"What is that?"

"It's a grocery store a few blocks from here." Michael stood up. "Let's go."

Before Nia could say anything, he had taken hold of her arm by the elbow and was leading her out the room toward the front door. He grabbed two coats, not caring whom they belonged to.

"What are you doing?" Nia pulled her hand away as soon as they got to the front porch.

"I wanted to get you out of there before you exploded." He thrust a coat at her. She was constant attitude, this woman.

"You were going to make a fool of yourself. I was doing you a favor."

"I don't need your help, Michael." Putting the coat on, Nia realized he had saved her just in time. She bit her lower lip to stop the tears, but it was no use.

"Nia." Michael couldn't ignore this strange sense of compassion he was feeling for her, for no real reason or purpose. She was really hurting, and he felt bad for her. Usually he would get far away from a crying woman, but something compelled him to stay, to want to help her.

Nia held her hand up to stop him. "Just . . . don't . . . say . . . a word."

Arms wrapped tightly around herself, she walked down the perfectly shoveled steps. She looked at the massive front yard of the house with its manicured bushes half-covered in snow. She was crying completely now, unable to stop herself. What was the matter with her?

Michael waited in silence as Nia worked through her tears. This tough woman who had read him the riot act and reamed him good more than once yesterday was a completely different picture now. She was vulnerable and very fragile. He was overcome with the desire to take her in his arms and hold her.

But he just waited. He waited for her to stop crying and gather herself together. When she had, he approached her again, placing a hand tenderly on her shoulder.

"There's a café at the grocery store. A warm cup of coffee sounds really good right now."

"Yes," Nia said, feeling a strange sense of comfort at his touch. She took a deep breath. "That sounds good."

Not a word was spoken as they walked the three blocks to Noss's, a tiny boutique neighborhood grocery store. It was quaint, yuppie to no end, and the kind of place where a pint of milk went for five dollars and no one complained. Nia headed for the small café area and ordered a coffee while Michael picked up his mother's order. By the time he joined her, she had gotten herself together and felt as if she owed him an explanation.

"I'm not crazy," she said. "Even though it may seem like I am."

Michael smiled. "Actually, you are crazy. We all are. Some more than others, but don't worry. I never thought that about you."

"I know I seem like the jealous, bitter older sister."

"I have a feeling this is about a lot more than that," he said.

They held each other's eyes until Michael's smile became infectious. Nia couldn't help herself. He was a very attractive man.

"I'm not going to give you my sob story," she said. "No matter how nice you are to me."

"Doesn't matter. I'm not good at being nice anyway. I made you smile. That's really the best I can do. It's just sometimes it's nice to let it out."

After a short pause, Nia thought, *What the heck?*

"I broke up with my boyfriend a month ago." She let out an ironic laugh. "Correction. My boyfriend dumped me for a young model."

"I'm sorry, Nia." What moron would dump her? Yeah, she had an attitude, but she was beautiful and strong. And sexy. "He's a loser, Nia. An idiot."

"Thanks." She appreciated that more than she'd expected to. "I'm just hurt and I'm pissed. And I'm sick of getting grief from my parents."

"Why would they give you grief about this?"

"Because it's all my fault."

"Exactly how is a cheating boyfriend your fault?"

"I'm too focused on my career. I'm in public relations, and—"

"With your attitude?" he asked, amazed. "That's surprising."

She stared him down. So much for Mr. Nice Guy.

"Sorry." He smiled an apology. "I'll just shut up."

"My parents think my preoccupation with my career is what has sabotaged my relationship with Joe, just like it sabotaged my relationship with other boyfriends. They're certain I'm destined to be alone, which is apparently more than they can bear. And now, with Ellen getting married, I can feel the disappointment all around me."

"That's a bunch of bull, Nia, and you know it. You're supposed to have some inclination to sabotage your own happiness?"

"Hey, you don't get to be thirty and single just sitting around."

"A joke." He reached across and patted her on the shoulder. "You made a funny. See, it's not all that bad."

"I want to be upset, Michael. Can you let me wallow in a little self-pity, please?"

"I think there's been enough of that. Look, Nia. Any man worth his salt would respect your drive and support your career aspirations. Whatever your parents or anyone else says, your relationship with Joe ended because he wasn't good enough for you."

Nia was dumbstruck. She couldn't have spoken even if she had any words to say. She felt relief wash over her for the first time in the longest time, and she didn't understand it. Who was this man to soothe her better than her friends? Why were the words he said, which she had heard several times from others in the past month and told herself, somehow different now?

"Did I say something wrong?" Michael asked after a while. He wasn't able to decipher what that look on her face was. He thought it was good, but wasn't sure. He hoped it was good.

Nia's full lips slowly curled into a smile. "No, Michael. You . . . Thank you. That was nice of you to say."

"I wasn't trying to be nice," he said.

"That's right, I forgot. You're not good at that. But just for a second there, you had me fooled."

Michael laughed, happy that she seemed to be in a better mood. "You know I'm right, don't you?"

She nodded. "Yeah, I know. It just . . . takes time."

Nia wasn't sure what was happening to her, but she suddenly felt like giggling. Had she been wrong about Michael Vincent? She couldn't think that way. She had been wrong about Joe Milton and others before him. The last thing she needed was to be wrong about a man like Michael Vincent. God only knew how many broken hearts he'd left behind.

Nia stood up. "I'm ready to head back. Do you mind?"

Michael sensed a sudden chill between them. He was disappointed. He liked Nia a lot better when she wasn't on the offensive. And he was liking the flow of their conversation. It felt . . . right. "We haven't even talked about what we agreed to last night."

He stood up, grabbing the decorative food platter. They headed out of the grocery store.

"Oh, yes, last night." Nia was grateful for the memory. It helped block the little voice in the back of her head that told her she was having a good time with this man. "Our partnership."

"We shook on it." He remembered that shake very well. Especially how it made him feel. "At the rate of all this planning, we won't have enough time. Jamie is a follow-through type of guy. Things get to a certain stage and he'd never pull out. Even if he knew it was the right thing to do."

"With our mothers arguing over everything, we probably have more time than we think. They can't agree on anything.

Maybe that should be our strategy: keep them fighting, and the wedding will never happen.''

"A PR specialist slash comedienne." Michael was glad he had to carry the platter. If he hadn't he would have to follow his urge to take her hand in his. Walking with her, even in the freezing December air, was nice. Very nice. "But I don't think that will work."

"You were right," Nia admitted. "I was fast asleep before Ellen came home, and I wasn't alone with her for a second this morning. But I will get her alone today and work on her."

"Good. Jamie and I worked out together this morning while Mom and Dad were at church. I tried to bring it up, but he kept slapping me down. He didn't want to hear it. I'm going to have to try harder. He's really been taken."

"Hey." Nia felt her sense of family fuel her anger. "My sister has not taken him, nor has she ever tried to. If you knew anything about their relationship, you'd know it was Jamie who pursued Ellen. Pretty vigorously."

Michael smirked. "Yes, of course. She's very cute. I'm sure he was interested in going out with her. But marriage?"

"Can we make a pact?" Nia asked.

"I thought we had." She was getting spicy again. That was okay. He kind of missed it.

"A new one," she said. "Let's not talk about why we want this wedding not to happen. It's only going to lead to arguments."

"Who's arguing?"

"You and I in a few seconds if you keep insisting that my sister tried to trap your brother."

"For a tough girl, you're very sensitive."

He thought she was tough? Nia was a little flattered, but she wasn't sure if he meant it as a compliment or not. No telling with him. "I would question anyone who wasn't sensitive to insults to their family."

"Breaking up an engagement is an ugly thing to do. You can't take it personally."

"You have this wrong, Michael. I'm not trying to break up the engagement. I'm trying to prolong it, so Ellen has time to make sure she's made the right choice."

"Let's be serious, Nia. Right now, all you want is for Ellen to have time to realize that every man is the wrong choice."

"Are you calling me a man hater?" Nia's blood was boiling a little. It wasn't just what he was saying, but the nonchalant coolness with which he said it. "I'm not a man hater."

"You hate me," he said.

"That's because you're an ass." She found a quick hit of satisfaction in the unsettling effect her words seemed to have on him. "Besides, I don't hate you or any other man. Well, maybe Joe, but that will subside after a while. I love my sister, and all I'm doing is what's best for her. You're the one who's doing this out of anger, spite, and some type of misogynistic mistrust of women."

"Don't give me that." Michael was annoyed now. "I'm looking out for my sibling, just like you. I'm not going to apologize for that."

"Just forget it," Nia said. "We were stupid to think we could partner on this. Why don't you just do what you have to do and I'll do the same. We don't have to apologize to each other or say anything else to each other all week long."

"Fine."

It wasn't really fine. Michael realized that. As they walked in silence the rest of the way, he couldn't ignore his disappointment. He was getting to like Nia a little. *Let's face it: you're getting to like her a lot.* She was easy on the eyes and pretty complex, the latter being a quality he hadn't encountered in the last few women he had dated.

But in the end, what was it all for? He was leaving for

Denver Sunday, and if he did what he intended, the Randolphs and Vincents would not cross paths again. So maybe it was better if they stopped speaking. If his interest didn't go any further, he didn't have to like it.

Back at the house, some progress had been made, much to Nia's dismay. To make matters worse, Ellen had decided that the best way to deal with the differences in both families was to spend every waking moment together through Christmas. Nia felt her stomach get tighter and tighter as she was read the agenda for the Randolph/Vincent holiday season.

Dinner, volunteering, dinner again, dress shopping, tux shopping, dinner again, and a visit to both churches. To top it all off, Christmas morning together as a family. All Nia could think of was all that time spent with Michael and that annoyingly smug grin. She did not want this. And as she looked at his reaction, she realized he was thinking the same thing. What hit her hard was the anger that shot through her at the thought of his not wanting to be with her, even though it was what she wanted as well. How was she supposed to explain that to herself?

She didn't have time to figure it out. For the icing on the cake, Ellen made sure Nia and Michael were aware of their part in the distribution of responsibilities for planning this quick wedding.

"You two are in charge of the rehearsal dinner." She smiled, nodding her head as if this chore were a precious gift she had reserved just for them. "You don't have to do the invitations or catering or anything. Just find the place and book it for the night before, which we haven't figured out yet."

"I don't think—"

"Nia will be happy to handle that, won't you, dear?" Sharon gave her daughter a sideways glance. "Besides, she and Michael need something to do."

"I don't know about Nia," Michael said, stepping up to

the task with a wide grin on his face. "But I'm looking forward to it. Nia, if you don't want to, I can do it myself."

What was this? Was he trying to make her look bad? How dare he? She eyed him sternly, letting him know she was well aware of what he was up to. "Of course I want to do it. I want to help."

"Great." He nodded as if they had just solved a big problem. "We'll start tomorrow."

"Wonderful." Ellen applauded the decision, and returned her attention to a bridal magazine.

"Let's take a break and eat something before we go on." Jonelle stood up from the sofa, letting Michael take her arm and lead her to the kitchen. "Jamie, take everyone to the atrium. We'll be out in a minute."

Nia was certain Jonelle was asking Michael for gossip on her. She probably wanted to know what had caused Nia a near breakdown. She wondered what Michael would say. Would he be respectful and say, "None of your business, Mother," or spill the beans? She just wanted this day, which was already getting too long, to end.

It ended soon enough, with Nia making every attempt to avoid Michael. It wasn't hard. He appeared to want nothing to do with her, which unnerved her. What right did he have? She didn't want to care, but she did. And that became ever clearer to her as she felt the bolt of electricity run through her body when he showed up behind her in the foyer and touched her arm. It was a meaningless hey-I'm-here-so-turn-around touch, but it had a much greater effect on her.

"What?" She sighed as she spoke, not sure why. She was tired of the long day, and tired of not understanding why she was so preoccupied with Michael.

"I wasn't trying to show you up earlier," he said, not certain that he really wanted her to go. Even though she wouldn't talk to him, he enjoyed having her around. She was something to look at and interesting to watch.

"Yes, you were," she answered back.

"I just wanted to make sure no one got suspicious of your attitude."

"My attitude?" She refused to let him make her angry again. "You've got some nerve."

"Yes, Nia. You may not notice, but your attitude stinks. And as long as everyone thinks so, everything that comes out of your mouth is suspect."

She rolled her eyes, turning away to grab her coat. "Leave me alone, Michael."

"Self-pity doesn't flatter you, Nia. You have too much character for that."

Was that a compliment or an insult? She wasn't sure, but it made her feel better. How did he do that?

"If we both at least appear to have an optimistic attitude about this engagement and wedding, it won't look suspicious when we try to talk Jamie and Ellen out of it. It will make more sense to them."

She turned back to him, acquiescence on her face. He was right. "When do you want to meet tomorrow?"

"How about noon? Let's meet at Houston's. A friend of mine had an engagement party there a few years ago and it was nice. Make a list of places you'd like to see. We'll move on from there."

"Fine."

When his hand came to her shoulder, Nia inhaled sharply. She felt her entire body tingle at the deliberate softness of the touch. She was compelled to look into his eyes, those dark eyes that gave away nothing.

"Nia." Michael didn't know why he cared so much. There was no reason for it. "Just ... you know, all things come with time, like we talked about earlier. Don't let anyone tell you that because you're a woman you can't have it all."

Nia opened her mouth to say thank-you, but nothing came

out. She just stared at him. She couldn't recognize her feelings until those secretive eyes of his blinked and his hand on her shoulder tightened a bit. It was clear to her now that she wanted to kiss him, and she felt helpless against her desire.

"Nia," he whispered, stepping closer to her. Those magical green eyes were pulling him in, lighting a fire inside of him that centered in the pit of his stomach.

The footsteps and high-pitched chatter of Sharon and Ellen coming brought Nia back to a reality she had fallen frighteningly quickly away from. Something snapped, and she stepped back. Michael's hand fell from her shoulders, and a cold chill of regret swept through her.

"You get your wish, Nia," Sharon said, passing her daughter, completely unaware of the bewildered look on her face. "We're all tired, so let's go. Your father is coming."

"You all drive carefully," Michael said, his voice cracking just a bit.

He watched as Nia practically knocked her sister and mother down to get out of the house. Not sure what had just come over him, Michael chose the easy way out and decided to forget it. At least, he planned to forget it.

On the ride home, Nia stared out the window as her mother and sister talked endlessly about the small accomplishments of the day. Her father was, as usual, completely silent. She savored the familiar sights of Chicago, a city she loved with all of her heart. Her heart. *Just concentrate on the scenery,* she told herself—begged herself.

It didn't snow in Alexandria, Virginia, until January. She had gotten used to that after living there seven years now. Part of her appreciated that fact, making it easier on the day-to-day travel. But there was a part of her that had grown up with snow everywhere by Christmas, and that was what made it special. But then again, there was snow and there was temperature. A give and take.

Everything was a give and take in life, Nia realized. It just seemed like lately she was all give. She knew what she was feeling now was temporary, and she tried to remember that every time she wanted to break down and cry. It was easier said than done. Right now, all she felt was waste.

She would get over this mess with Joe. Even in one month she had made significant progress, in her own opinion. She would recover and get back on her feet. She just had to ride it out, and take what little bits of happiness and relief were afforded her until then.

What she never expected, though, was that in the last month, the only bits of happiness and relief she felt had come today from the most unlikely source—Michael Vincent.

DAY THREE—
MONDAY

"You're late." Michael tapped at his expensive watch as Nia made her way into the lobby of Houston's. Houston's was an upscale chain featuring American fare. Its Chicago location was similar to many others across the country, with tons of wood everywhere. The food was good. Nia had enjoyed the occasional dinner here during her postcollege, pre-Virginia days when she worked downtown.

"It's almost twelve-thirty. I don't like waiting around. I look like an idiot."

"You look like an idiot whether you're waiting or not," Nia said. "I had to take public transportation here, and there was a . . . Oh, just don't start with me."

Nia was somewhat grateful that he was being a jerk right off. She had been wondering how she would handle seeing him again, after having been able to think of nothing else but him all night and all morning. If he had been nice, it would have been harder on her. It was bad enough that he looked incredible. A well-built man in a turtleneck was hard to deny.

"I was kidding." He had hoped to lighten the mood, to make up for the heaviness with which they had left things. But she was already pissed off. So much for that. At least he wasn't to blame. "Alissa is waiting for us."

He gritted his teeth as she took off her coat, revealing a red sweater dress that fit her shapely curves as though it had been made just for her. Why did she have to look so good?

"Alissa?" Nia asked.

"About the party room? Come on." As if by instinct, he went to take hold of her arm, but Nia pulled away. He registered the sense of rejection. "I'm not going to bite you."

"I don't need to be led anywhere, Michael. I'm an adult." In actuality, she was scared of his touch, but she could never tell him that.

"There she is." An attractive blond-haired woman with large blue eyes and legs a mile long smiled wide, showing perfect teeth. She held her hand out to Nia, and shook hands vigorously. "We were waiting for you."

"Sorry I'm late." Nia knew the type: always happy, always perky. Much like Ellen. The opposite of herself.

"Don't worry about it." She looked Nia up and down. "She's beautiful. You two make such a gorgeous couple."

Nia's jaw dropped. She looked at Michael. "What did you tell her?"

"Nothing," he answered with a shrug. "I swear. Alissa, we aren't a couple. Our siblings are getting married and we're helping them out."

"Oh." She looked a little deflated. "Okay. Well, still. You look good together. Let's go."

"After you, sweetheart." Michael waved Nia passed him, smiling at the rolling of her eyes.

"Just behave," she said, trying to hide her smile.

Better, Michael thought. *Much better.*

As Alissa showed them the room and spoke of the romantic ways in which they could decorate it, Michael entertained Nia with an array of expressions from nausea to horror to distaste. She had to bite her lip to keep from laughing out loud. Alissa seemed annoyed with them toward the end of her presentation, which might explain why she stopped the sell shortly, gave them pamphlets, and sent them on their way.

"This is all your fault," Nia said as they got outside. She waited for Michael to give the valet his ticket. "If you hadn't been acting like a teenage boy back there, Alissa wouldn't feel like her time was wasted."

"My fault? It's your fault. If you hadn't had such a frown on your face, I wouldn't have felt compelled to cheer you up."

"Stop it." Nia wasn't a fan of the "nice" thing. It made him too easy to like, and that was dangerous.

"Did you eat before you came here?"

"Didn't have any time. But we're working here, Michael."

"I'm hungry. I want something to eat."

"Fine, we'll just eat at one of the restaurants on my list. I made this list that—"

"Screw that." He stepped forward as he saw his car coming around the corner. "I haven't been in Chicago in two years. They don't make food like this in Denver. I've got my own list I've got to get to."

"Michael." Nia placed her hand on her hip with an impatient sigh.

"It's just down the street here."

"Just down the street, my . . ." Nia unwrapped her hot dog and fries. "The object was to stay in the downtown area. Is there a reason why they wrap the fries up in the same wrapping as the hot dog? It makes a mess. There's ketchup all over—''

"That's the point." Michael dug into his food. Man, this was good. There was so much he loved about this city. "You wrap it all up together so you get fries in the hot dog, and ketchup, mustard, onions, relish, all that on the fries. This place is the best."

This place was outside the city limits on the south side— more than a few miles from downtown. It was a whole culture away from downtown.

Nia was hungry, so she ignored the presentation and dug in. It was good. "I guess I'm just surprised that you would choose this place."

"Because I'm a spoiled rich kid from the suburbs?" He washed his food down with an orange pop. Just like the good old days.

"Well, this is off the beaten path of what I'm sure the Vincents are used to." Nia wasn't sure if she had offended him or not. His posture said no, but his eyes wouldn't give anything away.

"Well, despite my austere upbringing, I was an expert at finding ways of keeping in touch with the common folks. You know, keeping it real."

Nia smiled. "I know all about keeping it real. I'm one of those common folk, remember?"

"It may surprise you to know that this perfect image of a man you see before you wasn't always so."

"I think this will be the first time I actually throw my lunch up while at the same time eating it."

He smirked at her sarcasm. Despite what he kept telling himself, he knew he really liked her spicy mouth and attitude, and preferred it when she had them going. "I spent my youth doing everything I could to be the black sheep in the family. I ran with the wrong crowd. Well, wrong in my family's eyes. They were regular guys. The only thing wrong with them was that they didn't come from wealthy families. So I'm well aware of all the flavor this city has to offer. Not just what's downtown.''

''Why were you so intent on being bad?'' Nia wasn't really so surprised. As perfect as he appeared to be, there was a hint of bad boy to Michael. It was a little exciting.

Michael shrugged. ''I don't know. I've always been curious as to how other people lived. Jamie was perfect—the real kind of perfect—so I guess I didn't think I needed to be.''

Nia knew all about playing favorites. She knew her parents loved her, and that was enough. ''Do you regret that?''

''My childhood? No way. I guess the only regrets I have are in the present.''

''Like what?''

''It's a long story. You don't want to hear it.''

''Hey, wait a second. I bared my soul to you yesterday.''

''Sobbed like a baby.'' He rolled his eyes. ''It was a pitiful scene.''

Nia reached across the small circular table and punched him in the arm. ''You're awful. Stop it.''

''Okay.'' He loved her smile. It was so . . . genuine. ''My history of coming home for Christmas hasn't been stellar. Three years ago, I showed up for one and a half days. Two years ago, I showed up for one day. Last year, I didn't show up at all.''

''Not everyone can be home every Christmas. I'm sure you had a good reason.'' Nia softened at the look on his face. He wasn't joking around. He felt really bad.

''I was in Aspen with a supermodel.''

Nia felt her entire body tense. Another model. ''Anyone famous?''

''I'd rather not mention.''

"You traded in your family for a roll in the hay with a two-pound clothes hook?"

"Hey."

Nia wrapped her food back up. Her appetite was gone. Another model. "Never mind. I'm sorry I asked."

Michael was confused, but only for a second, as he quickly realized what he had said. "I'm not Joe."

"I never said you were."

"You didn't have to. Nia, I—"

"Just forget it. Can we get going soon? I have this list of restaurants that we have to check out, and the day only lasts so long."

Michael sighed, realizing that the good times were over for the day. "How is this going to work if I can't even speak without analyzing everything I have to say first?"

"I've never asked anything of you, Michael. And *this,* what you're referring to, is just for one day. We have six places to visit, and I'll come up with a place."

"To have a rehearsal dinner that we don't even want to happen."

"None of this makes sense." Nia stood up. "This is too much drama for me."

"You're causing it all."

"All the better for you if we get this day over with. I'll be waiting outside."

He watched her leave, noticing the distinct sashay in her hips. "Fine," he mumbled under his breath. "Freeze your butt off; I don't care. I'm done being the peacemaker."

Man, she had a good walk.

"I don't understand," Sharon Randolph said, her eyes set on Michael in astonishment. "You and Nia were together, but she took the El train home and you drove?"

Jonelle Vincent made a smacking sound with her lips. "You could have given her a ride, Michael."

Michael should have known Nia had an ulterior motive. She had been cold and distant for the rest of their wedding mission, only making the already freezing day colder. He felt completely blameless, which only fueled his anger. Despite that, he had expected to give her a ride back to the Randolph house, since they were all meeting there for dinner and to decorate the Christmas tree. When she refused, he thought she was joking. In the end he'd let her go. He'd had enough of her attitude for the day anyway.

But the reaming he was getting as he showed up at the Randolph house sans Nia made him realize that this was her intention all along. He'd been in the living room listening to both mothers tell him off while his brother, his father, and Gene Randolph just sat in the kitchen playing cards. No sympathy. No backup.

He would get her back for this.

"Michael." Jonelle shook her head. "This is so like you."

"I'll say it one last time." Michael stood up, as if that gave him some authority. "I practically begged her and almost physically forced her to get into my car. She flat-out refused. She's being a baby."

Jonelle wasn't buying it. "I just don't see why she would do something like that. It's freezing outside. Unless, of course, you were being a jerk."

"Thanks for your support, Mom."

"Come on, ladies." Ellen called out from the kitchen. "Help me put this food on the table."

Jonelle paused a few more seconds to stare at Michael before throwing her hands in the air and walking out.

"Well," Sharon said as she opened a box of tree lights and laid them on the sofa. "I know that Nia can be difficult at times. That is why she can't keep a man. She never gives."

"I don't think that's fair, Mrs. ... Sharon," Michael

said. ''Nia is as stubborn as a mule, but I wouldn't fault her for whatever happened with her and Joe.''

''What do you know about Joe?''

''I know enough to know that he was a jerk.''

''I'm not defending Joe's behavior, but I have to say that this wouldn't have happened if Nia had put her man first.''

''Come on, Sharon. You know that's ridiculous. Men who cheat, cheat because they're cheaters. They could have the best of women or the worst. They'll still cheat, because that's what cheaters do. I haven't known Nia a long time, but I sincerely doubt she's the type of woman to treat her man like a side dish. I'm sure she gave him all she had. She has a right to a career, and a right to a man who respects and supports that career. And she has a right to a mother who tells her so.''

Sharon blinked, but showed no other signs of being affected by Michael's words. He figured he had gone too far, and wasn't sure why he'd even started down that path. He was being disrespectful to this woman in her house.

''Mrs. Randolph, I . . .'' He shut up as she turned and walked away. *That went well.*

''Thank you.''

Nia threw her coat and purse on the chair as she entered the living room. She fought back the tears, scared of the emotion that was welling up inside of her. She couldn't believe what she had heard him say. How he had stood up for her in a way she couldn't for herself. Why had his simple words moved her so much?

''Nia, I . . .'' Michael felt himself touched deeply by the fragile posture she held. He wanted to hold her. ''I hope I haven't made things worse.''

''You shut Sharon Randolph up.'' She tried to smile, but really couldn't. Her eyes smiled. His words were still sounding in her mind. In her heart. ''That puts you in a class of one.''

"I got a good thrashing for showing up without you. I get the feeling you aren't too surprised about that."

This time she was able to find a smile. "I'm sorry. Can we call a truce?"

He titled his head to the side. "Why don't I get my revenge and then we'll call a truce?"

Nia held her hand out to him, knowing what the consequences might be. "Why don't we just call a truce now?"

He took her hand, his gut feeling making him want to pull her to him and kiss her. Just like he'd felt last night—kiss her good and hard. She was a hurting woman, and he wanted to do his part to help heal her.

Nia felt a rush of energy surge through her from his touch, but she didn't fight it. She welcomed it. It felt good, and it was what she needed right now. "Let's go eat."

Dinner was drama-free, and Nia felt relaxed for the first time in a long time. Not a word from her mother mentioning Joe or anything related. It was nice. Ellen and Jamie seemed very pleased with her choice for a rehearsal dinner, and the others had made progress in whatever their duties were that day. Dinner was spent talking about Christmases past, the good, bad, and ugly—mostly good.

Nia sat across from Michael, and although they spoke very little during the meal, they exchanged glances, some friendly, some more than friendly. Nia faced facts: they were flirting and she enjoyed it. There was a sense of recklessness about it that made her feel young and free. Made her forget about all the negatives in her life.

Their flirting continued to the tree trimming as the entire family joined in. Well, it started out as the entire family, but quickly lost its fervor.

Edward and Gene were in the den watching Monday Night Football. Jamie and Ellen had gone to get eggnog for everyone. Sharon had taken a call from her sister in Las Vegas, and Jonelle excused herself for a cigarette, leaving Michael and Nia alone.

"Pass me that ornament." Nia reached down, not wanting to be too unsteady on the stepping stool. "I would have never figured Jonelle for a smoker."

"She only smokes when she's nervous." He smiled when their hands brushed as she took the ornament. She was very soft. "The holidays always make her nervous."

There was that little flutter in her belly again. He really had a great smile. "You know you don't have to stay and help me with this. I know you want to watch football."

"I'm not bailing on you, Nia." He looked longingly toward the den. As much as he loved Monday Night Football, there would be other Mondays. He doubted there would be plenty of times to decorate a Christmas tree with a beautiful woman who smelled like fresh flowers. "Besides, I'm a having a pretty good time."

"You don't seem like the tree-trimming type." She held her hand down for another ornament.

"Actually I'm not. I don't think I can remember trimming a tree. I don't have one in Denver, and the one at home is always done by the time I get there."

"If you show up at all."

He jabbed her in her thigh. "Low blow."

"Just kidding. Not even growing up?"

He shook his head. "Mother did it herself. I think I remember Jamie helping her once or twice. She never asked me, and I never volunteered. Didn't have the patience."

"So I should feel grateful then?"

"I think I'm the one who should be grateful. This view of your rear is better than Christmas morning."

With a gasp, Nia swung at him. She'd meant to do it gently, but had swung too hard and lost her balance. Before she could let out a yell, she was falling off the stool and hurtling helplessly to the ground. She felt Michael's hands grab hold of her waist with a hard, firm grip. As he tried to steady her, she took hold of his shoulders to keep herself up.

Suddenly she was facing him, and with her body tightly against his, the swirl of fear in her stomach quickly turning to something else. Looking in his eyes, she saw a cloud of desire form, and she knew what was coming.

His lips came down on hers with a force that took them both off guard. Michael felt an animal hunger rise up within him that erased all reality. His heart jolted and his pulse pounded as the touch of her soft lips made his body groan. He knew he'd wanted her, but hadn't realized how much until this moment.

It was like a maddening storm that raged in the pit of Nia's stomach, his lips sending a hot fire coursing through her veins. Nia wrapped her arms around his neck, clinging tighter to him. She let his lips open hers, and his tongue entered her mouth. A delicious shudder rushed through her at the taste of him, and she heard a faint moan through the thundering sound of her heart.

Michael felt an aching in his groin as his mouth left hers and went to her neck. Her skin was so soft, smelled so good. He wanted to taste every bit of her. "Nia."

"Michael." His name came as a whisper as she felt his hands slide up and down her hips. His touch was almost painful, it felt so good. "Kiss me again."

His lips recaptured hers, more possessive now, as if he knew they belonged to him. She was making him drunker than any wine. Her soft curves tantalized him. She was thin, but she wasn't bony. She had a woman's body, and he wanted to get to it. But for now he just drank in her lips, her warm tongue. Tasting her, he wanted her more and more each second.

Just as Nia felt her mind about to leave her, she heard a

door slam, and her eyes flew open. She separated her lips from his reluctantly. "Michael, someone is coming."

Slowly, his mind taking a moment to return to him, he backed away. He let his hands fall to his sides, but wasn't happy about it. He could have gone on forever.

Their eyes locked on each other, neither of them certain how it began, but knowing they didn't want it to end. Jonelle's presence in the room lowered the tension only a bit.

"Where is everyone?" Jonelle threw her hands in the air. "This is ridiculous. I go out for five minutes and the crowd disperses. Honestly, I don't think Ellen and Jamie are ever coming back."

As she grabbed a box of colorful bulbs, she ignored Michael and Nia, who still stood there, arms at their sides, unable to do or say anything.

"Nia."

Sharon stood in the archway of the room. "The phone is for you."

Nia meant to ask who it was, but she just stared.

Her mother put her hands on her hips. "Would you get to the phone, girl? It's Joe. He sounded miserable. He was desperate to talk to you. That's a good sign."

"Joe?" That was enough to snap Nia out of her trance. What would Joe be calling her here for? Especially considering she had told him she would cut his you-know-what off if he ever called her again.

As Nia walked past him, Michael felt a pang of jealousy hit him. More than a pang, he had to admit. The way she'd changed when his name was mentioned. The way she had not been able to take her eyes away from him, but then suddenly didn't even see him as she walked by.

"What was I thinking?" he asked himself, stuffing his hands in his pants pockets. He felt like a fool. Why would he let himself kiss her? This was stupid. He was stupid.

"Did you say something, Michael?" Sharon asked, as she brushed by him and joined Jonelle at the tree.

He cleared his throat, knowing that the frustration was only going to build. "Look, ladies, I think I'm going to head out."

"Michael." Jonelle gave him her usual disappointed look. "Running off to meet a woman, I bet. I thought we talked about that."

"Old habits are hard to break, Mother." He leaned forward, kissing her on the cheek. "Mrs. Randolph, thanks for dinner and . . ."

Sharon pressed her lips together, letting him know she hadn't forgotten their earlier encounter.

"Thanks for everything," he added.

"Michael," Jonelle called after him, "remember tomorrow at the homeless shelter. We're giving away presents."

"More Randolph/Vincent family fun." He waved a goodbye with his back turned. He didn't have any more smile in him. Not even a fake one. He needed to get out of there and clear his head. He had come here to solve a problem, but all he was doing was creating an even bigger one for himself.

He was falling for Nia Randolph, a woman who was on the rebound. A definite no-no.

After taking a moment to compose herself, Nia returned to the living room. Her first thought, her only thought, was of Michael. They needed to talk. When he wasn't there, she was thrown.

"What did he want?" Sharon asked, hurrying to her daughter. "Does he want to get back together?"

Nia felt a full-on sense of disappointment. "Yes, Mother. He says he realizes the error of his ways. There is no way a twenty-two-year-old can be a life partner. I'm sure she just dumped him."

"Don't talk like that, Nia. She's out of his life. That's what matters."

"No, Mother. What matters is that she was in his life at all. That can't be undone. Just give it up. I told him to go to hell."

"Watch your language, young lady." Sharon sighed helplessly. "What did you do that for? You're not getting any younger, Nia. You don't have that option."

"I'll always have the option of not being with a man who cheats on me." She looked toward the den. "Did Michael join the guys in the den?"

"Forget Michael," Jonelle said, busy at the tree. "He's off to meet one of his ex-girlfriends. I knew he was going to do this."

Nia felt as if she had been socked in the stomach. "What do you mean?"

"He said he's off to meet a woman," Sharon answered, annoyed that the subject had changed. "What does it matter? I want to talk about Joe. What did he say exactly?"

Nia thought she was in the twilight zone. Had she imagined that kiss? Had she imagined the entire night? Anger began its early rise inside of her, but hurt had it beat by a step.

"Mama," she said, holding her stomach, "I'm not feeling well. I think I need to go lie down. I'm just upset . . . from talking to Joe. I . . ."

She didn't finish her sentence. She wasn't even really listening to herself. She just needed to get away from everyone.

In her bedroom, Nia stared out the window down the quiet Evanston street. The town rolled up the sidewalks by nine P.M. It always had.

What had happened? Nia knew she hadn't had the sanest of months, but she wasn't crazy. That kiss had been the most passionate kiss she could ever remember having—

and that included Joe. He was completely erased from her mind—until he called, that was.

And the second she stepped away, Michael left to meet another woman? Had he known he was meeting her all night long? During the flirtatious glances and smiles and suggestive words?

How could he have spoken so diligently about cheaters and done what he had done—kissed her and run off to another woman? *Men!*

She would *not* let another man hurt her. She would not be another sucker. *Forget Joe, forget Michael, forget everything.* Nia just wanted this week to be over so she could get back home.

DAY FOUR—TUESDAY

The Family Circle shelter was at the edges of the city and the western suburbs. It was one of the biggest in the Midwest, and required a great deal of community support. The Randolph family had been volunteering there for almost twenty years. They would come to feed the homeless, prepare food, give away gifts, and, of course, take part in the Thanksgiving and Christmas holidays with the residents.

Family Circle was for families, but mostly housed women and children—young children, and it broke Nia's heart to see such small children without a home to call their own. This shelter gave her an opportunity to give back to the community, but it also helped her keep things in perspective. She was blessed, and she needed to thank God every day for that.

And she had thanked him this morning for all of his blessings, making sure to add a little request for strength to get through another day around Michael Vincent. Nia found herself obsessed with thoughts of Michael and where he had gone last night. Had he planned it all along? Who was she? What did she look like? Was she the model type? What did they do? Why? Why? Why? She felt herself getting nauseous with humiliation at the thought of him.

Which made all the keener the confusion and the sense of deflation Nia felt when she didn't see him in the shelter at all. The place was bustling as usual. Jonelle, Jamie, and Edward were helping stack presents under the fake but wonderfully adorned Christmas tree while a big, fat Santa took a seat. There were at least a couple dozen other volunteers and workers running in and out of the kitchen getting lunch ready or trying to keep the children away from Santa and the presents until it was time.

No Michael. Why did she care? Nia didn't understand. Yes, she was attracted to him. Yes, she had feelings for him, especially after he had spoken up for her to her own mother. Not to mention that kiss. Man, that was some kiss. But he was no good for her. He wouldn't treat her right. Last night had told her that.

No, he wasn't her boyfriend. But a man who went from one woman's lips to another woman's bed in the same night was not one who could be trusted. But here she was, full of anxiety, hoping and wishing that he would come from the kitchen, the bathroom, or anywhere else.

"Take that frown off your face, Nia." Sharon gave her a jab in the ribs. "Smiles for the kids today."

Nia pasted a smile on, doing her best to remind herself why she was here. This was more important than a stupid kiss from a selfish man.

"Feeling better, Nia?" Jamie asked after giving her a hug.

"What do you mean?" She got right to work, hoping for anything to take her mind off of Michael.

"You were sick last night. Mother said that's why you

went to bed early. I'm assuming you're better now that
you're here.''

"Yes.'' She nodded. "I'm much better now. I wouldn't
miss this for anything in the world. I'm glad you guys could
come.''

"I've actually been here before,'' he said. "Ellen brought
me. She told me about what you guys do here every Thanksgiving and Christmas, and I thought it was great. We're all
happy to be here.''

"Too bad Michael couldn't join in.'' She bit her lip for
even mentioning it, but couldn't help it. "I guess he had a
late night.''

"I wouldn't agree with that.''

Nia's eyes widened as she swung around. She had heard
Michael's voice, but there was no . . .

Santa. There had never been a Santa with eyes as angry
as this one's. They stared her down, the only image that
was recognizable as Michael.

So he was here. And he had heard her ask about him.
*Good job, Nia. Now he knows you cared. So much for your
plan to seem unfazed.*

"I . . .'' She pressed her lips together, frustrated at her
speechlessness. "Never mind.''

"That sounds better,'' Michael said. She wasn't anyone
to pass judgment on him. She had no idea what he had been
doing last night. Whatever it was she thought, it couldn't
have been farther from the truth.

He had driven around to a few neighborhoods where he
knew women who would be very receptive to his surprise
visit. But he didn't go in. He didn't want to. In his mind,
there was nothing more pitiful than a man who had to sleep
with random women to prove his manhood. So he just went
back to Jamie's apartment and watched football. He let his
pride crush any bit of pity that wanted to come. Every time
he thought of Nia on the phone with Joe, knowing she still

cared for him, he was awash with anger and jealousy, which he vowed he would never let any woman make him feel. No woman was worth as helpless an emotion as jealousy.

But Nia was not just any woman. He was reminded of that the moment she walked into the shelter. But he vowed to stay away from her. *Just keep your distance. A week goes by in the blink of an eye.*

Jamie laughed uncontrollably. "I swear, man, every time I see you in that outfit I . . . Hey, there's got to be a store with a camera around here."

"If you take a picture of me," Michael warned, "I'll rip it apart."

"Keep your voice down," Ellen whispered. "You're Santa, remember? Stop being such a spoilsport about it. The other Santa couldn't make it."

"Dad or Gene would have been much better than me." Michael scratched at his ribs. This suit was itching the heck out of him.

Ellen shook her head. "Daddy has to leave in an hour to get back to work, and your father has that condition. He can't have kids hopping up and down on his lap like that."

Michael rolled his eyes. "There are other people. . . ."

"Just stop it, Mike." Jamie was still laughing. "Two hours, tops. Then you're done."

It was more than two hours. It was closer to three before the last child had sat on Michael's lap, received a present, had their picture taken, and gone on their way. Nia couldn't help but be touched. It was a special scene. The smiles on those kids' faces were priceless. What really touched her was Michael. She knew he was annoyed by the duty bestowed upon him, but she couldn't have told if she didn't know. He smiled, told jokes, made fun, and the kids laughed at it all.

She was falling for him, and she knew it. It was this side, the side that peeked out from that emotionless exterior, that really got to her. And she was helpless to fight it. Her heart had a mind of its own. What was she to do?

"Look what I got!" Jamie held up a disposable camera with a flash. "For our private collection."

"Jamie." Michael was already standing up after the last kid had finished. His legs were killing him. "If you take a picture of me . . ."

"What's the problem?" Jamie said, aiming the camera. "You've just had about a hundred pictures taken of you."

"Those will never be seen by friends of mine." Michael watched as Ellen and Nia cleaned up stray papers and wrappings.

He had found an unsettling pleasure in watching her the past few hours. And those moments, those few moments when she had looked at him made him feel so . . . so good he didn't know what to think.

"Sit down, bro." Jamie ignored the threats, knowing they weren't serious. "I want a picture in action. Hey, Nia. Come and sit on his lap."

Nia froze as if she had been told to by the police. "What?"

Jamie gestured at her. "Go sit on Mike's lap. Mike, sit down."

"Go on," Ellen said, seeming excited by the idea. "Sit down, Michael. It'll be great. Come on, be a sport."

"No." Nia resisted as Ellen pushed her toward Michael.

"Stop being such a baby," Ellen said, giving her one big final push.

"No." Nia was already feeling the tension build up inside of her. She was frightened of it, knowing that she wouldn't able to control herself if she actually touched him.

There were those times when a man did something out of challenged pride when he knew with every bit of sense God gave him that he should let it go. For Michael, this was one of those times.

"Come on, Nia." He sat back down, waving her over.

She was acting as if she would catch something just from his touch. He slapped his knee. "What's the matter? Are you scared of me?"

She sneered at him, seeing his delight in her discomfort. He wasn't going to get the best of her. After all, she had prayed. God was on her side, right?

"Fine," she said, sitting down on his lap. "Let's get this over with."

"Loosen up, Nia." Jamie lowered the camera. "You look like you're frozen. Loosen your arms."

"Yes, Nia." Michael took offense at the way she so obviously was intent on not touching him. He wrapped his right arm around her waist. "Warm up. This ice-queen thing doesn't suit you."

"Shut up, Michael." She glared at him, turning to Jamie. How long could she last? "Take the picture."

"Try something more like last night," Michael said. "You were a lot warmer then."

Nia's stomach tightened, as she felt her body react to his mention of last night. The kiss was still with her. But so was her dignity, and he was offending it. No man got away with that.

Nia realized his body was covered in layers of thick fabric, but his hands were bare. Without warning, she grabbed a fingerful of skin off the back of his left hand and twisted as hard as she could.

Michael let out a curse so loud that the entire shelter went silent. Everyone stared at him. With a raging face, he looked at Nia.

She smiled victoriously. "So nice of Santa to teach all the little kids a new word today."

She stood up, head held high, and walked away.

"I didn't get the picture," Jamie said, as she passed him.

"That's okay," Nia answered. "Your brother got the picture just fine."

"Just bring it on," Michael said as he saw his mother heading for him. This scolding was going to take at least the next hour of his life.

Nia watched as Jamie and Ellen rocked back and forth in each other's arms. She was so torn. Part of her didn't trust any man, and her experience with Michael did nothing to help that. She and Ellen had never been incredibly close, but she loved her sister with all of her heart and didn't want her hurt by anyone.

But now, as she watched them stealing a moment in the back alley of the homeless shelter, she saw something that seemed genuine. *Seemed* being the operative word here. Who was she to interfere? Maybe Ellen was the exception to the rule.

For so long, Nia had thought *she* was the exception. She couldn't fool herself into believing that things were perfect until a month ago. Things had been falling apart between her and Joe for a while. But she never thought he would walk away from her. She always thought they would eventually work it out. They had time.

"There you are."

Outwardly, she ignored Michael's presence. She didn't even turn to acknowledge him. Internally, she felt her stomach flutter and her heart do a little flip.

Michael bit down the hurt he felt at her rejection, but didn't leave. He sat next to her on the steps. "You know that whole thing was your fault."

Nothing.

Michael did not like being ignored. "Nia, I'm the one who's supposed to be mad at you."

Nothing.

"Nia, look at me."

Slowly she turned to him. She saw the anger in his eyes,

surprised by its intensity. She had really upset him. Nia didn't want to feel guilty, but she did.

"What's the matter with you?" Michael couldn't ignore the feelings that stirred within him in response to the pained look on her face.

Nia turned away, shaking her head. She looked at Ellen and Jamie kissing. "Look at them. Do we really want to mess with that?"

He looked at his brother, who looked happier than he had ever seen him. "We're not messing with it, Nia. If its meant to be, it will happen. Just more like a year from now instead of four months."

"Who says they'll have a year from now? Everyone thinks there's always time. There isn't. Anything can happen."

There was a silence, with Michael not knowing whether she even expected him to respond to her. This was why he stayed away from these types of conversations with women. They were so complicated. And Nia was probably more complicated than most. But he wanted to talk to her.

"So you're giving up?" he asked. "You're going to let this happen?"

She shrugged. "I don't really care."

"Of course you do. She's your sister."

"She should be allowed to make her own mistakes. God knows I have."

"But that's part of being a big sister. Like being a big brother, we have a duty to spare the younger ones from our own mistakes."

"I have my own problems," Nia said, circling her neck to stretch it out.

The gesture had a dangerous effect on Michael. He wanted her so badly. "You're talking about me?"

She looked at him, wondering if he was joking or for real. It was hard to tell with him, and her heart was a little too fragile right now to guess. "I'm talking about me."

Michael was amazed at her ability to make him feel guilty for something that wasn't even his own fault. "Look, Nia, about last night—"

"Please." She held up her hand to him. "I don't want to talk about last night."

"Was it that bad?"

Her eyes answered that. She couldn't hide it. "It was just not a good idea."

"Obviously."

"What the hell is that supposed to mean?" Nia wasn't sure what she expected, but his brushoff was hurtful.

"I can't say anything right," Michael said, confused by her response and smarting from her insistence that the most passionate encounter he could remember having in a long time wasn't a good idea. "I've been thinking about last night."

"With me or with the other woman you were with?"

He frowned, wondering if she was crazy or what. Then he smiled. "Oh, you think I was . . . No, Nia. I wasn't with another woman last night. I just didn't feel like proving that to my mother, so she thought I was. I was by myself last night, and fast asleep by the time Jamie got home. You could ask him."

"I don't really care," she said, knowing she was a bold-faced liar. She cared a lot. But if he wasn't with another woman . . . "Then why, Michael? Why did you leave?"

"I wasn't sure you would've noticed after Joe called."

Was he jealous? She found it a little charming. "That's ridiculous. Joe is the past."

"Sure didn't look like it when your mother said he was on the phone. You had just been in my arms kissing me pretty passionately, but I felt like you didn't even know I was there."

"I was just surprised. It was nothing. I think I told him off well enough. He won't be calling again." She threw her hands in the air. "Maybe it's for the best, Michael. I mean, what we were doing, anyway?"

"Do we have to know?"

She nodded. "Yes, I do. I'm not a man. I can't just lip-lock with someone and walk away."

"Thanks for the gender jab," he said. "That was very appropriate and well deserved."

"You're very sensitive."

"Isn't that the pot calling the kettle—"

"I don't want to argue with you, Michael. Just forget it."

"Fine." He stood up, unable to think of anything to say to her. "No matter what that kiss was about last night, Nia, you're not available."

"For what?" she asked looking up. He was angry, and that hurt. "For a holiday affair? What more could it have been? I live in Virginia; you're in Denver."

"Get over it, Nia." Michael didn't need to listen to any more of this. "We only have four more days. Even I'm mature enough to control myself for that long. Then we'll go our separate ways."

Don't cry. Don't cry. Don't you dare cry or . . . . Too late. A runaway tear trailed down her left cheek. It was as if she had wanted that to happen. Her attitude stank; she knew that. As much as she wanted to blame Michael, she couldn't. And now her heart was involved.

Only four more days?

DAY FIVE— WEDNESDAY

Nia slept in all day Wednesday. She ignored her mother's complaints, her sister's concerns. She refused calls from old friends, and sustained herself on sunflower seeds and grape pop. It was a remedy that had worked her entire childhood, and she had faith it would work this time. She was sick of feeling like this. Her head was clogged, and she could muster only pity for herself and anger for everyone else. She needed to get everything out of her system: Joe, Michael, everything. She was no good to herself or anyone else until she got her head clear and got back on track.

Michael took a break from the world. He skipped out of the apartment before Jamie or anyone else could get hold of him. He drove to the old YMCA, where he used to hang out with his boys, and played hoops for hours. He stopped by a couple of old spots for comfort food, and did some last-minute Christmas shopping.

He wanted—needed—to get Nia off his mind. She was clouding his head up, and that wasn't fair. He'd done nothing to deserve this. He never anticipated anything happening between them. Nor did he feel responsible for it—not solely responsible, at least. Yet here he was, gnashing his teeth, going over every conversation and encounter they had had since meeting earlier that week. Nothing made any sense. Nothing.

DAY SIX—THURSDAY

"This one is perfect." Ellen turned around in circles with a satin-tressed wedding gown laid against her chest. "I want them to try this one on too."

"You've said that about the last five dresses," Sharon said as she handed the dress in question to the salesgirl. "Please get this in a size two. Thank you."

"I can't help it." Ellen rushed back to the rack of preselected dresses.

Delana's was an exclusive Chicago wedding boutique that, according to Jonelle, every fine girl used for a wedding dress. It was by appointment only, and Jonelle had set up that morning for them. There was no one else in the downtown store. No one else was allowed. Not only did the store proprietors have a veritable buffet waiting for the women, but they came prepared with a preselected suggestion of dresses and two models waiting to parade for them.

"Try this one," Nia said, holding up a wonderful off-white strapless number. "Look at it, Ellen; it's got an A-line like you want."

Ellen grabbed at it as if it were food and she hadn't eaten in months.

"What's gotten into you, Nia?" Sharon took a sip of champagne. "You're so . . . You're just different. I thought I was gonna have to call the pastor yesterday to exorcise you."

"Just had a few things I needed to work through my system." Nia smiled at her with a careless shrug of her shoulders.

"What things?"

"Not important." Nia returned to the dresses.

She was feeling much better now. Much better. The old-fashioned rituals were always the best. She was so clear about the situation with Joe that she amazed even herself. She was over it. Lesson learned, and, most important, it wasn't her fault. Mothers would always be mothers. That was a right they earned for all the work they put in. But it didn't matter.

"Well, it's a good thing, at least," Sharon said. "You were no good to anyone with that attitude of yours."

"Mama, you should be happy I come home at all. With all the grief you give me over my spinsterhood, it's a surprise I even consider coming home."

"You think that's funny? Spinsterhood. You looking forward to it? Because I think thirty is when you officially become one."

"She's right, Sharon." Jonelle sat delicately in a royal-crested chair, her legs crossed perfectly over each other. "I've got to hope Michael will come home at all now. Be happy she's here."

Michael. That was the only aside in Nia's life. She had been able to work everything out except for him. Michael Vincent. With all the other guck out of the way, Nia was able to see more clearly what was going on with her and Michael. That was, she was able to see more clearly that it made no sense. She had been attracted to him from the moment she saw him, even when she was reaming him for insulting her sister. When he danced with her, she had felt the sparks even through the insult of his presumption. And then later at the bar that night, there was that one moment there, when she was about to rip into him again, that she felt herself more inclined to rip his shirt off.

And so went every encounter since then. Add the few moments when he actually showed a heart, and it built up to a case of what? Something. She didn't know what, but could only hope that it would work its way out after she had gone back home.

As far as men in general were concerned, that was still an open book. She would have to open her heart again. Despite what her mother said, she was too young to She wanted to be in love. She loved being in love, and held on to the hope that all of these attempts at love would pay off in the end. How would she know? No telling.

"Ellen." Nia came around the side of the rack of dresses to her sister, who seemed entranced and overwhelmed. "I have to ask you something."

"I don't know what to do." She was biting her nails so hard, there was sure to be blood soon. "There are so many, and they're all gorgeous. Nia, I can't stand it. I'm going to go crazy."

"Calm down." Nia squeezed her shoulder. "They'll all look different on the models, and you'll see that most of them are putrid. It'll narrow down the field quickly. I have to ask your advice."

Ellen's eyes widened in shock. "You're asking me for advice? Well, this is a first."

"Whatever." Nia leaned closer, not wanting the mothers to hear. "How do you know?"

"I don't know," she answered. "That's why I want them to try every single dress on. Every one of them."

"No, Ellen." Nia grabbed her at the shoulders to keep her attention. "I mean Jamie. How did you know that he was different from all the other guys you've been in love with?"

Ellen seemed dumbfounded as she stared blankly at her sister. Her eyes squinted as she strained to remember something. Nia needed to hear a response soon. Something.

"We were at Starbucks." A softness and a sense of calm spread across her face. "The one next to the hospital. I got a café latte and he got a café mocha. I don't know why I got it. I always get the café mocha. He always gets the same drink too. I guess I thought I'd be adventurous. Anyway, we sat down over some general conversation. Then I took a sip of my drink. Didn't like it. Tried another sip. Hated it. So I just said, you know, not meaning anything by it, not expecting any response, but I said, 'I don't like this. It doesn't taste good.' That's all I said.

"Nia, he didn't even blink. He didn't even take a second to think. He just took my cup, and gave me his. He drank my cup, and I drank his, and he just went back to talking. Like it was nothing. It was like breathing for him to make me happy, to solve my problem. I knew at that moment that—"

"This was the guy you wanted to spend the rest of your life with." Nia was already in tears, just thinking of it. "And to think, I was going to try to talk you out of this. What a fool."

"Don't worry about it." Ellen leaned forward, kissing her sister on the cheek. "I know what you're going through right now. Remember Alex Cramer? Left me for the waitress."

Nia nodded, barely remembering. "I wish I had been there for you more when that happened."

"I know. We've never been that close. It's okay. There

will always be time for us to both make up for it in the future.''

''Everybody says that, Ellen. I don't want to think that way. We need to work at getting closer now.''

Ellen seemed a bit confused, but smiled nonetheless. ''Okay.''

''That's my new motto in life,'' Nia said. ''Live like you won't have forever to get something done.''

Her first thought went to Michael. She wanted him. Regardless of what he felt for her now, she wanted to be with him. That fact came through loud and clear, although all the points around how this fact came to be were everything but clear. He probably wanted nothing to do with her.

''Hey.'' She poked her sister for her attention. ''When are we meeting up with the guys again?''

Michael could tell Jamie was in a bad state. They were all, all the men at least, supposed to meet at Jets, the elite man's choice for tailored tuxedos. Michael knew he didn't want to go, but he did it anyway. He had bailed on them all yesterday and felt pretty much obligated to do whatever was asked of him. Besides, he had gotten everything out of his system yesterday. Well, almost everything.

In the end, Michael was the only one to show.

''I mean, I can understand Gene not showing up,'' Jamie said, looking through one of at least ten booklets given him by the salesman. ''I'm not his son. Personally, I'm surprised Mom even asked him. But I would expect Dad to show up. He's not working at all this week.''

''Jamie. We're not even doing anything but looking at tuxes.'' Michael held up a hand to ward off a salesman on his way. ''You know Dad. If it isn't about the law, he's not interested'

Jamie smiled. "I'm glad you're here, bro. I was afraid you wouldn't come home again."

Michael sighed. His brother deserved an apology. The whole family did. "I'm sorry about last year, Jamie. That was weak, what I did. Honestly, I'm sorry for the half-assed attempt I've made for Christmas for the last few years. I'll do better from now on."

"Meaning my wedding? It's in four months, man. You have to come back."

"Jamie, have you really thought this through?"

Jamie slammed the magazine closed. "Don't start this!"

"Just hear me out," Michael said. "I'm only trying to help you."

"Help me with what? To end up alone like you probably will."

"That was a low blow, man."

"Well, maybe everyone doesn't want to be a bachelor for life."

"Neither do I, Jamie, but you need to take time to know—"

"Don't you ever think about coming home to a woman who loves you, who has your back no matter what? Getting out of that high-rise condo of yours and moving into a house with a den and a backyard where you barbeque? A table in the kitchen where your kids drink their juice and you read the paper?"

Michael paused, dealing with the reality of the situation. "I think about it a lot. More than I'll admit to you right now. I'm just not going to let my desire for that trick me into marrying the first—"

"That's not what this is about. I've been in love before Ellen. It was never like this. And don't tell me I need more time to be sure. Time is for people with insecurities and uncertainties. There's a way that a woman touches something inside of a man. The only thing that keeps a man from knowing it is being open to it. Guys like you are so mistrusting. You see a woman, and the first thing you do is start protecting yourself.

"If you just let it go, like I did, you'll know. I let all that crap go long before I met Ellen. And I went out with a few women. It wasn't there. But when I met her . . . when I first met her, I knew. She made me completely frustrated and excited at the same time. I cared about her with no rhyme or reason. From the first moment I saw her, I wanted to save her from everything in the world, but I was in awe of her strength at the same time. I wanted her in my bed immediately, but knew that her mind was going to blow me away. If you ever feel that way about someone, you'll know. And you won't need a two-year courtship to figure it out."

No rhyme or reason. Frustrated and excited at the same time. Nia. Michael was going to go crazy over this woman. No matter what he did to get her out of his system, it wasn't working. He was wound up so tightly over her, wanting her, hating her, worrying about her, wanting her again. He'd thought a couple of days away from her would help, but it only made things worse. It only made him more eager to see her, touch her. And how he wanted to kiss her again. Every time he remembered the sweet taste of her lips, he had to close his eyes, it affected him so much.

He would never escape, no matter how far west he went after this holiday was over. Was he strong enough to let it go, as his brother said? He had met a lot of women in his life who made him second-guess the entire sex. But Nia wasn't like any of those women.

Was it too late for him to convince her that he wasn't like any of those men who had disappointed her so much in the past? Would she even care?

"Hey," he asked, "when are we hooking up with the girls again?"

* * *

"Hey," Nia said as she saw their exit off the Kennedy Express pass by. "You missed the exit."

"Let's not go home just yet." Ellen winked at her sister, turning up the volume on the radio.

Nia turned the volume back down. "Ellen, Mama wants us home tonight to finish the invitations. We haven't even finalized the list."

"So what if we're a little late?"

"We promised her we would be there. That's the only reason she let us separate in the first place. Besides, you're not the one she'll blame."

"I already thought it out. I'll tell her that I made us stop by Courtney's place to pick up some pictures of bridesmaid's dresses that she had. You know she just got engaged too."

Great, another one. "I'm happy for her. So what are we actually doing?"

"We're stopping by Jamie's. He lives right on LSD."

LSD was short for Lake Shore Drive, one of the most expensive pieces of real estate in the country. The Gold Coast, as it was called, stretched for several miles along Lake Michigan, with old hotels, quaint bed-and-breakfast inns, and high-rise apartments and condominiums. Prime property. Just a parking space cost in a month what most people paid in rent. It faced the famous lake that seemed as big as an ocean, lined by Oak Street Beach, leading to Michigan Avenue, that magnificent shopping mile.

"What's at Ja—" Nia suddenly remembered: Michael was staying at his brother's place. "No, Ellen. Wait. No."

"What's the matter with you?"

"I don't know. But I . . . Why are we going there?"

"I need to spend some time with Jamie. You know how crazy doctors' hours are. Besides, tomorrow the families will be together all day, and then it's Christmas. Tonight we have to do the invitations. We have a short window. I want to be alone with him.''

Nia cleared her throat. ''Hence the question, why are *we* going there?''

''I need you for cover. Come on, Nia. What is it, Michael?''

Nia's head could have snapped, as fast as she turned to her sister. ''What? What do you mean? What do you know?''

''I'm not blind. I can see that you two don't get along well.'' She made a sharp turn. ''You guys are going to be family, so you'll have to get along. Now is as good a time as any.''

''There's nothing wrong with the way Michael and I get along,'' she lied. ''Are you planning on leaving me with him? Don't tell me: you're kicking us out to walk the freezing streets while you two get it on.''

''No. Jamie and I will leave. Are you sure there's no problem? I sense something really strong when you're both in the room. You always look like you're pissed off when he's around you.''

''I've been in a bad mood. But that's all over. I'm renewed.'' Then why was her stomach in a knot?

''Good, 'cause Jamie said Michael can be a bit of a jackass sometimes.''

''Michael Vincent doesn't get to me.'' Nia wondered how she could make a sweatshirt and jeans look good. Her hair was in a ponytail. Slowly she raised her hand and pulled the scrunchie out, making sure Ellen wasn't looking. ''I'm not even thinking about him.''

As soon as Ellen hopped out of the car, she could check her makeup and give her hair a quick brushing.

*   *   *

Jamie and Ellen were in each other's arms, lips locked even before a hello could make its way out. Nia's entire body tensed up, but she kept a smile on her face. She felt some activity already happening inside of her just in anticipation of seeing him—excitement and fear.

Realizing this embrace could go on for several minutes more, Nia squeezed past them into the apartment and put her purse down. She checked herself in the hallway mirror. *Not bad. Not great, but not bad.* She played with her hair a bit, not sure whether she made it better or worse. Where was he? *Let's get this over with.*

"Sorry, Nia." Jamie laughed, with Ellen draped around him. "Hate to include you in the deception, but this is really the only way we can be together."

"No problem." Nia inched farther into the apartment.

It was typical Lake Shore Drive. Externally, the buildings had an old-time look to them. Inside was a different story. Modern design, mixed with a little bachelor hodgepodge. All masculine colors, black, forest green, deep purple mixed with the typical browns. It was obvious a man lived here, and it needed a woman's touch big-time. Still, Nia didn't doubt that when she got the full lay of the land, it would end up being bigger than any place she had ever lived in.

Where was he? The big-screen television was blaring a college bowl game, but there was only one can of beer on the table.

"Make yourself comfortable," Jamie said as he passed her. He reached for the remote and handed it to her. "Two hundred and eighty channels. Got about twelve HBOs and nine Showtimes. Anything you'd want."

"Why do I get the feeling I'm going to be here awhile?" she asked, wondering if she would be giving too much away by asking where Michael was. "What are you two planning on doing?"

"We're going to the clubhouse." Ellen had a mischievous

smile on her face as she stood in the archway. "We have a special place."

"Ellen, that's a public place for everyone in the building, isn't it?"

"It's closed for the holidays and only Jamie has a key. He knows the landlord."

"Never mind." Nia held her hand up to stop her. "I don't want to hear any more."

"Oh, yeah," Jamie said as he grabbed his keys. "Michael's in the shower. He doesn't know you're coming, so be my guest and scare the hell out of him."

Shower. Naked in the shower. Nia jumped as the front door slammed shut behind them. She was alone in this apartment with Michael, who was naked in the shower. She felt a tingling sensation run through her body, and felt her control slip just an inch away from her. She couldn't ever recall being so aware of her sexuality and her womanly reaction to just the thought of a certain man.

What was happening to her? He was just a man, after all.

She didn't even know where the bathroom was. Would he see her when he came out? Would he have clothes on? What would she say? What would he say? Would he speak to her at all? There was no guarantee after the way they had left things.

That seemed like such a long time ago. So much had been satisfied in Nia's mind since that moment behind the shelter. She was in a better place now. And even though she didn't know exactly what was happening to her body—or her heart, for that matter—with Michael, she knew it made her feel good. She wanted to feel good. She deserved it.

"What did I miss?" With nothing but a towel wrapped around his soaked waist, Michael appeared in the entrance to the living room.

When he saw Nia, he had to blink. He had dreamed about her last night, and it seemed so real. So sensual and passionate. He'd been thinking about her in the shower. But now, could she really be here? It didn't make sense.

That body. Nia bit her lower lip as she took it all in. Wet, dark, smooth chocolate skin. Muscles ripped through his flat stomach, up and down his arms, and those pecs. Her body jumped into position. She wanted him.

"T-they're gone." She could barely speak. The towel gave a peek at thick thighs she wanted to wrap her legs around. "Ellen and Jamie are—"

"What are you . . ." She was real, and Michael heard his body growl in confirmation. "Where are . . ."

"They went to the clubhouse." She pointed to the ceiling as he took a step toward her. *Oh, my God, oh, my God, oh, my God.* Her body forced her to take a step forward. Then two steps.

"The roof?" It had seemed like a year since he'd seen her last. He'd become so obsessed with thoughts of touching her, kissing her again. Doing more.

"Do you know what they do up there?" Had she just asked that? She wasn't sure. It sounded like her voice.

There was a thick silence as each of them stepped forward a couple more steps until they were barely a foot from each other.

Michael's lips formed a wicked smile. "The same thing we're going to do."

They practically lunged at each other, falling to the floor. His lips ravished hers in a brutal, needing kiss that sent Nia's body from fire to lava hot in zero to one seconds. She wrapped her arms around him, pulling him closer. Her mind was gone; her reasoning was gone.

His towel was gone.

As she ran her hands all over his moist, tight skin, Nia's tongue wrapped around his. As he grabbed at her everywhere like a rabid animal, she was hearing herself make sounds she had never made before.

Feeling possessed by an uncontrollable demon, Michael pulled at her clothes. Off came the sweatshirt. She had no bra on, which only allowed him quicker access to her lovely full breasts. He was starving for her, his mouth taking in her left breast. He felt her body arch beneath him, and he begged himself to stay under control. With his tongue, he circled her breast before tenderly biting at her fully swollen nipple. Her skin was softer than silk.

''Oh, God!'' Nia felt as if her body had melted into a tide of fire as his mouth took her breast. She dug her nails into the top of his back. Waves of desire threatened to drown her. Her heart was beating so hard, she felt as if it would burst through her.

Passion surging through him with a force greater than he'd known to exist, Michael reached down, taking hold of her jeans. As he left possessive, wet kisses over her warm, soft belly, he unbuttoned and unzipped the jeans and pulled them down. He made sure to get the panties along with them. He had to have her. He knew that more than he knew anything in this world.

Her pants off, he returned to her mouth, wanting to drink in all of her sweetness. He positioned himself between her legs, calling out her name as her hands squeezed his buttocks. He looked into her eyes, seeing that she, like him, knew there was only one thing left. One thing, and they could have it all.

He lifted her fully into his arms, driving her crazy with teasing kisses to her lips, her neck and shoulders. Nia relished the feeling of her naked body against his, the strength of his arms only making her more eager to feel him inside of her.

As he laid her on the bed he had been sleeping in all week, Michael had to look at her. She was a work of art, something to behold. A smile formed at the edges of his lips.

"This is gonna be good," he said, shaking his head. "This is gonna be very, very good."

When he returned a second later, there was no hesitation. As soon as he applied protection and got on the bed, Nia jumped on top of him. She pinned him down, this time taking his mouth with hers. She felt as if something had taken her over, and it threatened to destroy her if it wasn't satiated.

Straddling him, she leaned back. Michael took hold of her hips to keep her still. His hands kneaded into her skin; he loved the feel of her. He guided her and lowered her onto him.

Tremors of ecstasy rolled through Nia as she welcomed him. She let out a groan, feeling almost faint. Her head fell back as her hands covered his to keep her balance.

She was so warm, so welcoming. Sensations of fire and ice ripped through him at the feel of her so tight around his manhood. He'd said it would be good. He'd underestimated it. It was better than good. Better than anything.

Nia set the pace as she moved up and down, each movement bringing a new burst of fire through her body. When she could open her eyes, she watched as he stared up at her. His eyes were clouded with desire as his hands slid up her hips to her waist. He pulled her down to him. His hands closed over her breasts; grabbing them was a harshness that served only to increase this wanton spirit controlling her.

They built a rhythm together, Nia moving up and down. Michael's head thrashed from side to side as he said her name, not to mention other choice words. Nia picked up speed, going faster and faster, screaming and crying out in pleasure.

When the explosion began to build, Nia grabbed at Michael's arms. She let out a final, wild cry as her whole body jerked and vibrated. It was so shattering, she felt certain she would pass out.

Michael surrendered to his own tide, his eyes shutting tight, his teeth gritting as a gut-wrenching moan left him. He shook all over, feeling as if he were swirling into insanity and being drained of his life. He was floating, gliding in a lake of fire, and it felt better than life itself.

Nia fell on top of him, exhausted to the core of her soul. He wrapped his arms around her. Their heavy breathing could have been heard from the clubhouse.

After lying on top of Michael for several minutes, Nia felt reality begin to settle back into her head. Her eyes opened wide. "The clubhouse!"

"What?" Michael was too tired to react quickly. He was confused as Nia lifted up and rolled over off the bed. "Nia, what are you doing?"

"Ellen and Jamie could come back any minute." She stepped backward, her head feeling light. She was dizzy. She held on to the wall to steady herself. "Where are my clothes?"

"Are you leaving?" Michael slowly sat up in the bed. He enjoyed watching her, and still felt a little weak in the knees himself. He'd stay there for a while.

"Do you want them to catch us?" she asked. She looked at him sitting there, completely naked and wet from sweat instead of the shower.

"Of course not." He got up, reaching for a pair of sweatshorts off the chair next to the bed. "Your clothes are in the living room. Don't you remember when I took them off you?"

"Not really," she said, hoping she could walk without falling.

"Hey, Nia," he called after her as she wobbled to the doorway. "It was better than good, right?"

She warmed to his comforting smile as he slipped into his shorts. "I can't remember it ever being good enough to erase my memory. Where . . . ?"

"In the living room," he answered, his ego the size of a football field now. "On the floor."

She hurried her clothes back on as Michael made his way to the living room after a quick stop by the kitchen. He handed her a bottle of beer.

"I thought you might be thirsty," he said. "I know I am."

She took the bottle with a thank-you. What was she feeling? Her mind hadn't completely returned to her, so there was no telling. She watched as he flopped onto the sofa, grabbing the remote to turn up the volume on the television. He wouldn't stop staring at her.

"What?" she asked, still a little breathless.

"Nothing." He smiled with a shrug. "I'm just waiting for you to explain what just happened."

"Me?" She sat on the sofa next to him, giving him a good sock in the elbow. "Why don't you explain it? You practically threw me to the floor here."

He laughed, hoping that he could make her feel more comfortable. He was a little nervous himself. "Whatever. Do you have any regrets?"

She thought about it. She felt better than she'd felt in years. "Not at all. You?"

"Are you kidding?" he asked. "Toward the end there, I was ready to call you Daddy."

She laughed, taking a sip of the beer. "Seriously, though, what just happened?"

He turned to her. "Something that I think we've both been wanting for a while."

"I . . . I don't do stuff like that. I just—"

"Don't worry, Nia. I don't think you jump into bed with anyone. I know you better than that. What happened just now was something neither of us has experienced."

"So I shouldn't try to figure it out," she said.

"We don't have to right now. I've got an idea. Why don't we just enjoy it?"

"Okay." She faced forward, staring blankly at the television. She took a sip of beer, unable to piece half a thought together. Something told her that her life had just changed forever, but she wasn't ready to accept it.

"Oh, by the way," Michael said, trying to push off his emotions for a second. He wasn't sure he could handle them right now. "That was your Christmas present, so don't expect anything under the tree from me."

Their laughter lightened the tension, allowing Nia to let go of her self-nagging nature. Still, deep inside she knew this was really no laughing matter.

"What's so funny?" Ellen asked as she and Jamie entered the living room.

"Oh . . . nothing." Nia felt as though she should tidy things up around her. Do something. She looked guilty; she knew it. Ellen would figure it out.

"It was a funny commercial on television," Michael said. "Why are you two back so soon?"

"My beeper went off," Jamie said, looking at the television. "I've got to get to the hospital ASAP. So what have you two been doing?"

"Watching the game," Michael answered.

"What's the score?"

"I don't know." Michael took a sip of beer.

"Why don't you—"

"Nia?" Ellen looked at her sister, confused. "Are your clothes wet?"

"No." She looked down at the wet spots left from rolling on the floor with Michael. "Yes. I mean, yes."

"I got her wet," Michael said.

Nia swung around to face him, her mouth and eyes wider than saucers.

He winked at her. "I spilled my beer on her by accident."

"Aw, man." Jamie looked around the sofa. "Where did you spill it, Mike? This is the second time today you've spilled something here. You're such a slob."

Nia hopped up from the sofa. "Let's go."

"Where is your shirt, Michael?" Ellen smiled flirtatiously. "Walk around bare-chested like that and you're liable to turn my sister on. Then who knows what would happen?"

Michael shrugged innocently. "Well, actually I had a shirt on, and Nia ripped it off of me. Good thing you two came or she would have ravished me."

"You're such a kidder," Ellen said.

"Isn't he?" Nia grabbed her by the shirt, pulling her. "Let's go."

Nia looked back at Michael just before turning the corner. He sent her a little wink, and she couldn't help but smile in response.

"So I guess you and Michael got along well," Ellen said, as she pulled out of the garage.

Nia tried to keep a straight face as she pulled her hair back into a ponytail. "I guess."

DAY SEVEN—FRIDAY

When the Vincent family showed up at the Randolphs for Christmas Eve dinner, Nia felt like Ellen looked. Ellen was jumping up and down as soon as the Lincoln showed up in the driveway. She acted as if she hadn't seen Jamie in a year.

Nia kept her posture in reserve as Michael entered the living room. She nodded a hello as he waved to her. He was such a devious one, giving polite smiles and hellos to everyone. He seemed so nonchalant. If it weren't for the rakish look in his eyes as they did a quick once-over of Nia while he headed for the kitchen, no one would have known. But she knew.

Nia had replayed their lovemaking over and over again all last night and all day today. It had been the best sex of her entire life. And whenever the questions came as to what came next, she wiped them away with another replay of the encounter. She woke up feeling alive this morning, remembering there was one thing even better than sunflower seeds and grape pop.

Her mother had her and Ellen running around like hyenas helping to prepare the Christmas Eve dinner for both families. This was part of the agreement: Christmas Eve dinner at the Randolphs, and Christmas dinner at the Vincents. This was how they would compromise.

Despite the fever pitch of activity, Nia still felt Michael's lips on hers, his hands everywhere, and the core of him inside of her. Her mother caught her daydreaming with a smile that required explaining. But she gave no explanation. This was her secret.

Their secret.

The second she saw Michael again, Nia's temperature rose and her pulse began to pound. She joined him in the kitchen with everyone else, as he laid big pots of whatever on the table and reached for another pot from on top of the cupboards. She watched his rear as he moved, remembering how it felt in her hands. He winked at her without checking to see if anyone was watching.

Almost a half hour—the most agonizing half hour of Nia's life—went by before the members in the full house dispersed to separate areas and Nia and Michael could be alone.

Without words, he grabbed her, pulling her with him into the pantry and sliding the door closed. With only a bit of light peeking through the door, their bodies were smashed against each other.

His lips barreled down on hers, taking them as a trophy for a warrior who had fought the greatest war. Their hands were crazy, everywhere, grabbing, pulling, and caressing. A sense of madness took them over as they ached to quench this thirst that seemed only to consume them more every second.

Finally, reluctantly, Nia pushed away. She gasped for air, feeling as though she'd been stuck in a sauna. "Michael, we have to stop."

"I can't stop, Nia." He touched her cheek gently, turning her face to him. "All I could think of since yesterday was getting my hands on you again. My family dragged me on these stupid visits to their friends' houses, dropping off presents to people I haven't seen since I was twelve. All I wanted was to feel you, touch you, be inside of you."

"Oh, God." Nia held on to the cabinet to keep from falling down. "I know, but we can't. Mama isn't giving me a second's peace. I'm her workhorse today. She'll come looking for me any second."

"Then when, Nia?" Michael felt as though he would go crazy if he didn't have her soon. "After dinner we have to go to your church."

"After that," she said. "I'll think of something. Just go. If we're missing long, they'll get suspicious. They're probably all sitting down now."

She turned to reach for the door, but he pulled her back. His lips claimed hers in one long, hard kiss that set her stomach swimming and her heart pounding through her ears.

Dizzy, she made her way back to the dining room in time for everyone to take their seats at the table. For safety purposes, she sat as far from Michael as she could. She was right to do so. Even from across the table he sent her looks and made expressions with his face that had her gripping the edges of the table to keep from responding.

Squeezing her rear end on the porch before they went off in separate cars was the last straw. Nia was certain that her mother saw that. Her stomach as tight as ever, she waited in the car for her to say something, ask something, or scold her. But nothing came. Maybe she had thought wrong. Either way, she felt wicked, and that only enhanced her excitement.

Second Baptist was packed to the hilt on Christmas Eve— so full that the Randolphs and Vincents had to separate. Nia

was grateful for that, since it allowed her to see Michael clearly. She was preoccupied with him, barely listening to the sermon, until she heard some choice words that caught her attention. Somehow words of family had found their way to relationships in general, and suddenly Nia felt as if the pastor were speaking directly to her.

"There is no surprise," he said in an inspiring tone, "that the holidays can be a straining time on relationships. It seems as if it would be the opposite. Because the rest of the year, we go about our lives. Our work and other distractions preoccupy our lives. Having a good time and living for the moment seem to be enough to define a relationship."

Nia looked at Michael, who glanced back at her. Their eyes both held the guilt of their feelings. They looked away.

"Because," he continued, "when we're caught up in things, that seems to be enough. But when you're around family and friends, true friends, you remember what makes a real relationship. You see couples who have been together for a long time, married for decades. You see friends whom you've had since you were in Sunday school. You see the family who has been there for you through thick and thin. And you realize that a good time and living for the moment just aren't enough."

Nia lowered her head. What was she doing?

"What we see"—the pastor picked up the pace of his words—"is that real relationships, the ones that leave us feeling complete and satisfied, are the ones in which we invest time and emotion. The ones filled with emotional risks and sacrifices and guided by Christian principles."

Shouts of "Amen" spread throughout the church. Nia looked at Michael again. His head was lowered. He was feeling just as she was—like a selfish fool.

"A relationship without this level of commitment," the pastor concluded, "no matter what kind, isn't worth having. That's why we come home for Christmas. We need to be reminded of what real relationships are, and why Christmas just isn't Christmas without them.''

"Amen,'' Nia whispered with a sigh.

They stood outside the church in silence, watching the members as they walked by. Nia watched as couples walked hand in hand. Children clung to their fathers' coat jackets, and husbands warned their wives of patches of ice in their path.

"I don't belong to a church,'' Michael finally said, digging his shoes into an icy snow mixture. "In Denver, I don't even go.''

"My church is nice.'' Nia's voice was high-pitched, giving away her discomfort and nerves. "It's a Christian-based nondenominational. You know, not conforming to any organized religion. My mother thinks that makes me a pagan, but I like it.''

"Sounds nice.''

Nia sighed. "What are we doing, Michael? You heard that sermon.''

He nodded. "I heard him. Someone has been watching us.''

"We're being selfish and stupid. We're doing what feels good without care for the consequences.''

"I wouldn't say without care.''

"Without thought then,'' she said. "You live in Denver. I live in Virginia. We don't even know each other.''

"Our siblings are getting married in four months.''

"Exactly. All the more reason for us not to take this lightly. We could be a part of each other's lives forever whether we like it or not.''

"So,'' he said, thinking he would like it, "what's next?''

"Let's just think, Michael. We've just been feeling, enjoying this thing that has taken us over. But is it real? I need real. As much as I've enjoyed being with you, sex isn't what fulfills me.''

"Maybe there's more than that." There had to be, he thought.

"It's all I can think about right now." She slapped him on the arm as the edges of his lips formed a smile. "Be serious."

"I am serious." He looked up at the sky. "You can see tons more stars in Denver than here. I'm supposed to know what to say, but I don't. I want real too. I've had all that other stuff, and I'm sick of it."

"So this is good, right?" she asked, knowing that right now all she wanted was to kiss him. "That we stop this for now and take some time to think. We need to know what we want from this, and if it's the same thing. Because if its not, we could get hurt. And I don't think I can go through that again."

Michael took one glove off and touched her cheek with the back of his hand. "You are a beautiful woman, Nia."

She smiled, her eyes closing gently. "I know."

"Okay," he said. "You're right. I know you're right. Even though my body says forget all that, I know in the end . . . I couldn't live with myself if I hurt you."

As his hand left her cheek, Nia looked away. She felt a tear coming on and didn't want him to see it. That was right, what she'd just done, wasn't it? She wasn't sure. She only knew that this was happening too fast, and she still didn't know where it was coming from. She owed it to herself to think it through, because something told her that if she threw caution to the wind with a man like Michael Vincent, and it ended up blowing up in her face, all the sunflower seeds and grape pop in the world couldn't bring her back.

DAY EIGHT—
CHRISTMAS MORNING

"Hey, baby girl." Gene Randolph winked at his older daughter as she sat down next to him on the living room sofa. "Glad you could join us. We're almost through opening up the presents."

"I'm sorry, Daddy." She leaned over, giving him a kiss. "Had a hard night last night."

That was an understatement. Nia would be surprised if she had gotten even a half hour's worth of sleep. She had gone over the scene with Michael outside the church over and over again, wondering what he really took from it. Wondering what she really meant by it. Wondering if she had made a horrible mistake.

She tried to convince herself she was doing what was right, but that argument wore thin as the night and the early morning wore on. What did and didn't make sense faded into the background. The bits and pieces that did or didn't fit together mattered less and less. In the end, all Nia wanted was Michael's arms around her.

It was simply all she wanted.

"I could hear you tossing and turning from next door," Ellen said, wrapped comfortably in a terry-cloth robe as she sat on the coffee table. "By the way, thanks for the gift certificate to Barnes and Noble. I can't wait to get there tomorrow. I'm buying up the whole store. Open yours."

"Yes, dear." Sharon, sitting on the floor next to the tree, reached up and handed her a gold-wrapped square box.

"Thanks."

Nia always loved Christmas morning. Everyone seemed happy, in a good mood. But right now her heart was breaking just moments after she had gotten it back together again. One more day. Then what?

"Nia," Sharon said. "Where are your manners? Open the card first."

"Sorry." Nia hadn't remembered her mother being so into cards, but her mind was really all over the place right now. She put the small box down and opened the card that had been taped to it.

"Cute." She smiled at the picture of two chocolate stick-figure women hugging. It was when she read the words that her heart stopped. She read them out loud.

" 'Holiday good cheers this time of year sound cliché. So if you don't mind, I have something else to say. I'm proud of your strength, your resolve and determination. I'm proud of your heart, your hope and human kindness. And although I don't tell you, you should know: a Randolph Christmas without you is like a Chicago winter without snow.' "

Sharon tilted her head to the side, lowering her eyes a bit. She smiled sheepishly and shrugged her shoulders. "A peace offering and an apology of sorts."

"Mama." Nia's voice caught in her throat. "I don't know what to say."

"You don't need to say anything." Sharon cleared her

throat. This was obviously difficult for her. "This week I found someone standing up to me to defend my own daughter."

"Michael." Nia remembered the scene between the two of them. How could she have forgotten that?

Sharon nodded. "I tried to brush it off, telling myself that he didn't even know you. But it stayed with me. I'm your mother. I should never be saying anything to anyone that would make them need to defend you to me. I just want you to know that, even though I haven't been in the past, I'm on your side now. Now and forever, no matter what you have to go through."

"Wow." Ellen wiped a tear from her eye.

"That doesn't mean your mother isn't entitled to her opinion," Gene said, leaning back on the sofa. He winked at his wife.

"But I'm still on your side," Sharon said, tears already streaming down her face. She opened her arms wide.

Nia went to her, hugging her tightly and sobbing deeply. She had tried to push back how much this meant to her, but she couldn't anymore. It was a small gesture that meant so much.

"Are you okay, baby?" Sharon held her daughter away, looking concerned at her continued emotional display. "Have I upset you that much?"

Nia shook her head. "No. I'm fine. This is about more than that."

"What are you talking about?"

Nia sat back down on the sofa, reaching into her heart. "I've been fighting something. Fighting my feelings because I just felt . . . I needed to be right. I just hope its not too late."

"Too late for what?" Ellen asked.

"For love," Nia said just as the doorbell rang.

Her heart leaped almost out of her throat. He was here!

"Finally," Gene said, standing up. "We can eat."

Sharon was up and running for the door as Nia and Ellen stood up.

"What are you talking about?" Ellen asked. "Love? Is this about Joe?"

"God, no." Nia felt butterflies in her stomach, waiting for him to come around the corner. What would she say? "I can't really explain it to you yet, Ellen. I have to explain it to someone else first."

Ellen appeared to want to know more until Jamie came around the corner. She was in his arms with one leap. "Merry Christmas, baby!"

When he turned the corner, Nia saw Michael in a different light. Yes, there was still that flicker of heat lighting a flame from her belly to the tips of her toes. That was undeniable. But now there was something else. There was love, that feeling that had been creeping up on her all week, knocking at her door ever so lightly. She had been falling head over heels for Michael Vincent, and had just landed face-first on the ground.

"Hello, Nia." Michael nodded to her, keeping his distance. He wasn't sure he could keep himself from touching her if he got any closer. What was that look on her face? Surprise?

"Michael, I—"

"Come on, everyone." Sharon waved them all in with one hand, pushing Nia along with the others. "Let's go to the kitchen. It's buffet style, so you're helping yourself. We only have a couple of hours before we have to be at the Vincents' church service."

Michael followed behind, doing as he was told. He wanted so badly to give Nia the room she asked for, but it was hard. All the thinking he had done after she walked away from him in front of the church last night had him wound up. He was scared of what he'd come to realize, but could not deny it. He had so much to say, but he knew it would only make things worse if he forced his feelings on her.

The spread on the kitchen table was appealing. The plates were at the beginning, and the utensils at the end. In between were baked ham slices, cheddar grits, homemade biscuits, and scrambled eggs. It smelled great, but Nia didn't have an appetite at all.

She felt silly letting her mother push her into line behind Michael. She avoided eye contact with him as he looked back at her. *Not now,* she told herself. *Not in front of everyone.* She wasn't sure how long she could keep it in. Sometimes having family around was a pain in the rear.

She felt like a fool, taking one baby step at a time and filling her plate with things she had no desire to eat. She felt completely immoral, feeling her body being aroused by his mere closeness. She had been a fool to think that she could be near him and not want him.

It was almost over. Michael stood at the end of the table, reaching for his napkin. Nia reached for the utensils. It was simple enough. Knife, spoon, fork. Well, at least the knife and spoon.

How one fork could make so much noise, Nia wasn't sure. But hers sure did as it slipped from her hand, seeming to hit every loud object on the table before hitting the floor.

Then it happened.

Michael turned to her, and his hands slowly hovered over his plate. He delicately picked up his fork. Nia's lower lip dropped as she watched him place the fork on her plate. He stretched forward, grabbing a fork from the table for himself before going for the napkin.

Everyone's head turned as Nia's plate hit the table. Food splattered just about everywhere, but she didn't notice. Her life had just changed forever.

"That was it!" she said, feeling joy overwhelm her.

"What?" Michael's brow raised as he backed away, confused. She looked as if she were about to blow.

"That was it," Nia said, having to catch her breath before speaking. "That was my café mocha."

Michael put his plate on the table, taking hold of her shoulders. "Nia, what is the matter with you?"

"Ellen said she knew Jamie was the one for her because he gave her his café mocha and took hers. You just did that. You gave me your fork and got another one." She noted his reaction. "I know, it's stretching, but it's what I've got to work with. So just trust me. It doesn't matter anyway. It means I love you."

She heard gasps around her, but none of that mattered. Michael's reaction was all she cared about. And as his look of confusion turned to a smile, she realized she wasn't a fool.

"You . . ." Michael couldn't find the words to explain how he was feeling. "You love me?"

"Yes, I do. Oh, Michael, I thought this was just about sex, but—"

"What?" Sharon and Jonelle spoke at the same time.

Nia ignored them. There was no one else in the room except Michael. "But it wasn't. I was just doubting myself because of Joe and Mama, and how fast everything happened. Stubbornly, I refused to admit that I was, but it was true. I just couldn't believe that there would be more to this than sex. But there is. At least for me."

"At least for you," Michael said, shaking his head in disbelief. "Nia, you have no idea what it means to me to . . . I love you. I realized that last night when you asked me to back off. I didn't want to. My body didn't want to, but my heart told me to. My heart told me that nothing I wanted was worth it, no matter how good it felt, if it meant I might hurt you. Then I realized that one night, one week, or one year with you would never, ever be enough. Not for me."

"So I'm not crazy?" Nia's heart was overwhelmed. She felt like crying. She didn't know what she expected, but not this. He loved her too! "I'm not crazy to think that you can fall in love with someone in the blink of an eye?"

"And you have to keep trying," he said. "No matter how many times you make a mistake. Because one day, you'll find that person who—"

"Gives you his fork without blinking an eye." Nia wrapped her arm around him. "Michael, what are we going to do? Denver? Virginia?"

"We'll do whatever we have to," he said. "As long as we're together."

When his lips came down on hers, Nia felt her body release. Her feet felt ten feet off the ground, and her mind began to sway back and forth. This was worth coming home for.

"Michael," Jonelle said. "What have you done now?"

EPILOGUE

You may now kiss the bride.''

Whistles and applause filled the church as Jamie Vincent wrapped Ellen Randolph in a loving embrace and kissed her passionately. A smile wrapped around Nia's lips as she felt Michael's hand grip her knee and squeeze. She looked at him with an admonishing stare.

"We're in church, remember?" she whispered as they all stood.

"It's just a touch," Michael said. But he knew there was no such thing as "just a touch" between him and Nia. Every touch led to something more between them. It had been that way for the last four months.

Nia clapped with honest joy as her sister, the new bride, made her way down the aisle. She felt tears well in her throat. She was so happy for Ellen. She was so happy for herself.

The last four months had been more of a fairy tale than

Nia could have ever imagined if given the chance. For as much as she had led herself to believe that you couldn't know immediately that you were meant to be with someone, it was almost scary to her how much she knew Michael was the one for her.

To the utter surprise of their families, they had resolved to make something of this relationship, and make something they had. Upon returning to Virginia, more than one of Nia's friends informed her that she shouldn't get her hopes up. Long-distance relationships were doomed to fail.

"Girl, you just don't know," Nia had told her. And she just didn't.

They couldn't stand to be away from each other. They talked on the phone for hours every night, sent E-mails to each other all day. They took turns each weekend, one flying to the other. They didn't get out much. They were unable to take their hands off each other, and their lovemaking always began in a greedy, starved fervor, and ended with a tender, gentle warmth.

Getting to know each other was an effortless process. They connected so well, and realized that although their relationship began in a combative manner, they actually had so much in common. There definitely was that fraction of competitiveness and challenge that they both presented each other. They were both determined, stubborn, and difficult in their own ways. But there was a mutual respect that was new to Nia.

She had never been with a man who didn't make her prove she was his woman. She was his, and she didn't have to give up parts of herself to show him that. Not only had he been more supportive of her career needs than any man she'd been with before, but he went out of his way to give her advice on how to get what she wanted out of business.

In return, Nia had been able to soften Michael. As she learned more about him from his family and his friends, she realized Michael needed softening. His heart had always been in the right place, but there was more to it than that. Michael needed a reminder of what was important, and she was more than happy to be a part of that: family, love, and friends, just as the pastor had said that Christmas Eve in church only four months ago. Relationships.

And Nia practiced what she preached. While building a loving, lasting relationship with Michael, she reached out to Ellen and found out it was never too late to form a sisterly bond. It was a natural thing that came from love and shared experiences. It was the strength of women to know that relationships were above all else. Sisters, brothers, mothers, fathers, friends, children, and lovers—that was what it was all about. And it was a year-round job, not something left over from Christmas or other holidays. Nia had found perspective in life, and she had found it through her relationship with Michael.

Nia loved Michael more than she could have imagined loving anyone. There had been a time not too long ago when she thought that either love wasn't real, or it was real, but wasn't for her. That second fact would have been unbearable, if she'd been destined to watch others fall in love and find mates, while she made mistake after mistake.

Not anymore. Nia took hold of Michael's hand as she joined the rest of the family when it was their turn to walk back down the aisle.

Michael held his head high and walked with confidence down the aisle with Nia at his side. No one was looking at him; he knew that. He had gotten used to being invisible next to Nia. She caught everyone's eye. But little did they know how much more there was to this woman than her exceptional beauty.

Michael knew he had to let it go with Nia. He couldn't hold back as he had with other women, deciding when and where it was appropriate to give more or open himself up to more. He let it go, and the result was a love that he had never imagined. The vulnerability that he had always feared didn't scare him at all. He was so confident in his feelings for this woman, he couldn't believe it himself sometimes.

Michael knew he had a lot of faults, but he was no fool.

"So we were supposed to talk about living arrangements last night," he said as they reached the outside of the church.

Nia took a deep breath. It was an average Chicago spring day, windy and a little nippy, but sunny and beautiful. She missed a lot about her home. She looked at her sister, who was already surrounded by bridesmaids and well-wishers.

"We never got around to it," she answered, turning to look at Michael's handsome face. He was really a good-looking man. And she loved him.

He smiled wickedly and leaned forward until his face was only a few inches from hers. "That's right. We were busy doing other things last night."

When he kissed her, Nia felt a swirling sensation in her belly, and she squeezed his hand. Reluctantly, she pulled away. "We almost got caught by your parents."

"Only adds to the excitement," he said. "Besides, they like you so much more than the other girlfriends I bring home."

She popped him on the shoulder. "Stop it. If there were any other women, you wouldn't have been able to crawl, let alone walk down that aisle today."

"After last night with you, I didn't think I could walk down that aisle today anyway."

"Stop making me laugh," she said, knowing that she didn't mean it. He always made her laugh, and she loved it.

"So, are we going to talk about it or what?"

"I've already offered to move to Denver, Michael." Nia appreciated his consideration. He didn't want to reinforce her feelings from the past. "I can get a job there."

"And I've offered to move to Virginia," he said. "I'm certain my clients will come with me anywhere. They've all but said so. And you know I've been ready to go off on my own for over a year now. I could move without a hitch."

"Michael—"

"No, Nia. Listen to me. Your career is on a roll. You've reached a point where you could make director in less than six months. If you leave now, you might have to take a few steps back."

She looked up at him, knowing his words were true. But it didn't matter. "I'm willing to do that for you. For us."

"I know that." He touched her cheek gently, loving how much she would sacrifice for him. For them. "And that's all I need. To know that you would. But that doesn't mean you have to."

She rested her face in his hand, loving the touch of him—so strong, yet so gentle.

"I'm moving to Virginia," he said with finality. "And I'm moving there as soon as I get back from this wedding. I can't wait to be with you all the time."

"I guess that's final," she said. The excitement of being with him all the time was more than she could handle. "It's going to be so great. All the time, Michael."

"We'll see if you're still saying that sixty years from now."

A smile formed at the edges of Nia's lips as she read his reference. He was sly like that. He always hinted at something incredible with the meekest of words. She knew how to play: act like it was nothing.

"We'll see," she answered, her demeanor betraying the somersaults her heart was doing in her chest. It wasn't as if she knew it wasn't coming, but still . . .

There was no way she wasn't marrying this man.

A Christmas wedding sounded perfect.

About the Author

Angela Winters is the national bestselling author of eight romantic suspense novels, one romance novel, and one holiday novella. Her first novel, ONLY YOU was released in 1997, followed by SWEET SURRENDER, ISLAND PROMISE, SUDDEN LOVE, A FOREVER PASSION, THE BUSINESS OF LOVE, KNOW BY HEART, and LOVE ON THE RUN. Her novella, NEVER SAY NEVER in MAMA DEAR, a Mother's Day Anthology was released in 1997. Angela's novels have received great reviews from *Romantic Times,* The Romance Reader, Romance in Color, *Affaire de Couer,* and the Romance Connection.

Angela's next romantic suspense, DANGEROUS MEMORIES, is due in November 2002. Her tenth novel is a romantic suspense and the third installment in the Hart Family series, due in the fall of 2003.

A native of Chicago, Illinois, Angela received her bachelor's degree in Communications from the University of Illinois at Urbana-Champaign. Angela now makes her home in the D.C. Metro area. She is currently a member of Romance Writers of America and Washington Romance Writers. More information on Angela and her novels can be found at *www.tlt.com/authors/awinters.htm.* You can contact Angela at *angela_winters@yahoo.com*

THE GIFT

Niqui Stanhope

Dear Readers,

I hope you have a very merry Christmas, and a happy Kwanzaa! Here is my gift to you.

Take care,
Niqui Stanhope

Chapter One

Nathaniel Hawkins got to his feet, adjusted the rumpled tie at his neck, and then called a brisk, "Come in."

The door pushed open, and despite every effort he made to control it, his heart pounded heavily in his chest at the sight of her. Noel Petersen. All grown-up. But, still the same Noel he remembered.

"Mr. Hawkins? It's so nice of you to see me at such short notice. I can imagine how very busy you are."

She came forward with such confidence that for a brief moment he just stared at her without responding. She had grown into a beauty. No one would debate that. But it was not a warm kind of beauty. It was cold. Distant. Broken in some way.

His brow furrowed in thought. She had suffered in the years she had been away from him. Now here she was, back home, and she didn't even recognize him.

He gestured to the dangerously rickety chair before his

desk. "Of course I made time to see you. I wouldn't have missed this opportunity for the world."

Noel gave him the kind of seductive smile that worked such magic on difficult male clients.

"You speak as though we've met somewhere before . . . ?"

There was the hint of a question in her voice, and she looked at him with the same sinfully beautiful black eyes that had caused him many a sleepless night in high school.

"You don't remember me then?" His eyebrows lifted in slight inquiry.

Noel gave the almost threadbare chair a dubious look, and then perched herself very gingerly on the edge of it.

"Your face does look familiar," she lied. "But . . . I can't seem to place you."

Nathaniel smiled. "Well, I guess I couldn't really expect you to remember me. It was a long time ago."

Noel's brain charged over the many men she had met in the past years. She prided herself on her memory. It was definitely not like her to forget a face. And she never forgot a name. But somehow she couldn't seem to remember him at all.

He allowed her to struggle for only a moment more, and then he said with a rueful twist of his lips, "Carver High. The old red and gold. I was a few years ahead of you."

Noel sat back in the chair, genuinely surprised. "Oh, my God," she said. "Now I remember. You . . . you were voted most likely to succeed or something like that . . . weren't you? You were the jock, and the high school president."

She laughed in a delighted tinkle of sound. "I can't believe it. Imagine running into you again after all of these years. And under these circumstances too. It's almost too incredible."

Nathaniel leaned forward. "Not so incredible, really. I went off to college. But when I finished up, I came right back here to the old neighborhood. I had to give back what I could . . . you know?''

She nodded, but Nat could see that she really didn't understand a single thing he was saying to her, and it pained him to see the cold materialism in the flimsy smile she gave him in response.

Noel spread her fingers and said in a manner that told him quite clearly that she was ready to get down to business, ''Well, to each his own. That's what I always say. If this makes you happy''—she shrugged—''then who am I to object to it?''

Nat met her eyes for an instant, and it pleased him to see that she became strangely restless during that brief glance.

''Yes,'' he agreed, reaching forward to arrange the stack of papers before him. ''But I know you didn't drive all the way to South Central to reminisce about old times.''

Noel reached into the satchel sitting beside her chair. ''Actually, my staff has been trying to get hold of you for weeks. But it's been a bit difficult.'' She drew a neatly put-together proposal from the black leather bag at her side, and placed it before her on the scratched lacquer desk.

''This,'' she said, tapping the paper with a beautifully manicured nail. ''This is why I'm here.''

Nat said nothing in response, and Noel ran an assessing head-to-toe glance over him. He was obviously not doing well financially. His office was an absolute wreck. And his clothes looked as though he had picked them out of the discarded leavings at a bargain-basement sale. It was obvious that he was in need of money. But it was also clear that he was a proud one, so a straight sales pitch, emphasizing the financial benefits of accepting her offer, would not work well with him. She knew this instinctively. There was something else that made him tick. *But what?*

Noel's brow wrinkled in thought. He didn't appear to find

her attractive either. So an overtly flirtatious approach would probably not work.

"You've heard of the Windsor Hills condominium project?" Her mouth tilted seductively at one corner, and Nat gave her nicely shaped lower lip a thoughtful glance before resting long fingers beneath his chin.

"I think everyone in this city has heard of it."

Noel bit the soft inner curve of her mouth. Not an encouraging response. It would seem that he was opposed to the project. But if he was, that was just too bad.

"I did a little driving around before coming here. And I noticed how run-down the old neighborhood is—"

"We're trying to build things up again," Nat interrupted. "But it's going to take more than just money to do it."

"Oh, I agree," Noel said, leaning forward to give him a deliberate glimpse of soft, golden bosom. "It requires vision. A plan. Someone who understands the area. The people."

A smile flickered in Nat's eyes. "Someone like you, you mean?"

Noel's heart leaped in her chest. She hadn't expected it to be this easy. "Exactly. I'm so glad you understand . . . ."

"I didn't say I understood. In fact, you'd be hard-pressed to find a less understanding person." He paused to give her a steely look. "And what I find hard to believe is that you— Noel Petersen, a girl from this very neighborhood—you have no feelings at all for the people you've left behind here."

Noel's mouth sagged open, and her elegant fingers curled about the arms of the chair.

"You know nothing about . . ." she began, and then very deliberately checked the angry flow of words. This would achieve nothing, she knew. She had to stay focused on the reason she was there. She had to get him to sell his piece of land. The project could not go ahead without it.

"You were saying?" Nat asked with slightly raised brows.

Noel forced a smile to her lips. She had negotiated with difficult customers before. He was obviously just trying to push her buttons. But he would soon come to realize that she was not like any woman he had ever come into contact with. She could control her emotions just as effectively as he. And she never, never did or said anything without thinking it out thoroughly first. She was no impulsive, irrational female.

"You judge me too harshly. I've worked very hard for everything I have today. Nobody gave me anything. And just because I no longer live in the neighborhood, don't think I don't care about what goes on here." She paused for breath, and then charged on.

"What this community needs is a serious face-lift, if you ask me. It's the only way to attract big-business concerns to the area. The only way to bring jobs back to the neighborhood."

Nat got to his feet, but Noel remained determinedly seated. If he was going to throw her out, he would have to do so bodily. She absolutely refused to leave until he had at least given her a fair hearing.

"So this luxury condo project that your company is in charge of . . . is basically a Good Samaritan type of venture?" His lips twisted mockingly, and he literally glowered down at her.

Noel gritted her teeth and carefully considered her response. It was all she could do to remain calmly seated. He was quite obviously playing a cat-and-mouse game with her. But she was no mouse. No, indeed.

"It is not a nonprofit venture . . . but I'm sure you already knew that." She held up an imperious finger, as he appeared about to speak. "It will, however, result in a complete image readjustment for the entire area. Windsor Hills will become the place to live . . . a hip, happening place to be. It'll be more than just your ordinary exclusive condo complex."

"And what will become of the people who live in the designated image-readjustment zone?"

Noel came to her feet now. She couldn't make herself sit still any longer, not with him looking down at her as though she were some particularly distasteful form of bug life.

She drew a short breath, and noticed with a flicker of interest that his gaze skittered across her chest before returning to her face.

"My company is offering a more than fair price for every piece of land that we acquire. And not only are we doing that, but"—she jabbed a finger at him—"we are also providing relocation assistance to anyone who desires the help. Really, Nat," she said now, and her tone softened with deliberation, "this project is going to be a very good thing for everyone concerned. The homeowners we buy out will get some money—a nice little nest egg—and a much better place to live. The entire neighborhood as it stands now is nothing more than a collection of—"

Nat's voice cut neatly across what she had been about to say, and for a moment shock stilled her tongue.

"What . . . what did you say?" Noel managed after a moment spent groping for the right words.

He came to stand directly before her. Although she was, by any description, a tall woman, she was still six or so inches shorter than he.

"I said"—and he bent toward her—"I won't sell."

Noel's eyes sparkled up at him with suppressed rage, and she said as crisply as she could, "What do you mean, you won't sell? Did you understand a thing I just explained?"

Nat stroked a finger around the soft curve of her chin, and she held her ground without moving a single muscle. If he thought such behavior would intimidate her, he was in for a big surprise.

"I always knew you would've grown into a bad-tempered shrew."

Noel's nostrils flared. A bad-tempered shrew? She was nothing of the sort. In fact, if the truth were known, she had one of the most pleasant and calmest dispositions around.

"I have no idea what you're talking about. I've been nothing but sweet-tempered since I got here." And she raised a hand to ward off any attempt at further touching on his part. " You, on the other hand, have been surly . . . difficult . . . mean-spirited . . . ."

The skin around his eyes crinkled, and then he laughed. And it was a hearty, totally masculine sound that caused the baby-fine hairs at the nape of her neck to twitch in the most peculiar way.

"You don't know mean-spirited . . . if you think that's what I was being."

He stuck his hands into his pockets, and Noel tried her best not to notice the way the muscles in his chest flexed beneath his cheap cotton shirt. The way his thighs bulged as he shifted his stance before her. He was exactly the kind of man who attracted her. And exactly the kind she wanted to have nothing whatsoever to do with. She liked men she could handle. Men who needed her more than she needed them.

"Anyway," she said, interrupting the wayward direction of her thoughts. "We seem to have gotten very successfully off track somehow." She tried the kind of smile that always worked so well on her many male conquests. "Why don't we begin again? Can we sit?"

Nat glanced at his watch. "As much as I'd like to do just that, I'm afraid I can't."

Noel's mouth opened and closed soundlessly. He wasn't going to say no, he wouldn't sell, and then just show her politely to the door. She wouldn't let him. She couldn't let him.

"You must have some extra time this evening . . . or

maybe tomorrow? I'm completely at your disposal. Just say when, and I'll meet you wherever . . . ."

He slanted a glance at her and then walked to his battered chair to retrieve his equally shabby jacket. Noel turned her gaze away from the horrible polyester garment with its faded elbow patches and hanging multicolored threads. Good God in heaven, didn't he have a woman to look after him? And if he did, how could she let him out on the streets dressed like a homeless person?

"You can come with me right now, if you like. I teach an after-school class every day at the community center."

Noel's brows rose. The community center? Was he really calling that run-down piece of property she had passed on the way in a community center?

"Ah . . . well, I was really hoping—"

"It's up to you," he said. "Don't let me force you. But since you're so interested in closing the place down and throwing the kids out onto the streets, it might be a good idea for you to at least see what it is you want to destroy."

Noel's chest rose and fell, and heat shimmered before her eyes. How dare he try? He would not make her feel guilty about her condominium project. She had struggled for years to make such a thing a reality, and no Nathaniel Hawkins or dilapidated community center would be allowed to stand in the way of progress.

"I'll come with you," she said tightly. "But I'd also like to make it abundantly clear that my intention is not to throw the children out onto the streets, as you so nicely put it. I'm sure there are other community centers close by where . . . where they'll be able to go."

He opened his office door and waved her into the hallway.

"You've been away from here for far too long," he said. "This isn't Beverly Hills."

"I don't live in Beverly Hills," she said with rising heat.

He pressed the elevator button and gave her a baffling grin. "Oh, no? Where then? Brentwood? Bel-Air?"

"You're bitter," she said, forgetting for just a minute that she was supposed to be pleasant to him. "You're just a shabbily dressed, very bitter little man."

And at that he threw back his head and guffawed in a manner that made Noel want to kick him solidly in the shins.

In the creaky elevator, with what looked suspiciously like tears of laughter glittering at the corners of his eyes, he finally said, "Are you trying to tell me that you don't like the way I dress?"

Noel's nicely shaped brows rose a fraction. "Is that a rhetorical question?"

"I never play verbal games. They take too much effort. If I ask a question, I always expect an answer."

A frown huddled between Noel's brows. Never before in her thirty-three years had she ever—ever—met a more disagreeable human being. Here she was, trying to be conversational, and at every single turn he slapped her down. If it weren't for the fact that she really needed his piece of land, she would walk away from him now without even a backward glance.

"So what does this silence mean?"

The elevator doors groaned at that very instant and Noel ignored his query to ask in a voice that was a trifle high, "Is this thing safe?"

Nat gave her a dark look and said in an abrupt manner, "Of course it's safe." The elevator gave an almost human cough in response to his confident assurance, and spat a rainbow of sparks for good measure.

Noel watched the entire performance with mounting trepidation. She could just see the newspaper story now: *Wealthy developer Noel Petersen perishes in fiery inferno in South Central Los Angeles. An unknown homeless man was found at her side. The man also lost his life.*

She cleared her throat as the doors made a valiant attempt at opening midway to their ground-floor destination.

"Look," she said, and there was a definite thread of fear in her voice now. "I really think we should get off—"

But the elevator prevented her from saying more by shuddering to a sudden and very certain stop. Nat pressed a large thumb against one of the buttons, and grumbled something unintelligible beneath his breath.

"We . . . seem to be stuck," Noel ventured as the elevator gave another shriek and an uncertain wheeze.

"Just a minute," he said, stepping before her and treading very heavily on the tips of her designer shoes. "It's nothing to worry about. It does this sometimes. It just requires a little help." And he gave one wall of the elevator a mighty blow. The machinery groaned in reply, and then said no more.

Noel stood firmly on the panic clawing at the back of her throat. This was no time to become hysterical. It was abundantly clear that Nathaniel Hawkins was mental. A complete lunatic. And if she managed to get out of her current predicament without being burned or suffocated to death, she would be away from this place—and from him— as quickly as she could make her legs carry her.

"We're going to have to climb out." His voice brought her back to the problem at hand.

Noel turned an incredulous glance in his direction. "Climb out? What do you mean, climb out?"

He removed his jacket and shoved the offensive garment at her. "Just what I said. Unless you want to remain in here for the rest of the afternoon?"

"But . . . but what about the maintenance people? Won't they come looking for you after a while? When you're missed?"

He smiled at her. "Oh, we don't have a regular maintenance staff. And actually, this elevator is really never used.

I like the stairs. Keeps me in shape. But because of your shoes''—and he gave her three-inch heels a dubious look before continuing—"I thought you might prefer this method."

At the expression of dumb unconcern on his face, Noel felt the barrier of polite behavior that always kept a civil tongue in her head splinter.

"You have to be one of the most . . . the most . . ." She struggled for a suitably vicious word and then gave up when none struck her as severe enough. "I mean," she spat with dangerously sparkling eyes, "anyone with even an ounce of common sense would not continue to use such a questionable contraption. Not to mention the fact that it's probably against the law to keep this thing in service. And to think I risked my life a while ago coming up in this piece of junk. I could've fallen to my death in this thing—"

"Now, now," he said, holding up a hand to stem the flow of words. "Let's try to focus on getting out of here. OK? Once we're out, we can both collapse into screaming hysterics."

Noel nodded. "Screaming hysterics? I'll give you screaming hysterics, you—"

"Don't forget who you're supposed to be, Noel Petersen," he said, neatly cutting her off. "Ladies of good breeding don't use that sort of language. No, they don't," he said as she drew breath again to tell him exactly what she thought of him and of ladies of good breeding.

"Now, remove your shoes. I'm going to hoist you up onto my shoulders so that you can shift that panel above us."

"I'm only going to say this once," Noel said in a very sturdy voice. "I am not climbing onto your shoulders, or anywhere else on your person."

He gave her a look of exaggerated patience. "Well, one of us has to climb up to that panel. Do you think you can support my weight? If you think so, I'll quite willingly climb onto your shoulders."

Noel gave her beautiful Milanese sandals a glance and then bent to remove them while muttering vile things about Nathaniel Hawkins, and about men in general, beneath her breath.

"OK. Good," he said when she was through. "Just step onto my hands, and I'll lift you so that you can reach my shoulders. You don't look as though you weigh that much."

"I'm not leaving my shoes behind in this place," Noel said as she placed her right heel in his cupped palms and steadied herself by resting a hand against the flat of his chest.

"You can always buy another pair if you lose these," he said as she wobbled a bit and then clawed at his shoulders for balance.

"I got these shoes in Italy." *You idiotic bum.* "And they cost me a small fortune. So"—she panted, placing a stockinged knee on his collarbone—"there is no way on this green earth that I'm losing them."

She heard him mutter something about women being such vain and trivial creatures beneath his breath, and she kneed him very deliberately in the neck. He grunted in response and said, "OK, now, hoist yourself onto my shoulders."

Noel grabbed his ears and pulled herself up. Her long legs wrapped themselves around his neck, and for a brief instant his face was buried somewhere in the folds of her stylish skirt. A hair-fine shiver rattled Noel from head to toe at the feel of his slightly grizzled jaw against the soft skin of her thigh. Good God almighty, what was the matter with her? This was totally out of character. She never, ever lost control of herself in this manner. Shivering just because a man's facial hair brushed against her. How ridiculous. How insane. Especially since the man in question was completely out of his mind.

His voice was slightly muffled beneath the voluminous folds of her skirt.

"Are you all right up there? What're you doing? Stop daydreaming and haul yourself up."

"Well, I'm sorry I'm not going at the proper pace," she said, a quick dart of sarcasm creeping into her voice. "But it's been a little while since my last mountain-climbing class."

"That's nice to know," he said, deliberately disregarding her meaning. "But now is really not the best time to discuss your extracurricular activities."

Noel gave the crown of his head a look of dislike, and heaved mightily. The elevator chose the exact moment that she was getting both knees properly settled atop his broad shoulders to lurch into sudden movement. She made a little sound of dismay as she teetered with legs splayed on either side of his neck, and then cringed inside as the doors sprang open on the ground floor to the startled cry of, "God. I'm so sorry."

Chapter Two

Noel twisted around so that she might properly explain. She fully realized how it must look. Here she was with her legs wrapped very securely about Nathaniel Hawkins's neck, literally hanging from his shoulders, his head buried beneath her skirts. What else would anyone think?

"We were stuck," she said, beseeching the onlooker with smoky black eyes. "So we ... I was just ..."

The man grinned at her. "I know," he said. "You decided to pass the time as best you could."

"No," she said with a hint of desperation in her voice. But before she could say any more, the man was chuckling with an amused, "Have a merry Christmas ... and a happy Kwanzaa. I think I'll take the stairs." And with no more said, he was gone.

Noel slithered in an ungainly manner down the front of Nathaniel Hawkins's chest and stood in her stockinged feet before him. She had suspected that it was amusement that had kept him silent through the entire thing, but now she had proof positive that she had been completely right.

"I don't think it's funny," she said, staring up at him without even the whisper of a smile. "That man thought—"

"Oh, you mean our local councilman?" He chuckled.

Noel drew a tight breath. "Please tell me you're joking. That wasn't the man I'm supposed to be pitching my proposal to later this week."

Nat gathered up his jacket from where it lay on the dusty floor. "Oh, were you supposed to talk to him also?"

He was all innocence, and as Noel continued to stare at him she couldn't help wondering if he had somehow managed to stage the entire elevator incident, just so she would be suitably embarrassed before the councilman. She wouldn't put it past him for a second. He was certainly devious enough. But if that was his game, she would soon put an end to it. He would not sabotage her delicate negotiations with the city. She would have to do some damage control, but the project would not be sidelined because Nathaniel Hawkins had managed to give a key member of the city council the impression that she was some sort of a raving nymphomaniac.

"I'm going home," she said. She had to think—think of a way to get him to sell, and think a way out of the current mess she was in. Besides, her panty hose were now riddled with assorted runs, and she felt sure that she had also torn various other undergarments.

"But I thought you were coming with me to the center?"

She shot him the kind of look that again caused deep laughter lines to crease the skin about his eyes.

"OK," he said. "So you're not coming. But . . . what about the land you want to buy? Doesn't your project depend in some way on it?"

Noel slapped on her shoes, struggling a bit with the straps. Let him have his fun now, she fumed. She would have hers later.

When she was finished, she said in a sharp voice, "I will

call and make another appointment with your office, Mr. Hawkins.'' And she stalked from the elevator without a backward glance.

Later that evening, as she stood on the sweeping veranda of her beach house, she was still in a total quandary as to what exactly to do about things. It was completely unlike her to be so conflicted. She hadn't built her business into a multimillion-dollar concern by being soft and sentimental. She had been featured in *Fortune* magazine, for goodness' sake. They had called her velvet steel—had said that she was the face of the twenty-first century's new entrepreneur, a real estate developer with vision as well as creative genius. Why couldn't Nathaniel Hawkins understand that her condo project would completely revitalize the neighborhood? Why couldn't he see that with such a stylish community of professionals in residence, the entire character of the area would change? She intended to bring lawyers, doctors, engineers, as well as others to live in Windsor Hills. Graffiti-scarred buildings, liquor stores on every corner, these would be things of the past. What could he possibly have against such very positive progress? Why could he not see it? Was he completely mental?

Noel took a sip from the crystal wineglass in her hand and squinted at the foaming waves. Her stomach ached, but she couldn't work up the enthusiasm to eat anything. It was almost exactly four weeks before Christmas, and she wished, really wished, that it were somehow possible to skip the holiday season entirely. It was a time of year she had come to dread. The bright lights. The happy people. The shopping. It was the only time of year she really felt completely empty. Completely alone.

She put the half-full glass aside and drew in a deep breath. If life were fair at all, she would be completely happy. This was what she had always said she wanted. A beautiful house right by the ocean. More money than she really knew what to do with. The power to make things happen with just a phone call. A gorgeous European sports car. She didn't have a man in her life, but that was OK. Life was less complicated that way. She answered to no one. She was free, unencumbered. Completely independent. And, if she really wanted a steady man, she could get one. Sure, there was a shortage of eligible bachelors, but that was not really a problem for her. She had never had trouble getting men. She just hadn't made time in her busy life for one in the past few years. She had dated, yes. But she had never let things go beyond the casual. She should be happy. Her shoulders squared as her indomitable spirit rose again. She would be happy. She would make a point of being happy this holiday season. No matter what happened. No matter what Nathaniel Hawkins did to ruin things for her.

Her stomach rumbled in agreement, and she pressed a hand to her firm abdominals. She would have to eat something. But what? An omelet maybe? She nodded at no one in particular. Yes. A couple of glasses of white wine and a thick cheese omelet with mushrooms, tomatoes, and all of the fixings, and she'd be feeling as right as rain in next to no time at all. What did Christmas matter? It was all pure commercialism anyway.

Noel wandered into the kitchen and began to open drawers and cupboards. She pulled out a deep saucepan and set it on the stove. Once upon a time she had been a very good cook. She had loved to experiment with flavors and textures with different dishes. But over the years she had gotten busy with other things. And she had put the cooking aside. It was not nearly as interesting cooking for just one person as it was preparing a good meal for a family. For kids.

She cracked an egg against the edge of the pan, and rubbed at the corner of an eye with one of her long, stylish sleeves.

It was so silly getting so worked up. She hadn't cried in years. Why did Christmas have to come around and mess everything up?

Noel sniffled, cracked another egg, stirred in a helping of milk, and then set to work on the mushrooms and tomatoes. Before long, the warm smell of good food filled the kitchen. She stirred in butter, grated the cheese, and added a touch of red pepper. When the omelet was nicely golden she added a final grating of cheese to the softly pouting top of it, and turned off the stove. She hardly ever had bread, but tonight was special. She deserved a little treat. She would have two thick slices spread with good yellow butter. She would have enough wine to help her sleep through the entire night without waking, and in the morning she would awaken refreshed. She'd be better able to deal with Nathaniel Hawkins then. She'd be ready to fight again. To win.

She arranged the omelet nicely on a plate and noted with some satisfaction that she hadn't lost her touch. She could still knock out a darn good meal if the urge took her. She wasn't just a heartless career woman who could do nothing more than make money. Hadn't Nathaniel Hawkins implied just that today? Her brow wrinkled. Maybe he hadn't said that exactly. But whatever it was he had said, it was something pretty close to that. She opened the fridge and selected a chilled bottle of white wine. What did he know about anything? What did he know about her? She had never let anyone get under her skin like that. Why had she let him? Why did it matter what he thought of her? It had never mattered before.

She went out to the veranda again and began turning on the lights. It was a beautiful warm, breezy evening. The sky was softly pink, and there was the scent of ocean salt and that special fragrance of nighttime in the air. She dragged a table across to one of the softly padded chairs, and then went about arranging things. A knife and fork, a fresh wine-

glass, a good linen napkin. Her plate of omelet and bread.
And a final trip back inside for the bottle of wine.

She settled back in the chair and stared out toward the
horizon at the slowly sinking red sun. She had always thought
that she was happy. She had never had these deep and
turbulent feelings before. And it was strange how very suddenly they had come upon her too. Maybe her biological
clock had started ticking just like that. Maybe that was the
problem. Her hormones and all of the other chemicals in
her body were beginning to rear their ugly heads.

Noel took a bite of omelet and chewed slowly. Delicious.
Really, really good. It had just the right degree of cheesiness
with that necessary hint of hot pepper. And the mushrooms
were succulent and soft. The tomatoes . . . just right.

She was in the middle of taking a very hearty bite of
butter-spread bread when the front door chimes sounded.
She chomped on the bread and cast an irritated glance at the
face of her watch. Who could it be at this hour? Admittedly, it
wasn't yet dark, but still, it was a little late for door-to-door
salespeople to be calling. She took another bite of omelet and
closed her eyes. She wouldn't answer. Maybe they
would just go away, whoever they were. Her car was in the
garage and most of the interior lights in the house were off,
so there was little sign that there was anyone at home. She
poured herself a glass of wine with a very steady hand, and
tried to ignore the incessant ringing of the bell. They
wouldn't ring forever. She took a sip of wine and massaged
the tense spot at the base of her skull. When the ringing
continued unabated, she slapped her wineglass down. *Who
was that?* She stood in a sudden movement. They weren't
going to stop ringing, it would seem. Well, they were going
to be sorry that they hadn't just given up and gone away.
She cast a quick glance down at her ragged denim shorts
and incongruously elegant long-sleeved blouse. She was
decent enough. With a heavy frown in her eyes, she padded

on bare feet to the front door and yanked it open without even bothering to check the peephole first.

"What do you . . . ?" But the rest of her diatribe faded into silence at the sight of the man standing as large as life in the middle of her doorway.

"You . . ." she sputtered. "What are you doing?"

"Good," he said, taking his thumb from the bell. "You're finally awake."

Her eyebrows climbed toward her hairline. "I'm in no mood for any more of your jokes," she said. "And it's too late for a social visit, so unless you've come to tell me that you're willing to sell me your land, I have nothing to say to you."

Nat leaned a large shoulder against the arch of the doorway and said in a lazy voice, "If this is the way you treat all of the people you do business with, it's a miracle you're not living in a shack out here at the beach."

Noel drew a tight breath and attempted to close the door on his large foot. She wouldn't talk to him. He had just shown up to give her more hell. He had decided not to ever sell, but for some demented reason, he wanted to have a little fun with her.

"I know your mother taught you better than that," he said, resisting her efforts by placing more of his body in the mouth of the doorway.

"Don't you dare say anything about my mother," she said, her voice beginning to wobble a bit. "You know nothing about her . . . nothing about me." He didn't know her mother had died a slow and lingering death from a largely mysterious illness that the best doctors in the world had struggled to even define. He didn't know how that had crushed her—having all of that money, and not being able to help ease her mother's suffering. He didn't know that.

Nat's demeanor changed immediately at the sound of the slight tremor in her voice. "Noel. Sweetheart. Let me in. I have something to say to you. Something I think you'll want to hear.''

The businesswoman in her made her hesitate for a moment. Could he want to talk to her about selling the community center? Maybe she should listen to what he had to say. If it wasn't anything of relevance she could always show him politely to the door.

''Will it take long? I was just in the middle of having my dinner.''

His eyebrows lifted. ''Really?'' And he smiled. ''You know, I thought you might be doing exactly that, so I brought a little something.'' He raised a finger. ''Don't go away. I'll be right back.''

Noel watched in bewilderment as he walked back to the battered pickup truck parked in the middle of her driveway. Her gaze flickered in an analytical manner over him. He really needed some new clothes. And he needed someone to help him pick some things out, because he apparently had no color sense at all.

He was walking back toward her before she could even think to change her mind about letting him in. He had what looked like two shopping bags in his hands.

''Dinner,'' he said once he was close enough. ''Thought you might be more receptive to our little talk if your stomach was full.''

Noel closed the door behind him without uttering a single word. He was obviously a very strange, color-blind man.

''I was eating out on the—''

But he was already walking into the kitchen, laying things down, and hunting in drawers and cupboards as though he did this every day.

''I got us some Chinese food and soda.''

Noel's brows lifted. *Soda?* She didn't drink soda. She hadn't had it in years. She had only wine now. But, of course, someone as basic as Nathaniel Hawkins would never even think of that.

Nat opened up the second bag and gave her a little wink. "And I got pound cake, chocolate fudge, whipped cream, and strawberries for dessert."

She folded her arms before her and considered how she might break it to him that she had no intention of eating any of the greasy food he had shown up with. Just the thought of how many calories she'd be wolfing down made her stomach cringe.

"Look . . . ah, Nat . . ." She had almost called him Mr. Hawkins, but given the present circumstances, it seemed silly to be so formal. "I appreciate the food, but I was really . . ."

He looked up at her, and for some strange reason the expression in his eyes stilled the words on her tongue.

"You'll like this," he said. "I made sure that I got a good variety. All of the favorites, like beef and broccoli, orange chicken, peanut chicken, and some of the more exotic dishes, too."

Noel swallowed. He looked so eager and . . . kind. Was he faking it? She couldn't tell. But still, she didn't have the heart . . . .

"Thank you," she said, and accepted the heaping plate of food that he handed her.

"We'll eat out on the balcony?" he asked, nodding toward where her stone-cold omelet now sat.

"Veranda," she muttered beneath her breath. It was a veranda, not a balcony. Though he couldn't be expected to know that.

"What?" he asked. "I didn't hear that."

She walked rapidly ahead of him. "Oh, nothing," she tossed over her shoulder. She put the plate down beside her half-eaten omelet. It was such a pity that it was ruined now.

It would never taste the same heated up. An omelet was at its best only when it was fresh from the pan.

Nat put his plate down beside hers, then dragged up another chair. "Looks like a good omelet," he said, hunkering down in the chair.

Noel sat too. "It was," she said. She knew she was being obtuse, maybe even rude, but she couldn't seem to help herself. He just seemed to rub her the wrong way. Even the most innocent-sounding comment he made seemed to be laced with some sort of an accusation.

Nat dug a fork into his food, placed a hearty quantity into his mouth, and then waved his fork at her.

"Eat. Eat," he said. "Don't be shy. I won't tell anyone you actually do have a good appetite."

Noel looked down at the mound of food, and then up at him. "What was it you were going to talk to me about?"

"Not until you've eaten. That's the deal." He cracked the large bottle of Coke, then picked up her half-finished glass of wine.

"White zinfandel," he said, taking a swig from her glass without asking. "Good, but not great."

"Is that so?" Her eyebrows lifted in surprise. She was shocked that he even recognized the fact that it was wine, let alone anything else.

He speared a thick chunk of orange chicken and held it out to her. "That is so."

"No," she said, backing away from the fork. She didn't eat this sort of food.

"C'mon," he coaxed. "Just a little bite. It's really good."

She hesitated for a moment more, and then bent quickly to take the piece of chicken off the fork. Maybe if she ate a little bit of the food, he would get on with what he was really here to discuss with her.

He leaned forward, and before she could guess his intention he wiped a trickle of juice from the corner of her mouth with a gritty thumb. Her lower lip trembled in response, and it was all she could do not to back away from his hand.

"Good?" And he gave her a very direct, black-eyed look.

Noel swallowed the chunk of chicken without the benefit of proper chewing. She was unsure of what he was referring to—the chicken or the touch.

"Don't you think," she began hoarsely, then paused to clear her throat. "Don't you think it might be a better idea if we talk about your . . . idea while we eat? I mean it *would* be more efficient."

He shoveled some more food into his mouth, and then inquired in a casual manner, "Are you lonely?"

Noel blinked at him. *What?* Had he heard her suggestion? What was he asking her? What did his question have to do with anything?

"I'm sorry? What?" She was confused.

He speared a piece of broccoli and a sweet chunk of beef, and again offered her his fork. This time, because she was so disturbed by his question, she took the food without even thinking.

"I just wondered," he said. And again his fork was poised before her with more for her to eat.

"I don't understand what that has to do with anything." She shook her head, refusing the next forkful of food, and he turned the utensil and placed it neatly in his mouth.

"It actually has a lot to do with what I want to talk to you about."

"But you said you were going to talk to me about the community center." Had he tricked her just to get into her house to talk to her about loneliness and other such nonsense?

He sampled another forkful of food before saying, "I have a proposition for you . . . and you will soon see how everything ties together."

Noel leaned forward. "OK. I'm listening."

Nat smiled. "But not eating, I see."

Noel picked up her fork. Fine, if he wanted her to eat, she would eat. Maybe that might urge him into the discussion that much faster. She would just have to work off all of those extra calories later. She popped a bit of orange chicken into her mouth, and tried not to notice how very succulent it was.

"I'm eating," she said after a moment, "but you're not talking."

He swallowed his entire glass of soda without pause, and Noel watched him with pursed lips. He was stalling very deliberately, and she was beginning to get the feeling that whatever it was that he wanted to say to her, it was probably something that she didn't want to hear.

He put the empty glass back on the table, and tapped himself in the middle of the chest. Noel sucked in a breath. If he even dared to release a belch, she would have to get up and show him to the door.

"Good soda," he said. "Now," he continued, leaning backward to prop his head against folded arms. "What do you know about Kwanzaa?"

Noel blinked. Good God almighty, what was he talking about now?

"Kwanzaa?" she asked in a strained voice. "I really don't understand you."

He closed his eyes, and Noel held on tightly to a tide of rising anger. She knew he wasn't about to fall asleep in the middle of everything.

"You want to buy my community center. Right?" He opened an eye.

Noel looked at him for a long moment without saying a word. It was no wonder he hadn't managed to make anything much of himself. He definitely had a good brain, but that certain something that burned in the hearts and souls of all high achievers was sadly absent in him. He would probably live his entire life barely eking out a living, scrabbling from month to month to make ends meet, going from one doomed project to the next. He just didn't have any of the right stuff.

"Yes. You know I want to buy your property," she said with great patience.

Both eyes were open again, but he still reclined against his hands as though he hadn't a single care in the world.

"And you know I don't support your project."

She forced herself to smile and say in a calm voice, "I was beginning to get that impression. So what is it you propose?" In her line of work, she had negotiated with high rollers and sleazoids. And one thing she had learned and learned very well was that every man had his price. Every man. Even a softheaded idealist like Nathaniel Hawkins.

Nat looked at her for a long moment. "I'll sell you the community center—"

Noel barely managed to conceal her start of surprise. "Well, that's great," she began, her heart thrashing heavily at her rib cage. "I'll come by early tomorrow and we'll start the paperwork. I can promise you a price that's more than just fair—"

"You didn't let me finish." He was sitting up again, and Noel was surprised by the change in his expression. In just an instant he had undergone a complete transformation. There was a shrewd, seasoned look about him now, one that Noel had come to recognize and respect. In her experience, only the most hard-nosed and cold-blooded businessmen ever wore that particular expression in their eyes. But this was Nathaniel Hawkins, not some hotshot dealmaker.

She laced long, elegant fingers together. "I'm sorry. You're right. I cut you off. Please finish what you were saying." Her mind was already moving on to other things. With this property in the bag, things could finally move ahead as scheduled. She would get all of the legal angles with the city nicely wrapped up. The councilman who had witnessed the embarrassing elevator incident would not be a problem either. She would send him a gift. A nice expensive one. And maybe season tickets to the Lakers or any other team he might prefer.

"As I was saying, I will sell you the community center." Nat held up a hand as she got ready to interrupt yet again. "If . . ." he said, and he gave her a moment to absorb the impact of the word. "If you agree to a little stipulation of my own."

Chapter Three

Noel eyed him warily. Stipulation? She always got nervous when a word like that drifted into any negotiation she was in charge of. It usually meant that the person was going to be completely inflexible about something or other. But no matter, she was good at ironing out inflexibilities. In fact, it was one of the things she did best.

She was poker-faced as she leaned toward him. "I'm sure we can work out whatever it is. Tell me about it."

Nat smiled, and Noel wondered for an instant whether she had misjudged him.

"Good. Good. That's what I was hoping you'd say."

She nodded and waited for him to continue. He was certainly taking enough time to get to the point.

He reached for one of her hands, and Noel allowed him to hold it. "The community center throws a Kwanzaa festival for the neighborhood around this time every year. All of the kids get involved. It's usually lots of fun for everybody."

Noel stared at him, not understanding a single thing he

was saying to her. At the back of her mind a little voice was whispering to her, *This is what happens when a man's brain has been idle for too long.* He had no ability to concentrate at all. Here he was in the middle of an extremely important discussion, one that could possibly net him a nice seven-figure chunk if he played his cards right. And in the middle of everything, he just up and forgot the discussion entirely and began to speak about some completely irrelevant Kwanzaa festival.

"Right," she said. "But getting back to what we were discussing . . . I think you were just about to tell me what I needed to do in order to make this deal happen."

He smiled at her as though she were a particularly dim-witted child. "I'm right in the middle of telling you all about it. But you keep interrupting me."

Noel waved a hand. "Sorry. Go ahead then." Let him ramble if that was what made him happy. She would just have to pick the pertinent morsels out of the jumble of words.

"To cut right to it," he said, and again Noel noticed that same shrewdness in his eyes that she had seen before, "the only way I'll sell the community center to you is if you agree to take charge of the Kwanzaa festival."

Noel stared at him for a second without uttering a single word. Take charge of a Kwanzaa festival? He *had* taken complete leave of his senses. There was no doubt about that. She didn't know a thing about Kwanzaa, and even if she did, she certainly had no interest in mucking about at a derelict community center with a pack of screaming kids. Didn't he know who she was? She was a high-powered executive. Her time was extremely expensive. Every minute she spent on other pursuits meant less money for her. Didn't he know that?

She racked her brain for an appropriate response and finally settled on, "So . . . that's your stipulation? That I take charge of this festival? And if I do, then you'll sell?"

He shrugged. "That's it. But you have to run everything from start to finish. You personally. Not a member of your staff."

Noel rubbed a hand across her forehead. The things she had to do for her job.

"I don't understand why this is important at all."

"It's what I want. Call me eccentric." And he undid the first three buttons on his shirt. Noel's eyes followed the movement of his fingers while her brain worked frantically. She had to find a way out of his ridiculous requirement. Every man had a price. Nathaniel Hawkins had to have one too.

"What if . . ." she began, then thought about it for an instant more and went on. "What if I sweetened the deal by adding, say . . . I don't know . . . fifty thousand to your asking price? Could we get around your little stipulation?"

Nat's eyes brightened and a smile bloomed inside Noel. Greed was a wonderful thing. She could see the pure avarice in him now. He had probably never had that much money at any one time in his entire life.

But his next words had her mouth bobbing open soundlessly and then snapping shut again.

"I . . . I don't understand you," she finally croaked.

"Well, let me repeat it for you then," he said with a nice note in his voice. "I said—"

"I know what you said," Noel interrupted hotly. "And it doesn't make any form of sense. Who in their right mind would turn down a chance to make an extra fifty thousand dollars on a deal . . . on any deal? Are you completely without any business acumen?"

And when he continued to stare at her without saying a single word, another possibility occurred to Noel: maybe he was a drinker. Although she hadn't detected the smell of the bottle on him, it was entirely possible that he was just stone-cold drunk.

"Look," she said. "Maybe it might be best to continue this discussion tomorrow." Once he'd had the time to sleep off the effects of whatever it was he might be under.

"This is the only shot you'll have at getting the center. My offer is nonnegotiable and is only available tonight. So . . ." And he shrugged. "If you want to pass on it I'll understand."

"You can't mean that," she almost bellowed. "You can't just ask me to . . . to run some . . . some festival, and expect me to go along with things just like that. Don't you know how busy I am? Even if I wanted to run your festival, I couldn't. I just don't have the time to do it."

He stood and began to clean up. "OK. Believe me, I understand."

"You understand. What do you mean, you understand?" This time she was shouting, and she didn't care. The man was crazy. He couldn't just get up and leave as though there were nothing more to say.

"I don't see what you're getting so worked up about," he said blandly. "I made you an offer and you turned it down. You can't say that I didn't try to be reasonable."

Noel clamped her lips together and tried to hold on to her rising temper. Why, *why* did this man and no other manage to push all of the wrong buttons in her? It just didn't make any sense at all. She was never like this with other clients. And she was always especially polite when she was negotiating a deal of this importance. She had to be calm. She just had to be.

"Don't go," she said. "I'm sorry. I'm . . . I'm not usually like this." She turned away to stare at the dark body of water. If she rearranged a couple things in her schedule, maybe she might be able to squeeze the festival in. She'd be overworked, but that couldn't be helped. If she dropped dead from exhaustion in the middle of everything, then he'd at least have to live with the guilt of that for the rest of his life.

She took a breath and then plunged. "OK. I'll do it."

"Good," he said, and he looked at her in such a very pleased manner that Noel raised a hand and chewed on a knuckle. There was something more to his offer. She was no fool. Something that he hadn't yet revealed. Something that had nothing whatsoever to do with money.

"I want it in writing though," she forestalled him as he lifted the stacked plates from the table and headed for the kitchen.

He turned back to look at her. "What?"

Noel glowered at him. What? What did he mean, "what?"

"I want you to put in writing the fact that you will sell me the center if I take over the running of this Kwanzaa festival." And at his expression, she said, "It's not that I don't trust you." It was, really. She had learned the hard way not to trust anyone.

"My word is my bond," he said. "But I'll put it in writing for you if that'll make you happy. I know that's the way you do business in that wheeling and dealing high-finance world of yours."

Noel gathered up the bottle of soda and the wine bottle and followed him. That was the way all normal people of good intelligence did business. It had nothing whatsoever to do with the fact that she worked in a high-finance area.

Nat scraped the remaining bits of food into the garbage can, set both plates in the sink, and then began rolling up his sleeves.

"Oh, you don't have to do that," Noel objected immediately.

"Where's your Christmas tree?" he asked, ignoring her completely.

Noel's heart shuddered. "My . . . what?"

He turned on the faucet full blast and began to apply dishwashing soap with tremendous gusto.

"Your tree. Isn't it about time to begin putting it up?"

She looked down at a dirty spot on the counter and began polishing it with the edge of her sleeve. She didn't want to talk about Christmas. She just didn't like the time of year at all. It filled most people with love and the softer emotions. But it made her deeply, deeply sorrowful. It reminded her of all she didn't have. All she might never have.

"I . . . I never put one up." And she looked up with eyes that had suddenly gone fierce. "It's too much of a hassle to go through for just one day. All that effort . . . dragging trees in, putting up ornaments, pine needles everywhere. Then you have to take everything back down again after Christmas day." She let out a tight breath. "What's the point?"

Nat handed her a clean plate. "Happiness."

She accepted the plate and gave him a heavy frown. "What?"

"That's the point. It makes you happy, so you do it."

Noel stared at him, not knowing exactly what to say to that. He handed over another plate and then began on the glasses.

"Happiness is a very important thing, you know," he said in a conversational manner. "If you have that, then let the world bring it on . . . because there'll be nothing you won't be able to face. Trust me. I know."

Noel dried the plate with a bent head. What did he know about anything? Telling her about happiness and how important it was. Didn't he think she knew that? Who wouldn't know that? But not everyone was fortunate enough to be happy. Sometimes in life, it just wasn't possible to be happy. Life came along and got in the way.

The water was off now, and he was drying his hands with a dish towel.

"Do you know what love is?" he asked, and her head bobbed up again. What was this? Some sort of sermon?

"It means different things to different people." She was

pleased with her reply. It was clinical. Almost academic. What could he possibly say in response to that?

He leaned back against the counter, folding his arms across his chest. "A good answer. But not exact enough. Love is nothing more than harmony. Being in perfect synchronicity with another soul."

"Whatever you say," she said, closing the cupboard door and walking out of the kitchen. Maybe he would take the hint and go. She really had no interest at all in discussing love, happiness, Christmas, or Kwanzaa.

She walked out to the veranda again and went to stand at the railing. It was completely dark now, and the moon shimmered white and mysterious just over the horizon. A beautiful breeze ruffled her soft bob of black hair. It was a perfect night. Not too warm. Not too cool. She could almost imagine that all was right with her world. Almost.

She felt Nat come to stand beside her, and reluctantly she looked up at him. And as she did, an errant thought ran through her head. He had good lips and a nice face. Kind eyes. If you believed in that sort of thing.

"What has happened to you in the years I haven't seen you, Noel?" His voice was soft, and the sound of it was almost blown away by the gentle breeze.

Noel turned back to stare blindly at the water. What made him think that he could talk to her in this manner? As though . . . as though it really mattered to him? His hand came up to brush back a hair from the corner of her eye, to curl the strand about an ear. And she flinched before she could prevent herself.

"It's OK," he said. "It's just a hair."

But his fingers lingered to stroke the whorls of the very ear he had just tucked the strand neatly behind. A sudden and totally unexpected rash of goose bumps flooded her arms, and she shivered.

"Want to use me as a jacket?"

She shot a sideways glance at him. If he was about to make a move on her, he would be sorely disappointed at the results. She absolutely did not date men like him.

"I'm not cold," she said, and her voice was brisk. She was tired, maybe. Confused, definitely. But certainly not cold.

He ran a thumb down the flat of her arm. "You shouldn't be so wary of me," he said. "I'm not the kind of man you might think I am."

She pursed her lips. There was really only one kind of man. They came in all sizes, shapes, colors, persuasions. But really, there was only one kind of man. For a minute she wondered whether she should even bother with a conversation of this sort. He was just baiting her, she knew. And really, where could such a conversation go?

"And what kind of man are you?" Now, why did she say that? She didn't want to know what kind of man he was. It didn't matter at all to her. Not at all.

Nat turned toward her, leaning an elbow on the rails, and in the half light she admitted reluctantly that he was handsome. Not model beautiful. But solid and definite, with good, warm features that were almost indescribable in some strange way.

"This isn't a good way to live. Not for you."

He had deliberately not answered her question, Noel noticed. Her brow furrowed for an instant. He obviously felt completely comfortable asking her just about anything under the sun, but when it came to her questions, he felt just as comfortable ignoring those.

"What are you talking about now?" She knew exactly what he was referring to, but he had no right to criticize the way she lived. This way suited her completely. And was his life so much better than hers?

She met his dark eyes and saw a flicker of something there she hadn't noticed before. Compassion. And something else she couldn't quite define. She blinked and her throat went suddenly dry. Was he sorry for her? Was that why he lingered now, instead of going home, or wherever else he might go?

"You live out here," he said in a voice that was soft and deep. "All alone. No friends to speak of. No . . . man."

Noel's body snapped to attention. "Why . . . whatever . . . whatever you think you know about me, you're wrong. I have many friends. Good ones. And . . . and if you must know, although I really don't think it's any of your business, the reason I don't have anyone in my life right now is because . . ."

"Yes?" And he seemed to lean even closer to her. "Because why?"

She gritted her teeth. She really, really should not even be having this kind of conversation with him. It was ridiculous. Silly. Pointless.

"I don't have the time for it," she finally said. "Relationships take time. Lots of it. And that's one thing I don't have a lot of. Besides, they're a distraction anyway."

"So," he said, flexing the fingers on one hand, "you intend to go through the rest of your life exactly as you are now? Without any significant person in your life?"

Attack. Her brain almost screamed the word. She had to attack him too. That was the only way to make him abandon his current course of questioning.

"I suppose your life is perfect? You have everything in place, right? All the friends you need. A good woman. Everything."

"No," he said. "My life isn't perfect. I don't think there're many out there who'd actually be able to make that claim. There's always something missing. I know what's missing in my life. I've waited a long time for it . . . because I never gave it enough importance. Or maybe . . ." And he frowned now, looking away from her, and out at the ocean. "Maybe the right motivation just wasn't there."

The anger that had flared so suddenly in Noel died away just as quickly. She hadn't expected him to respond with honesty. With sincerity. He made her ashamed of her behavior, of her antagonism toward him. Maybe he was lonely too. Maybe that was the reason he had shown up at her house unannounced, with dinner to boot. He didn't have a steady woman in his life. That would certainly explain the kind of clothing he wore.

She cast a sideways glance at his face and her heart softened a little. *Poor guy.* She would try to be friendlier. Maybe there was more to him than she had originally thought.

"Don't you . . ." And she stopped to think. She hadn't tried this soft approach in a long while, and the right words were hard to find. He was looking directly at her again, and for some inexplicable reason, she felt nervous.

"Don't I what?"

He was so calm. So collected. Noel swallowed and then laughed self-consciously. "It's not like me to be at a loss for words. But I didn't want to ask any presumptuous questions."

He shrugged out of his threadbare jacket and draped it about her shoulders. "You look cold." And when he was satisfied that she was properly covered, he said, "You can ask me anything. And I love presumptuous questions."

Her lips twisted, and a genuine chuckle bubbled from her throat. "I should've known you'd say that. But . . . OK, what I was going to ask was . . . don't you have someone in your life right now?"

A smile flickered in his eyes. "No one."

She sucked in a breath. Yes. It was as she had thought. The clothing had given him away. Should she press him further? He was a good-looking man. Surely he would be pursued? Surely he would have to beat women off him with a broom?

"Why don't you?"

He appeared to consider his words carefully before saying, "Work. Not getting out enough. Not running into the right person."

It was her turn to smile. "Now, that I don't believe. You're pretty well known in your . . . our old community. You mean to tell me that with all of the people you work with, all of the women you must run into, you've found no one at all interesting?" She chuckled again, amused. "Don't give me that. I think I know why you don't have anyone. If that's true at all."

His eyes became bright and watchful. "You've got me all figured out then?"

She put her arms into the sleeves of his jacket, and noted absently that although it was shabby, it was quite warm.

"I wouldn't say that exactly." She smiled. "But I think that maybe the reason you don't have anyone at the moment is because you don't really want to." She narrowed her eyes playfully. "You like having an entire pack of women constantly wondering. Right?"

He laughed and his eyes glinted at her with dark lights. "Just goes to show how little you really know about me."

Her eyebrows tilted. "Oh, yes?"

Nat tapped the rails with a hand. "Yes. But"—and he released a breath—"I've got to get going. Besides, I've probably long overstayed my welcome . . . ."

Noel just barely managed to prevent words of denial from tumbling into sound. It was strange and totally unexpected how it had happened, but she had begun to enjoy his company. And she suddenly didn't want to be all alone with herself again so very soon . . . .

Chapter Four

Noel took her time removing herself from his jacket. What was it he was rushing off to do? Surely it couldn't be anything of earth-shattering importance. Why didn't he want to stay any longer? Had she somehow given him the impression that she was getting tired of his company?

She handed the jacket back, holding it out so that he might slip his arms into the sleeves. He did this with quick efficiency, shrugging so that it fit his body again in that snug and compact manner that somehow managed to emphasize the firm muscles just beneath the cloth. Noel found herself wondering how he came to be in such good shape if he ate so poorly. Junk food and soda were notorious for putting pounds of unwanted fat on the best frames around.

"Well," he said looking down at her, "I'm sorry you didn't enjoy the food."

Noel blinked at him and then rushed into immediate speech. "No, that wasn't it. It's just that, I don't ... I don't ..." She couldn't think of how to put it.

But he helped her, his lips twisting a bit at the corners. "You don't eat poor people's food?"

Blood rushed to Noel's face. Had he said this to her just an hour before, she would've jumped all over him. But now his words sank in instead of running off her back as they usually would. Was he right? Had she turned into some sort of pretentious snob?

"That's not the reason why," she said, trying to force some conviction into her voice. "I have to watch my weight all the time. I put on pounds very easily."

"Uhm-hmm," he said, and then changed directions on her. "What're you going to do for the rest of the evening?"

Noel wet her lips. She'd been trying not to think about it. In fact, she didn't want to think of the lonely stretch of hours ahead of her. She didn't want to think about tossing around in bed, unable to sleep. Of late, her insomnia had returned in full force. She sometimes found it impossible to get to sleep until the very wee hours of the morning.

She folded her arms about her. "I have lots of paperwork to do to prepare for this project."

He stuck his hands into his pockets. "It sounds completely responsible, and completely dull."

Noel opened her mouth to object, but he prevented her from speaking by saying, "Let's go shopping for a tree and some Kwanzaa candles."

Her teeth closed on the tip of her tongue, and for an instant she couldn't speak because she was in genuine pain.

"Shopping . . . for a tree?" she managed after a moment. Hadn't he understood her before? She didn't put up trees. She didn't celebrate the season. And she definitely didn't do the Kwanzaa thing. It meant nothing to her.

"You always do your research before starting a project . . . don't you?"

She nodded, already knowing where he was going with

that particular line of questioning, but not having the slightest idea of how to get out of the trap he was setting for her.

"If you're going to take over the Kwanzaa festival, then you have to know something about Kwanzaa. Doesn't that make sense to you?"

Noel held her tongue. It made sense to her. It made nothing but sense to her. But what did learning about Kwanzaa have to do with shopping for a Christmas tree?

"I can't go like this," she said, looking down at her long bare legs.

His gaze ran over her from head to toe, and then back up, and a wave of heat followed the progress of his eyes.

"Go change then. I'll wait."

Five minutes later, Noel was traipsing back down the stairs in a pair of faded boot-cut jeans, a tank top, and a sleek black leather jacket. She had run a comb carefully through her hair so that her shoulder-length hair framed her face in a casual windblown manner.

Nat watched her come toward him, and his right hand curled into a fist. She was so beautiful. So damn sexy. How was he going to reach her?

"How's this look?" Noel asked when she was close enough. But she regretted the words almost as soon as they were out of her mouth. Why was she asking him this? The poor man was completely color-blind and had absolutely no sense of style whatsoever.

"You should be warm enough in that," Nat said, after giving her a long and considering look.

Noel nodded. Just as she had thought. He had misunderstood. She'd been asking him a totally different question, and he had naturally assumed that she was concerned about warmth.

"Let's go then," she said. Already she was regretting the impulsive decision that had made her agree to go along with him. It was a spate of temporary madness. Loneliness. Something.

In his truck, she settled against the hard leather and waited as he struggled to get the engine going. After a few tries, he turned to give her a rueful smile.

"It does this sometimes. I won't be a minute. I just need to take a look under the hood."

Noel watched him through the glass windshield as he moved from one side of the truck to the other, fiddling with this, unscrewing that. She shook her head and muttered to herself. The man's entire life was broken down. He worked in a broken-down building. Rode up and down to his office in a broken-down elevator. Wore broken-down clothes. And drove around town in a seriously broken-down truck.

He was back in the truck less than a minute later, his hands dripping oily black fluid.

"Should work now," he said, and fumbled beneath the dashboard for an absolutely filthy piece of cloth. He wiped both hands on this, flung the rag into the back, and started the truck. Noel clung to the side of her seat as the engine roared into life. They sat there for a bit as the chassis jiggled from side to side, and Noel closed her eyes and remembered the elevator. Something else was going to happen; she just knew it. She was willing to bet that they wouldn't make it even two miles without breaking down or running off a cliff or something. If they did manage to make it out and back without mishap, it would be nothing short of a miracle. Every time she came into contact with Nathaniel Hawkins, she was literally taking a chance with her life.

"All buckled up?" she heard him ask. And her eyes popped back open. She fumbled for the belt as he threw the vehicle into gear. What difference did it make whether she was buckled in or not? With the kind of shape the truck was in, if they were involved in any kind of accident at all, neither of them would have any chance of surviving it.

"Buckled in," she said, and clung again to her seat as they roared up the driveway in reverse.

She said nothing more until they were rattling along on Pacific Coast Highway.

He shot her a sidelong glance. "Comfy?"

Noel almost laughed at that. There was nothing even remotely comfortable about the seat on which she was sitting. The leather was hard, cold, and cracked in any number of places. And she felt certain that a spring or other sharp object had lodged itself somewhere near the base of her spine.

"Have you ever thought of getting yourself some new stuff?" The question was out before she could even rethink the wisdom of asking it.

Nat shifted gears, and she watched in near fascination as his big fingers curled about the gearstick. Her brow furrowed. Hands like his were tailor-made for lovemaking. He had big, thick fingers. Strong hands. They were just perfect. Just perfect.

She made herself look out the window and away from the bothersome hands. What in the name of heaven was the matter with her? This was not like her at all. She was never this unfocused. Here she was asking him perfectly normal questions, and then what did her brain do? Throw her a curve about his hands.

"What's wrong with the stuff I have now?"

His question caused her to look at him again. What was wrong with his stuff? Was he serious? Was there anything "right" about anything that he possessed?

"Well . . ." Noel hesitated to put her thoughts into words. She wouldn't have done so earlier in the day, but somehow now she couldn't bear to be unkind to him. He shifted gears again as they coasted down a gentle swell in the road. She drew a little breath and said, "It seems like . . . some of your things could do with a little bit of sprucing up."

He smiled. "Like my truck, for example?"

"I'm sure it was a good truck once. But really"—and she turned to give him a direct look—"you have to admit that it's seen better days." She touched him lightly on the thigh and felt the muscles beneath his jeans tighten. "Maybe after we conclude this deal, you'll be able to buy yourself some new things. Spending money is not a crime, you know. It's nothing to be ashamed of."

"You think I'm ashamed of spending money?" he asked, a deep chuckle in his voice.

They were on a different freeway now, heading toward Los Angeles. Noel wound the window down and tried to settle herself more comfortably against the leather. She pulled her jacket closer and wished she had not started this particular conversation with him. She knew he had little money. He was not like her, a superachiever.

"I'm sorry," she said after a brief moment of silence. "I shouldn't have said that. I didn't really mean it the way it came out. I'm sure you would . . . would buy yourself things if you had the money." She paused to think, because that had come out all wrong, too. She hadn't meant to let him know that she was aware that he hadn't much funds. Most men were very sensitive about such things.

She shot him a quick sideways glance and was surprised by the look of great amusement on his face. Her brow wrinkled. What a strange man he was. He actually seemed to be happy about not having any money.

"Money's not everything, you know," he said. Because his voice was suddenly so serious, Noel's eyes darted to his face. And as though he sensed her eyes on him, he turned toward her.

Their glances collided and held, and a shiver she was barely able to conceal racked Noel from head to toe. The moment seemed to stretch for an interminable amount of time, and then she pulled her eyes away with a thudding heart and focused blindly on the road. There had been something deep in his eyes that she had never before noticed in anyone. There was a curious wisdom lurking in the depths of his black eyes. It was as though he knew or understood something about life that she didn't.

"Where're we going again?" she asked abruptly. There were goose bumps covering the flesh of both arms now, and it wasn't because she was cold.

"We'll get the Kwanzaa candles first, if that's OK."

She nodded. It didn't matter to her what they got first. She wasn't particularly interested in getting either the candles or the tree. But to get him to sell his property, she would play along. She would probably just throw all of the Kwanzaa paraphernalia he forced on her into a drawer anyway. The tree would be a bigger problem. Maybe she would hire a contractor and have him chop it into firewood. Who would know the difference? It wasn't as though Nathaniel Hawkins would be back at her house. Ever.

Nat fiddled with the ancient tape deck, and Noel gritted her teeth. It would be Christmas music, she knew. And she just couldn't stand listening to any happy carols about chestnuts roasting or bells jingling. She had some very serious problems to work through. And it wasn't fair that everywhere she turned, people were wishing her a merry this and a happy that. Why couldn't they just leave her alone?

Music squeaked out of the speakers, and Noel sighed. Just as she had thought. The singer's deep baritone rattled through her head. " 'Twas the night before Christmas, and all through the house, not a creature was stirring, not even a . . ." She blocked out the rest of it, and was unaware that Nat was speaking to her until she felt his fingers on her arm.

"I'm sorry . . . what?" She tried to avoid looking at him this time, until she figured out exactly what was wrong with her. Why he had this peculiar effect on her. It would be best if she kept the eye contact to an absolute minimum. Because

Nathaniel Hawkins was not a man she could have. She could never say to him, *How would you like to go back to my place for a nightcap, and if things move in that direction then . . . ?* He was absolutely off-limits for so many reasons.

"I was asking you if you liked this time of year." His voice rose above the music, and Noel used that as an excuse to reach forward and turn the music down.

"This time of year? You mean wintertime?" She was being deliberately obtuse, she knew. But she really didn't want to hear anything he might have to say about the holiday season.

"Ah," he said. "So that's part of it."

"Part of what?" She forgot her earlier decision about not making eye contact with him. He had guessed that she had understood his question, and her eyes bored into his, daring him to say again that she was lonely and that that was part of the reason why she didn't enjoy the season.

"Part of the reason why you're so unhappy. It's the time of year."

She fumed. "I don't know what you're talking about. Unhappy? Why should I be unhappy? I have everything that—"

"I know," he interrupted. "You have everything that most people think they need in order to be happy. Right?"

"Of course," she said tightly. "Do you know how many people would kill for what I have? My life is . . . is great. If I felt like it right now, I could be in Paris tomorrow. Or Rome. Or the Caribbean. Or . . . or just about anywhere at all."

He swung off the freeway, heading down an exit that said Figueroa Street. When they were again driving along the surface streets, he asked in a quiet voice, "Why aren't you happy then?"

"But . . . but . . ." she stammered for a few seconds. "Weren't you listening to what I just said?" Was he com-

pletely mental? She had just told him in very specific terms
exactly why it was that she was happy. Why didn't he believe
her?

They were pulling up to a small whitewashed building,
and Noel squinted up at the hand-painted sign just above
the door. It said, *First AME Church's Soup Kitchen and
Clothing Exchange.* She nodded to herself. Why hadn't she
guessed it? Of course he would buy the Kwanzaa candles
from a homeless shelter. He probably came here regularly
for his clothes too.

Nat cut the engine and turned in his seat, one arm draped
along the back of her seat. "We'll talk about things later.
OK?" He reached across to give her door a good thump
with his fist. Noel pulled herself back in the seat so that he
wouldn't brush against her by accident. "For now," he
continued once he'd managed to get the door open, "you'll
just have to enjoy yourself."

Noel stepped from the truck and slammed the door behind
her. Enjoy herself. *Right.* She would just have a screaming
good time shopping for secondhand candles and clothes at
the shelter. It would be an absolutely perfect night out.

Chapter Five

Nat stepped before her to open the door, and Noel noticed the peeling paint on and around the wooden frame. She suppressed a sigh. The whole place was a wreck. Why was it that everything in this neighborhood was in this horrible state? Did no one care?

"After you," Nat said, smiling down at her. Noel didn't return his smile. As far as she could see, there was absolutely nothing to smile about. This was the neighborhood she had grown up in. It had never been a wealthy area, but twenty years before it had never looked like this. So run-down. So completely devoid of hope.

She stepped into the little alcove that led into the belly of the building, and her eyes ran hurriedly over the slogan on one of the walls. It read, *For the Motherland, cradle of civilization. For the ancestors and their indomitable spirit. For the elders, from whom we can learn so much. For our youth, who represent the promise of tomorrow. For our people, the original people. For our creator, who provides all things great and small.*

An important message from the ARABESQUE Editor

Dear Arabesque Reader,

Because you've chosen to read one of our Arabesque romance novels, we'd like to say "thank you"! And, as a special way to thank you, we've selected four more of the books you love so well to send you for FREE!

Please enjoy them with our compliments, and thank you for continuing to enjoy Arabesque...the soul of romance.

Karen Thomas
Senior Editor,
Arabesque Romance Novels

Check out our website at
www.arabesquebooks.com

SPECIAL OFFER!
4 FREE BOOKS

ARABESQUE ®

A PRODUCT OF

★BET BOOKS™

3 QUICK STEPS
TO RECEIVE YOUR "THANK YOU" GIFT
FROM THE EDITOR

Send this card back and you'll receive 4 FREE Arabesque
novels! The introductory shipment of 4 Arabesque novels – a
$23.96 value – is yours absolutely FREE!

There's no catch. You're under no obligation to buy anything.
You'll receive your introductory shipment of 4 Arabesque
novels absolutely FREE (plus $1.99 to offset the costs of
shipping & handling). And you don't have to make any
minimum number of purchases—not even one!

We hope that after receiving your books you'll want to
remain an Arabesque subscriber. But the choice is yours to
continue or cancel, anytime at all! So why not take us up on
our invitation to receive 4 Arabesque Romance Novels, with
no risk of any kind. You'll be glad you did!

Call us
TOLL-FREE
at 1-800-770-1963

THE EDITOR'S "THANK YOU" GIFT INCLUDES:

- 4 books absolutely FREE (plus $1.99 for shipping and handling)
- A FREE newsletter, *Arabesque Romance News*, filled with author interviews, book previews, special offers, and more!
- No risks or obligations. You're free to cancel whenever you wish... with no questions asked.

BOOK CERTIFICATE

Yes! Please send me 4 FREE Arabesque novels (plus $1.99 for shipping & handling). I am under no obligation to purchase any books, as explained on the back of this card.

Name _____

Address _____ Apt. _____

City _____ State _____ Zip _____

Telephone ( ) _____

Signature _____

Offer limited to one per household and not valid to current subscribers. All orders subject to approval. Terms, offer, & price subject to change. Offer valid only in the U.S.

Thank you!

ANHL2A

Accepting the four introductory books for FREE (plus $1.99 to offset the cost of shipping & handling) places you under no obligation to buy anything. You may keep the books and return the shipping statement marked "cancelled". If you do not cancel, about a month later we will send 4 additional Arabesque novels, and you will be billed the preferred subscriber's price of just $4.00 per title. That's $16.00 for all 4 books for a savings of 33% off the cover price (Plus $1.99 for shipping and handling). You may cancel at any time, but if you choose to continue, every month we'll send you 4 more books, which you may either purchase at the preferred discount price. . . or return to us and cancel your subscription.

THE ARABESQUE ROMANCE CLUB: HERE'S HOW IT WORKS

ARABESQUE ROMANCE BOOK CLUB
P.O. Box 5214
Clifton NJ 07015-5214

PLACE
STAMP
HERE

Her eyes danced over the words, settled, and then returned to read more carefully. Nat came to stand at her side.

"It's a libation statement," he said.

"A what?" She looked at him, her eyes puzzled.

"It's an African tradition—and now an African-American tradition—to pour a libation, often water, in remembrance of our ancestors. It's usually done on special occasions. Like Kwanzaa, for example. And as the libation is poured, this"—he pointed at the wall—"is read."

"Oh," she said, and read the words again. For some reason, sudden tears pricked at the backs of her eyes. It was so profound. So . . . meaningful. Why had she lost touch with all of this? The question rattled around in her mind, and she didn't have an answer. Not a good one, anyway.

Noel bit down on the soft inner curve of her lip and tried to control the uncommon rush of emotion she felt. It was so silly to let simple words get to her like that. But they were more than just words. Confusion shone in her eyes. She couldn't exactly articulate what she meant. But the statement had touched something deep in her. Something she had thought was long dead.

"Come meet everyone," Nat was saying as she still stood staring at the writing on the wall. He laced his fingers with hers and pulled her along by the hand. At the feel of his skin against hers, Noel felt a warm glow light somewhere deep inside her. It had been such a very long time since she had held hands with a man. And even though they weren't really holding hands as lovers would, it was still his skin touching her skin. And the sensation of it was not unpleasant. Not unpleasant at all.

Nat pushed at another door, and noise and activity spilled into the quiet hallway. He ushered her before him, and as she stepped into the room, it was as though a wave of pure energy reached out and grabbed hold of her. There was suddenly color, light, laughter, song. It was almost overwhelming to the senses. And Noel stood like a rock right in the middle of the doorway, taking it all in. She hadn't expected this ... this happiness, not at a place like this one. She had expected a ramshackle room with hardly any furnishings. Maybe long wooden tables with large pots of soup or stew. Weary, worn-out women standing behind the tables with big ladles, slopping food into bowls. A shuffling line of homeless men and women with outstretched hands and rheumy eyes. But not this.

Her eyes sparkled as long-dead memories came to the surface. There was a choir singing. "Joy to the World," gospel style, hands clapping, voices raised in glorious song. She turned and said spontaneously to Nat, "This is incredible. It's ... it's just like my old church. The one my mom used to take me to every Sunday morning. She was a Baptist, you know."

And for some reason completely unclear to Noel, he bent and kissed her on the cheek. She looked at him with surprised eyes, and he smiled in a manner that caused her heart to begin a rapid pounding in her chest.

"Come," he said. "Let's meet some of my friends."

The next few hours passed so quickly that Noel was actually disappointed when Nat came to whisper in her ear, "It's time to go, I think. We have to get the tree, remember?"

Noel nodded. *Oh, yes, the tree.* How strange that she had forgotten about that. In fact, she had forgotten about everything. Not even once in the past hours had she even remembered that she was Noel Petersen, the wealthy business mogul. Here, it didn't matter who she was. What she did. How much money she had. No one cared about that. What mattered here was something deeper. Much deeper. She had blended right in with Nat's friends, laughing and joking with them. And she had pitched in too, serving juicy cuts of chicken, soft-baked potatoes topped with cheese, sour cream, and chives. Talking to the men and women who walked in off the streets, hoping for a warm meal and a measure of kindness. It had made her feel good about herself. Good about life. Somehow, in some strange way, she didn't feel nearly so empty now.

Noel glanced at her watch as Nat maneuvered her toward the door. It was almost ten-thirty.

"Are you sure there'll be Christmas tree lots open at this hour of the night?"

"Sure," he said. "Most of them don't close shop until at least eleven. Some stay open even later than that."

A short, plump little woman Noel had taken an immediate liking to bustled by with a dish of spongy corn bread as they had almost made it to the door. She gave Noel a warm smile and asked, "When'll we see you again?" And then to Nat, "Just see that you bring her back again soon. OK?"

Nat grinned. "Yes, ma'am."

Noel smiled at the little woman. "Don't worry, Sadie," she promised. "I'll be back."

"You two will see each other again anyway . . . whether you come back here or not," Nat added. And at Noel's questioning look, he said, "Sadie works at the community center too."

"Oh," Noel said. She had almost forgotten about that. About her luxury condominium project. Her multimillion-dollar venture. What she had learned here tonight had put all other thoughts out of her head. She had learned something so very important. Something that she might never have realized had she not had this experience. She understood now why it was that Nat had opted for this kind of life, instead of the one he could so easily have had. It was deeply rewarding to give. All the money in the world could not have purchased the wonderful feeling she now had.

As Nat opened the outer door, Noel turned one final time to look behind her. When she had arrived just hours before, she had seen the building as nothing more than a run-down, ramshackle wreck that was worthy of little more than demolition. Now . . .

"You know you can come back whenever you like?"

"I know," she said. "I can see why you do this . . . now."

He pulled his jacket closer as they stepped out into the night air. "I don't do any of it for myself, though. You know what I mean?"

Noel nodded, because she was really beginning to understand exactly what he did mean. He opened the passenger-side door and waited for her to climb into the truck and seat herself comfortably. He shut the door behind her, and then walked around to the driver's side.

"Hope we don't have any trouble getting started this time."

Noel chuckled. "Well, if we do, I'll get out and push." She was already thinking that maybe as an extra little gift to him, once the deal was concluded, she would buy him a nice brand-new truck. Maybe even an SUV if he preferred it.

He leaned forward to turn the key in the ignition just as the door to the building burst open and a tall teenage boy dashed out. Nat cranked down his window.

"Now, look at that," he said. "We would've had to come all the way back here if I'd forgotten that."

Noel squinted at the boy. "What? Have you adopted a kid now too?"

Laughter rumbled in his chest. "Funny girl," he said. He reached an arm through the window to grab what the boy was carrying. "Thanks, Aaron. Tell your mama I'll drop by next week. OK? And you stay out of trouble."

The boy grinned at Nat. "Cool." And he waved at them as they pulled away.

"What's that?" Noel asked after a moment of pensive

silence. The *I'll drop by your mama* comment had gotten her attention.

"Forgotten about Kwanzaa so soon?" And he handed her a beautifully carved object that looked to Noel very much like a Jewish menorah.

She turned it over. "Nice craftsmanship. Is this where the candles go?"

"Uhm-hmm," he said, and he slowed down to let a large Metro bus go by. "Aaron—the kid you saw back there— he carved it. It's called a Kinara. We need to stop and get red, green, and black candles."

Noel poked her fingers into the nicely carved holders. "He's very good."

"I know," Nat said. "I taught him myself."

Noel's brows lifted. "You?"

"At the community center. That's one of the classes I teach. Aaron's a really talented kid. But he's kind of high-spirited. What he needs is a strong male figure around all the time . . . to keep him in line. He's run into trouble from time to time with the PD."

Noel made a clucking sound with her tongue. "Anything major?"

"No. Not yet. I keep him really busy after school at the community center. His mother works two jobs, so she's not usually there in the afternoons when he gets in. She tries to be there for him on the weekends. Gets him involved in church activities, like the Feed the Homeless programs."

"No father?"

He turned into Jerry's Ice Cream Parlor before saying, "You know how it is. The father may have been around at one time. But he's long gone." He cut the engine and turned in his seat to look at her. "Feel like a cone? This place sells the best ice cream in the neighborhood. People come from all over the state for a taste of their chunky Midnight Magic. Or their Dark and Sexy."

At her unsure expression, he tapped her lightly on the arm and said, "Come on. You only live once. You can't miss a treat like this."

Noel placed the Kinara carefully at her feet. "OK, Mr. Hawkins," she said. "But I'm gonna be thinking of you tomorrow when I'm sweating it off in the gym."

"Fair enough," he said. And he was out of the truck and slamming the door before she could even think to say any more. "I'll get it," he said, leaning through the open window. "What do you like? Strawberry? Chocolate?"

She nodded. "My two favorite flavors."

"Good," he said. "You'll like Midnight Magic then."

Minutes later, Noel was making little sounds of amazement as she sampled the ice cream in her hand.

"This is," she said between swallows, "the most incredible-tasting ice cream I've ever had. How do they do this?"

"They're really good," Nat agreed. He proffered his cone. "Try this. It's called Orange Fantasy."

Noel leaned forward and ran her tongue around the entire rim of the cone. "Umm," she said, "good. Really, really good. Want to try mine?"

A little thrill went through her at the warm feel of his fingers holding her hand steady as he bent toward her. She held her breath as his tongue caressed the mound of red-and-brown ice cream. It was such a completely innocent act, and yet she couldn't seem to control the erotic wanderings of her mind. She could so easily imagine that she, and not the ice cream, was at the center of such loving attention.

"I think," he said, after taking yet another taste of her cone, "I think they somehow manage to get better each time. I don't remember this ever being so good." His thumb softly stroked the underside of her wrist before he let go of her hand.

And with her heart fluttering in her chest, Noel said, "With the right funding, they could be as big as that thirty-one flavors place." Then, because she was still so confused by her reaction to him, she asked the question she'd been mulling over since they'd left the First AME building.

"Do you visit Aaron's mother a lot?"

Nat hid a smile behind his half-finished cone and carefully considered his response. "Are you asking if Aaron's mother and I are involved?"

Noel swallowed a giant gulp of ice cream, and tried to gather her thoughts. She didn't want him to think that she had a personal interest in whatever his response might be. Because she didn't. It didn't matter one iota to her who he went out with. It was just that he had said very definitely earlier in the evening that he wasn't seeing anyone. So naturally she had wondered.

"I . . . I was just making conversation really," she assured him, a ring of ice cream lightly coating her top lip. "You don't have to answer. It was . . . it was probably not an appropriate question anyway."

He reached forward to rub a gritty thumb across her top lip. "You had some cream there," he said when she froze in surprise. And without giving her a chance to properly recover from that, he rubbed his thumb over her softly pouting top lip again. Noel took in a sharp breath, then stopped breathing altogether. There was no question about it, she knew. That last touch had been a definite caress.

"No more ice cream," he said softly. "Now," he continued in the same tone, "you were saying your question was inappropriate. Right?"

Noel crunched on the sugar cone. "I don't even know why I asked it."

"Well, I'm glad you did ask it. I don't want there to be any misunderstandings between us."

Noel gave him a steady black-eyed look. What was he talking about? There was no "them." Not in that sense anyway. They were nothing more than business associates.

OK, maybe she did find him a bit attractive, but nothing could ever come of it. Nothing *would* ever come of it. She didn't indulge in affairs with her clients.

She forced herself to concentrate on what he was saying, and tried to think of how exactly she might get things back onto a strictly business footing.

"I sometimes drop by Aaron's mother's place to help with things about the house that might need fixing. I'm good with my hands, and she seems to appreciate the help."

A slight ridge appeared between Noel's brows. Of course the woman appreciated the help. Sometimes men were so blind. So stupid. Couldn't he see what was going on? If he thought for even one second that Aaron's mother didn't have other intentions toward him, then he was even more mental than she had originally thought him to be.

"Is this . . . this woman a young one?" She ignored the whisperings of her conscience. The question did not qualify as a strictly business-related one. But she was curious. Nothing more. Just curious.

He shifted in his seat and started the truck, and as they puttered back into the flow of traffic, he said, "I guess she's young. Relatively young." He turned his head to look at her. "I never really paid too much attention, though."

"She might be a good choice for you then. Since she's young, I mean."

"I don't think she's a good choice . . . not for me anyway." And he slanted a glance at her before returning his attention again to the road.

"Well, it's not healthy to be all alone all the time. Trust me, I know. Besides, you definitely need someone around to take care of you." And as the words came out of her mouth, she cursed her wayward tongue. Now, why had she said that?

"You don't think I'm doing a good job of looking after myself?"

Noel's eyes flickered over his clothes. It wouldn't be out of bounds for her to tell him that his clothing needed some attention. She'd just be giving him some very helpful, practical advice that could possibly help him in the long term.

"I don't want to be too critical. But . . . as a man of some standing in the community . . ." Now, how could she say this gently? "Don't you think you should pay just a little more attention to how you dress?" There. She had said it. Now, if he didn't like her honesty, it was just too bad. A little truth never hurt anybody. It was for his own good anyway.

He was silent for a long moment, and Noel turned her head to look out the window. Well, she had offended him, it would seem. Or maybe he was hurt. She hadn't meant to hurt his feelings. She bit down on her bottom lip. Sometimes she was just a little too blunt. She had to learn to hold her tongue. She would tell him she was sorry. That his clothes weren't that bad.

She turned back and was surprised to see an indecipherable look on his face. She cleared her throat, thinking of how to begin again. Apologies did not come easily to her. In fact, she hardly ever made them.

"I'm . . . ah . . . I didn't—"

But her words were interrupted by his low, grating question: "Why don't you look after me? I'd certainly do a good job of looking after you."

Her mouth flopped open, wobbled for a bit, and then closed with a snap.

"What?" He had definitely gotten the wrong impression; that was certain. And here she had been worried that she had somehow carelessly hurt his feelings. He wasn't hurt at all.

"It makes sense, doesn't it? You don't have anyone. I don't have anyone. You need me. I need you."

Noel cranked down the window and let the night breeze

cool her face. She had never said or even hinted that she might need him. His assumption was presumptuous. Ridiculous. *And true,* a traitorous voice somewhere deep inside whispered. She ignored the voice.

"I never, ever mix business and ... and anything personal."

Nat turned into a giant Christmas tree lot and parked the truck in a patch of soft red mud.

"You never make exceptions?"

Noel swallowed. She couldn't believe she was actually having this conversation with him. It was entirely her fault, though. She had created this aura of false intimacy between them with her unwise questions.

"Hardly ever." And she fumbled with the lock on the door. She had to get out of the truck and away from him. Suddenly there wasn't enough air, enough space between them.

He reached across her to help with the door, and when the catch was free he straightened up to say, "OK. We'll just be friends then. Good friends."

Noel mumbled a brief agreement beneath her breath, and got out of the truck with a heavy feeling in the pit of her stomach.

Chapter Six

It was very close to midnight before they finally chugged back up the long driveway leading to Noel's beach house. They had spent more than half an hour at the Christmas tree lot, walking up and down rows and rows of fir trees. They had all looked more or less the same to Noel. But Nat had been on a crusade to locate that one special tree. It had taken them a good long while to find it. But then, suddenly, there it was. And Nat had inspected it from all angles before saying with deep satisfaction in his voice, "Now, this is a good tree. See how sturdy the branches look? And the pine is just the right color of green. The taper's not bad either. Very symmetrical. It'll look great once it's decorated."

Noel had looked at it, and agreed that it was indeed a nice looking tree. She hadn't the heart to tell him, since he was so very enthusiastic about finding it, that she had no intention of ever decorating the thing. She didn't know what she was going to do with it now. Somehow chopping it into firewood didn't seem so very appealing anymore.

They left the lot with the tree nicely tied and bundled in the back of the pickup truck. Then they stopped at an all-night convenience store for the candles. By then Noel was beginning to struggle against a wave of fatigue. It had been a very long day. Nat had insisted on paying for everything, even though Noel knew that he quite probably couldn't afford it.

Once back in the truck, he had invited her to rest her head against his shoulder. She had resisted the idea at first, but then, as the miles stretched onward, and the feeling of bone-weariness stretched along with them, she had given in and rested her head against him for just a minute. Just a minute.

She was aware of nothing more until a hand gently shook her awake.

"We're home," the kind voice in her ear said.

Noel muttered a response, and snuggled more deeply against the beautiful warm thing she was lying against.

"Come on, honey," the voice said. And somewhere in deep slumber Noel heard the endearment and smiled in response. It had been a while since anyone had referred to her in that manner, and she liked it. The voice had seemed so sincere.

"Just a minute more, honey," she replied. "I'm so tired."

An arm came about her, and she had the unsettling feeling that she was somehow floating. The voice asked her a question, and she rubbed her nose against something warm and prickly. It felt like a chin. *No, it couldn't be.*

"What?" she muttered, as her feet banged against a hard and smooth object. She opened an eye and then closed it again. It was all right; she was in her living room. She was just having a strange dream.

She floated again for a while, perfectly content and safe. Then the voice said, "You are a deep sleeper, sweetheart."

And she felt something soft and very comfortable against her back. She opened both eyes then, staring blurrily at the dark shape above her. Her heart pounded for an instant. Who was this in her bedroom in the middle of the night? Then, as the veil of sleep retreated, she sat up slowly with an embarrassed, "Oh. I fell asleep." This was totally unlike her. She usually suffered from insomnia. She never fell off to sleep this easily. Never.

Nat sat on the edge of the bed. "It was a long day, and you work a little bit too hard, I think."

Noel stared at him. "How did I get up here? How'd we get in?"

He shrugged.

"I found your keys in your pocketbook. And I carried you up."

"Up all those stairs?"

"I've carried much heavier than you." He stood with his hands shoved into his pockets. "I'll come by again tomorrow evening so that we can get the tree and the Kinara all set up. If that's OK with you?"

She swung her legs to the floor. Tomorrow? He was actually coming back then?

"Thank you for carrying me," she said, "but you really don't have to go to all that additional trouble over the tree and the Kinara; I can just—"

He jingled his keys. "I'd like to do it. Unless you don't want me to?"

She denied it immediately. "No. Of course you can, if you really want to. I was just thinking of you having to drive all the way out here again . . . ."

"I do a lot of driving in my line of work. Besides, it'll be fun. In life you should always make room for a little fun. Don't you think so? It shouldn't be all about work all the time." He smiled at her. "Well, I'll get going. See you at the center tomorrow? I'll call you and we'll figure out a time."

Noel walked him back downstairs, said "Good night, and

thank you again for . . . for everything tonight,'' and watched from the arch of the doorway while he removed the tree from the back of his truck and rested it just beside the stairs. She waved at him as he started the engine.

When he had gone, she closed and locked the door, and then leaned back against the polished wood. It had been nice having him around for a few hours. But he had left without even trying to give her a good-night kiss. Not that she wanted one. She had just expected him to try.

Noel straightened from her position against the door. It didn't matter. She had a lot of things to think about. She had to plan the Kwanzaa festival, and then really focus on what needed to be done to get the Windsor Hills project off the ground. Once Windsor was well on the road, her company would get many other such projects. Inner Visions Management Company, the multibillion-dollar conglomerate that had hired her to do the job, had assured her of it.

She walked slowly upstairs. Nat would come around to her way of thinking soon enough. Windsor would be good for the community. Things would work out. They would.

Chapter Seven

Nat called her at seven the next morning, just as she was stepping from the shower. Noel draped a thick towel about herself and ran to get the phone.

"Yes?" she said. No one ever called her this early in the morning unless there was some sort of emergency.

"Good morning. Hope I didn't wake you."

At the sound of his voice, Noel visibly relaxed. All manner of wild thoughts had been running through her head. For some reason she had expected it to be a call from Inner Visions Management saying that her company had been fired from the Windsor job.

"Oh. It's you." She sat on the edge of the bed. "I thought—"

"I said I would call you today. Remember?"

Noel rubbed at the wet ends of her hair with the towel. Yes, she remembered. But she hadn't expected him to be so very early about it.

"You took the Kinara with you," she said.

"I'll bring it back this evening. Don't worry."

"Oh, I'm not worried," she rushed to assure him. It had just been something to say. She had decided just before falling into a very peaceful sleep the night before that she would try her level best to make sure that things remained on a strictly business footing between them.

"So, how're you feeling today?"

The question puzzled her for a minute. He seemed to be asking her something deeper.

"I guess I feel all right." Just as she felt most days. Not up, not down, just somewhere in the middle.

"But are you happy though?"

Noel wrapped the towel a bit tighter about her body. Happy? Was he back to that again?

"What does it matter if I'm happy?" She looked out the window at the beautiful blue ocean. At the green palm trees waving softly in the breeze. "Most people aren't happy every single day of their lives. Don't you know that yet? I mean, most people are just . . . just living their lives, you know? Happiness really doesn't come into it."

"Hmm," he said. "Is that what you really think?"

"Yes. That's what I really think," she said in a firm voice. What did he think life was anyway? Some sort of trip through the Land of Oz? Life was hard. And in order to make it, you had to be similarly hard. People were cruel. Vicious. Deceitful.

"Maybe you've been all alone in the world for a little too long. Life is supposed to be happy, you know. So, if you've managed to convince yourself that it's not, you need to rethink that."

Noel sighed. He would never understand. He was living in some other galaxy. Not in the real world. Not in the one in which she lived. He was so convinced about this happiness nonsense that she could clearly see that there was little point in arguing. She would not be able to convince him otherwise.

"Whatever you say. Look," she said, "I'll come down to the center at about four this afternoon. OK? I've got to go in to the office first." She forced herself to laugh. "They can't do without me there."

She heard the smile in his voice as he said, "I don't doubt it. I'll see you later then."

" 'Bye," she said, and hung up the phone. She sat on the bed for a moment more, staring absently into space. Why hadn't she asked him if he was happy? That certainly would've dried up all of his future comments about happiness.

Noel stood and went across to one of the bay windows. It was going to be one of those gorgeous blue-and-gold southern California days. Sun. Sea. Surf. She frowned at a seagull sitting peacefully on the sill.

"One of these days," she muttered, "I'm just going to stay home and lie out on the beach. I can be irresponsible and happy too."

At a few minutes before four, Noel pulled into the little chained-off parking lot that sat directly in front of the community center. She spent a moment more gathering together the blueprints on the passenger seat. She stacked them all neatly, rolled them, and then fit the entire collection into a cylindrical leather-bound carrying case. She had had a very interesting meeting with the architects. The Windsor condominiums were going to be absolutely beautiful. They were going to be done in the ultramodern town-house style. Split-levels with curving staircases connecting the two floors. Fireplaces and balconies. And they were going to be able to get everything done under budget too.

A sudden thump on one side of the car brought her head up. She wound her window down.

"Sorry, Miss Petersen," the tall youngster said, bending to retrieve the basketball.

"Aaron," Noel said, and she smiled at the worried face just above her. "Have you damaged my car?"

The boy had a careful look at the paintwork. "Naw. 'Sall right," he said, and he stood back and began dribbling the ball as Noel stepped from the car. She closed the door and armed her car alarm.

"This yours?" the boy asked once Noel was through.

"Yes," she said. "Do you like it?"

Aaron bounced the ball some more. " 'Sall right for a girl," he said, looking her snappy blue BMW Z3 Roadster over with a critical eye. "But the 500SL is really a man's car."

Noel laughed. Now, that was something she had never heard before. "Is that the kind of car you want?"

Aaron loped along beside her, never missing a beat with the ball. "Yeah. I might get me one of those," he agreed. "Maybe two." He looked at her with serious eyes. "When I get me an NBA deal, I'ma take my mama right outta here. You know. Buy her a nice house up in Baldwin Hills or somewhere like that. But . . . "

Noel looked at him. "But?"

The boy gave her a pensive look. "But depends if we stay 'round here or not."

Noel stepped over a large crack in the sidewalk. "Why does it depend on that?"

Aaron dribbled the ball, then performed an amazing feat of aerial acrobatics and slam-dunked the ball through a nearby hoop.

Noel stood watching him. He was good. But then, he seemed to be good at a lot of things.

"Why do you have to remain around here?" she prodded when he returned to walk beside her.

"I work out couple days a week with one of the SC

coaches. Didn't Nat tell you?'' And at her blank look, he continued with a trace of pride in his voice, "Coach thinks with 'bout a year's more work with him . . . I might be ready to be drafted.''

"Well, that's great," Noel said, and there was genuine admiration in her voice. "Just imagine that.''

Aaron shrugged in a very adult manner. "Won't happen, though, if those Windsor condo people come into the neighborhood.''

Noel blinked rapidly several times. "What?" she managed after a bit. "Why not? What does that . . . do they have to do with your getting drafted by the NBA?''

"Simple," the boy told her. "My mama will go back to Louisiana to live with her sister if they buy our house. And back in Louisiana . . . in the backwoods, they only have pigs and cows and stuff. So I won't have a coach. Not one like Pete Phillips, anyway. He's trained many of the guys now playing pro ball.''

"Oh," Noel said, and she chewed on the side of her mouth.

They had reached the side stairs leading to the second floor of the building, and Aaron stopped and gestured with a hand. "You'll find Nat up there somewhere.''

Noel gave the boy a little pat on the back. "Thanks. But aren't you coming?''

"Later," the boy said, and he bounded away toward the cracked basketball court. Noel watched him go. For a moment, she had been tempted to say exactly what Nat had said just the night before: *Make sure you keep out of trouble.* He was a nice kid. Such a nice kid. And she suddenly felt protective of him.

Noel continued up the stairs, a slight frown in the depths of her eyes. Surely what Aaron had said to her about missing out on a chance to be drafted by the NBA if her project continued couldn't be true.

At the top of the stairs, she paused to knock on the closed door. When she got no reply, she opened it and stepped into a long tiled hallway. She stood there for a bit, looking around. There were closed doors lining either side of the corridor. She knocked on the first door, then opened it and poked her head around. Just as she had guessed: a classroom.

She spent a moment there lifting up the tops of the wooden desks, looking inside. Then she went to one of the windows. Her eyes fell on Aaron down below. Two other teenagers had joined him, and the three were now involved in a lively game of ball. A wistful smile twisted her lips. She could remember a time when she too had been that young. That carefree. A time when she had really believed the world to be a different place, one filled with good, decent people. But the years had taught her that none of those things were true. She leaned her forehead against the glass and then almost jumped out of her skin.

"So what do you think?" the voice behind her asked, and she whirled around with a hand pressed to the center of her chest.

"God. Where'd you come from?"

Nat strolled into the room, and Noel sat firmly on the thrill that rippled through her at the sight of him. "Thought you might've gotten lost. So I decided to come look for you."

She gestured toward the window. "Aaron . . . down there told me where you were, so I didn't go up to your office again in that death trap."

He laughed in a rueful manner. "Good. That elevator is out of service now, by the way. So . . ." He rubbed his hands together in an enthused manner. "Are you ready to meet everyone?"

Chapter Eight

The next weeks passed quickly, and Noel was thrown into life at the community center. On the first afternoon Nat had shown her around, and Noel had noticed immediately that although the external facings of the building were in need of several coats of paint, things were surprisingly well maintained inside the community center. On the upper floors there were rooms with computers, video games, potter's wheels. There were playrooms with balls and slides, and general-usage rooms where business, art, and science were taught. And in the basement of the building, there was even a nicely maintained racquetball court and a lap pool. Nat had introduced her around to the counselors at the center, letting them all know that she was now their resident expert on Kwanzaa, and as such would be the one in charge of organizing the annual festival. Noel had felt like a bit of a fraud, especially since she knew very little about the holiday, but everyone had been so friendly that she had felt at home right away. And once she met some of the kids, she had put down her carrying case, rolled up her designer sleeves, and dived right into things.

Nat had put her in the room used for craft instruction and, with a wink of encouragement, left her there with a circle of children around her. But Noel had enjoyed herself immensely. She had fielded almost every question under the sun, from "Are you uncle Nat's girlfriend?" to "Can we do something extra special for the Kwanzaa festival this year?"

Noel had answered all of the questions, shaking her head and saying in a somewhat mournful voice that no she wasn't uncle Nat's girlfriend, which amused them all. And then she had promised that they would have the biggest and the best Kwanzaa festival that year.

Later in the evening, Nat had arrived at her house with Aaron, and together they had moved the Christmas tree into the middle of her living room. After a bit of a struggle, they had managed to place it neatly in its stand, and Nat had spread a black, red, and green Kwanzaa blanket around its base. They hadn't stayed very long, though, much to Noel's disappointment. But Nat had given her a hug and whispered in her ear, "We'll decorate this on Christmas Eve. OK? And we'll light the Kinara the day after Christmas." She had nodded and held on to him for a second longer than was necessary.

Now, two weeks later, after much study and reflection on Kwanzaa, Noel had finally decided exactly what she would do. The festival would be big. Extravagant. Like nothing the neighborhood had ever seen before. And not only would it be a block party to end all block parties, but it would involve one of the key principles of Kwanzaa.

She glanced at her watch. Where was Nat? He was late, and she wanted to discuss the idea with him. Of late, she had come to rely on his little visits. She was even able to admit now that she looked forward to them.

Noel walked into the kitchen to check on the two steaks in the oven. She had them on slow grill so that they would cook to a succulent tenderness. When they were ready, she intended to steep them both in spicy barbeque sauce. She had also cooked a pot of white rice with corn and had an entire bowl of potato salad chilling in the fridge.

She smiled to herself as she opened the oven and spooned some juice over the meat. It was funny how just a mere two weeks before she would never have thought of eating such a dinner. Too many calories. But everything was changing. The way she looked at things. The way she experienced life. And all because of Nat Hawkins. She chuckled. And to think she had actually been worried about how he dressed. She didn't care now how he dressed. Her lips curled. Well, OK, maybe she still did, but it wasn't nearly as important as it had been. She could now see the man beneath the rags.

Noel closed the oven and wiped her hands on a towel. Things were just about ready. The phone rang suddenly, and she ran across to the wall unit, took a breath to steady herself, and then answered. And the smile in Nat's voice was reflected in Nat's eyes.

"I'm just a few minutes away," he said. "I got hung up in my last class."

"Oh, the arts and crafts one?"

"No. Business finance."

"You teach that one too?" This was news. It hadn't occurred to her that he would know very much about finance. Why hadn't he asked her to teach it? Surely, of the two of them, she would have been the better choice. It was, after all, what she did for a living.

"I have many talents." He chuckled. "There just might be more to me than you originally thought, Noel Petersen. Hmm? What do you think?"

He was playing with her, she knew. So she played right

back. "Well, I don't know," she said thoughtfully. "Your clothes still have me puzzled."

He didn't miss a beat. "Now, if you were looking after me, there'd be no problem."

She laughed, and it was a hearty, full-bodied sound that warmed Nat's heart.

"You're such a flirt." She chuckled. "I bet you say that to all the women."

It was his turn to laugh. "Such a disbelieving young lady you are."

Noel heard the sound of a truck, and she asked, "Are you here?"

"I'm here." He paused to turn the engine off and then said, "I brought you something too."

Noel cradled the phone at her ear and smiled. "Something for me? Nat . . ." There was slight admonishment in her voice. He kept buying her things, and she knew he couldn't afford them.

"Open the door for me," he said. "I'm coming up the stairs."

"OK," she said. "I'm going to hang up now."

"Wait."

She brought the phone back up to her ear. "Wait?"

"I want something from you."

"Oh," she said with a silky note of fun in her voice. "No free lunches, huh?"

"Didn't you tell me nothing was free these days?"

Noel gave an elaborate and very staged sigh. "Me and my big mouth. What do you want from me now?"

"A kiss."

Her heart gave a sudden thump and then began a frantic pounding. He had a way of surprising her. She hadn't been expecting him to say that. But what of it? It was just a kiss. A short little kiss. A hot little kiss?

"On the phone?"

"Open the door and I'll show you how I want it."

Noel grinned. "I'm hanging up."

She replaced the phone in its bracket, gave herself a quick look in one of the living room mirrors, and then went to the front door. She snapped the locks, and then pulled it open, eyes shining.

"There you are," she said.

Nat folded the cell phone he still held in his hand and placed it in his shirt pocket. "Here I am . . . again." He lounged in the doorway, looking down at her. "You must be tired of me, huh? You see me every single day, and in the evenings too."

"Yes, I know," Noel agreed. "You do seem to be around all the time." She tilted her head and considered him with slitted eyes. "Now, why is that?"

He laughed. "It must be the food. What're you cooking? I could eat the kitchen table."

"Come in," she said, stepping out of his way. Her heart beat heavily in her chest as she closed the door behind him. Had he forgotten his request? Or was he waiting for a signal of some sort from her?

"Feel like eating out on the veranda this evening?" she asked over her shoulder. He stopped before the Kinara, which she had placed on the mantelpiece.

"Sure."

Nat followed her into the kitchen after adjusting the candles. "So . . ." he said as she busied herself with plates, knives, and forks. "Am I going to get my kiss, or are you going to make me beg?"

Noel laid the cutlery on the counter carefully, then looked up at him.

"Were you serious about that?" She was stalling. Why? It was just a simple kiss.

He leaned against the counter. "I've never been more serious."

"Okay." Her heart had begun to flutter again. It had been a long while since she'd been held by a man. Two years, ten days, to be exact. Was that the reason why she suddenly felt so nervous?

He touched her arm, and his fingers were gentle. "Don't worry," he said. "It's just me."

Noel tilted her head up and closed her eyes. She allowed his arms to wrap about her. She felt his nose rub against hers. A little wave of electricity rattled them both as his lips settled on hers, and Noel's mouth parted in shock. What was this? What had happened? His lips were actually sweet. Sweet and warm, and infinitely right somehow. She sighed. This was what she had needed for so long. So long. Why had she been such a fool? No one could exist as an island.

Time seemed to tumble slowly to a halt, and all Noel's concerns of the day simply withered away to nothing.

She kissed him slowly, tentatively, and it was as though she had never experienced this before. Never been kissed before. Every sensation was new. Special. Wonderful. One of Nat's hands gently stroked the smooth skin of her back while the other held her firmly. And it went on, and on, and on, until they were forced to finally part from each other, breathless.

Noel stepped back, her eyes bemused. Could this be real?

"Wow. What a kiss." She tried to make light of it, but the truth was, the experience had shaken her. She had never reacted like that before. No one had ever been able to lift such emotion from her.

Nat ran the back of an index finger down the curve of her cheek. "I waited a ton of years for that."

Noel turned blindly toward the stove. What was he talking about? A ton of years?

"Oh, you . . ." she said, bending to remove the meat from the oven. "You're always funning me."

Nat took the oven tray from her and then swore softly beneath his breath.

"It's still a bit hot," Noel said. "I'm sorry." And she took his fingers and blew softly on them. "Are you burned?"

Nat rubbed his fingers across hers. "These hands are like old leather. I just wasn't expecting that degree of heat," he said, when she still continued to regard him with contrite eyes.

"You sit down while I get everything ready," Noel said.

And she busied herself with the many pots and dishes as Nat perched himself on the lip of a smooth counter. It was a trifle unnerving having him watch her like that, but she worked quickly, ladling the rice, then the potato salad. She poured the barbeque sauce over the meats, and then placed them on separate plates. The soda was next. She had gotten his favorite, Coke. And as she removed it from the fridge, he said, "Soda? But you don't drink that."

She tossed him a little look over her shoulder. "Now I do." And she was rewarded with a smile.

When she was nearly through, she said, "I think I know what I'm going to do about the festival."

"Tell me," he said. He slid from the counter and began helping her carry the dishes out to the veranda.

"Well," she said, close behind him, "how about if we have a huge block party? With fun rides and games for the kids. Vendors selling African products. And"—she paused to put down a dish—"a stage with professional musicians."

Nat offloaded the plates in his hands, then straightened. "Sounds like an excellent idea," he said. "But do you think we have enough time to plan and execute all that?"

Noel gave him a little tap on the hand, and he looked down at her fingers and then back at her.

"That's the beauty of the whole idea." Her eyes sparkled with enthusiasm. "What is the third principle of Kwanzaa?"

He smiled. *"Ujima."*

Noel propped her hands on her hips. "Uhm-hmm. And what does it mean?"

"Ah," he said, nodding. "I see where you're going with this. Since *Ujima* means collective work, you intend to get the entire—"

"That's right," Noel said, a note of glee in her voice. "I'm going to get the entire community involved in putting this festival together. That way, even though the time is short, we'll be able to do it. And it'll be fun for everyone."

Hmm," he said. "I like the way you think, Miss Petersen. But what about the professional musicians? How're you going to arrange that?"

She gave him an audacious wink. "Don't worry about a single little thing. I've got my contacts. Now," she said, "time for food . . . and my present."

Chapter Nine

It was Christmas Eve, two days before the festival, and Noel sat in her office at her desk. She'd been busy all morning making last-minute phone calls. Preparations for the Kwanzaa festival had consumed her days over the past weeks. And she would never have been able to pull everything together so quickly had it not been for the people in the neighborhood. She had gone to the local First AME church and, after services, had asked the pastor if she might address the congregation. She had done this with a pounding heart, not knowing exactly how everyone might respond to her audacious idea. But she need not have worried at all. Afterward, almost every member of the congregation had come up to her and, after showering her with congratulations, which she didn't really think she deserved, had promised their total support.

And they had been as good as their word. Noel had divided the work up into committees, and everyone had pitched in. There were many late nights. But it had been fun. And suddenly she had more friends than she really knew what to do with. The mothers knew her. The children knew her. Even the homeless people on the corners now called her by name. Suddenly her name, Noel, had assumed a totally different significance. Some called her their Christmas angel. And this humbled her.

In next to no time at all, she had become something of a legend in the community. And despite her every attempt to suppress the feeling of happiness that swept over her whenever she thought about it, she couldn't. These were her people. This was her neighborhood. They needed her. She needed them. And this good, solid feeling was something that all the money in the world couldn't buy.

There was a knock at her office door, and at Noel's "Come in," her secretary poked her head around.

"Oh, Sue," Noel said, looking up from the pad on which she'd been scribbling. "Leaving now?"

Her secretary smiled. "Yes. I just wanted to pop in to wish you a merry Christmas . . . and to give you this." She produced a very large package from behind her back.

Noel rose from her seat. "A gift? For me?" She was touched. Deeply. It was the first time any of her staff had ever given her anything. She had always made sure that they received their Christmas bonuses, of course. But since she had been no fan of the holiday season, she had never given presents. But this year, because the scales were finally beginning to fall from her eyes, she had.

"It's nothing much, really," Sue said, coming forward. "But I saw it in one of the stores a few days ago, and as soon as I did, I thought of you." She placed the package on Noel's desk. "I hope you like it."

Noel bit her lip and fought against the sudden rush of tears. How nice it was to have people really care about you. It really was the best thing in the world. Better than having money.

"Thank you, Sue," she said, swallowing the tears clustered at the back of her throat. "I'm sure I'll love it."

Her secretary beamed at her. "Well," she said, "have a merry Christmas. And a happy Kwanzaa."

"Yes," Noel said, and her eyes glittered with unshed tears. "You too." And she waved a hand. "Go on. Go home to your family."

Sue hesitated. "Do you have . . . do you have anything planned for tonight and tomorrow? I mean, if . . . if you're not doing anything special, we would love to have you over for Christmas dinner . . . if you can stand the kids. They get very hyper at this time of year."

Noel came out from behind her desk to give her secretary a warm hug. "That's probably one of the nicest things anyone has ever said to me. And ordinarily I wouldn't have had a single thing planned. But, Nat . . . you remember him? He's come here a couple times. Well, he's . . . I'm probably going to do something with him."

"Good." Sue smiled. "I like him. He seems like a very decent sort of person. A good man. The kind you don't let get away."

Noel returned the woman's smile. Her secretary was right. Men like Nathaniel Hawkins definitely did not come along every day. In fact, they hardly ever did come along.

"Merry Christmas," Noel said. "And don't worry about all the work still on your desk. We'll take care of the Windsor project once everyone gets back after New Year's."

Once she had gone, Noel returned to her seat behind the desk. She was awaiting a very important call. She'd been thinking about the Windsor condominium project over the past weeks. And the more she thought about it, the less she was able to convince herself that it would indeed be a good thing for the community, as she had originally thought. She hadn't considered the human element before. The project had made complete sense on paper. The numbers had made sense. But now that she was in the thick of the community, now that she had seen some of the problems firsthand, she knew that erecting a luxury complex and pushing the people out would solve none of them. The Windsor project would disrupt too many lives. Too many dreams. Aaron's dreams. All the dreams being spun by the counselors at the community center.

She rubbed a hand across her forehead. It just wasn't the right thing to do. It wasn't. And she had to find a way to stop Inner Visions Management from going ahead with the project. Because she knew that they would go ahead with it whether her company was involved or not.

The phone rang suddenly, and she reached for it. "Noel Petersen." She listened for a bit and then said, "Great. Let's meet on the third of January. I'll call you later to confirm the time. Right. No, no, everything's fine. I just need to talk ... Well, I don't want to go into it now. Okay. See you later then. And merry Christmas."

Noel hung up with a smile on her face. She hadn't expected to get a meeting with the CEO of Inner Visions so easily. But maybe God was in her corner, since her motives were purely selfless ones.

She grabbed her bag and stood. Now she could go home to Nat and decorating the Christmas tree.

Later that evening, she was perched on a ladder with reams of red and silver tinsel in her hands.

"I haven't done this in years," she said, laughing down at Nat. "Am I doing it straight?"

He stepped back, tilting his head. "A little more to the left, I think. Okay, right there. You've got it."

Noel hung the tinsel meticulously from each branch. "I'm gonna want some serious eggnog after I finish this," she said, wiping imaginary sweat from her brow.

Nat grinned. "And you shall have that and more, honey."

Noel wagged a finger at him. "Pass me those blue balls, sir."

He handed them over, and then busied himself in another box. He emerged with something green in his hand. "Mistletoe," he said, holding it above his head and wiggling his eyebrows.

Noel chuckled. "Later," she promised.

He winked at her and said, "I'm going to remember you said that."

When she was finally finished hanging all of the shiny balls, she looked down at him. "Do you think we really need the popcorn?"

Nat gave her a look of mock horror. "What? A fully decorated tree without popcorn? It's required by law, you know."

"Okay. Okay. Hand me the corn," she said, reaching for the long cord of strung popcorn. She pulled one from the very end of the string and popped it into her mouth.

"Delicious," she said, and pulled another so that he might taste too.

Nat came forward and deliberately nipped at her finger. Noel shrieked and pulled back her hand.

"Now you're getting vicious," she said. "And to think I was going to be extra nice to you tonight."

And so they continued, joking back and forth with each other until the tree was fully dressed and resplendent, a large, sparkling star positioned at the very top. Nat helped Noel down from the ladder and together they regarded the tree.

"It's beautiful," Noel said. And it was. The winking red, white, and gold lights. The shimmering silver tinsel. The gorgeous blue balls.

Nat wrapped warm arms about her waist, holding her

before him. "Let's go for a walk on the beach," he whispered in her ear.

Noel turned. "A walk on the beach? At this hour?"

"I'll protect you," Nat said, kissing the tip of her ear. And Noel smiled because she knew that he would.

"Let me grab a jacket then."

Minutes later they were walking hand in hand in the crunching sand. They walked for a good stretch up the beach, not saying a word, just enjoying the sound of the foaming waves and the pull of the wind. Finally Nat spoke. "It's nice out here," he said. "Maybe I'll buy a house somewhere along the coast."

"Hmm," Noel agreed. She hadn't the heart to tell him that on his salary, he probably would never be able to afford a place like hers.

She looked up at him. "How come you've never invited me over to where you live?" she asked. As far as she could see, there was little point in encouraging him to dream of owning a beach house. It would never happen.

He smiled at her and tickled her nose with a finger. "I will. Soon."

"Such a cryptic response," she teased. "What's the matter? Don't you want me to see your place?" She didn't care if he lived in a hovel; didn't he know that?

He laughed and transferred her arm to his waist. "Over the weeks, we've gotten closer. Wouldn't you say so?"

She poked him in the side. "You made me break my rule about never mixing business and play—sure," she said, stretching the syllables deliberately.

He grinned at her. "You never stood a chance."

She chuckled. "You're so conceited."

"Not conceited, my love," he said. "Just determined. You know I've been seriously into you since we were kids."

She glanced at him with shining eyes. "There you go funning me again."

"I'm serious," he said. Noel met his eyes and her heart shuddered. He *was* serious. She looked down at their sand-encrusted feet and tried to calm her roiling mind. Could two people fall in love with each other so quickly? In mere weeks? Was that possible? She had strong feelings for him; there was no doubt about that.

"How come you never said anything to me in school then? Or even after that? I was always in the news. You could've found me."

"You were too young in school. And afterward I had to wait until the time was right," he said.

Noel had no idea at all what he meant by that, but she smiled up at him and said, "Well, I'm glad we ran into each other again." Was she ever glad. He didn't know it, but he had changed her entire outlook on life.

Nat shifted her to stand before him, and there with the ocean curling about their ankles, he kissed her. And as he did, Noel was certain she heard bells jingling. A choir singing. And she sighed and held him tightly, because she knew that something strange and wonderful was happening.

Christmas day came and went quickly. Too quickly, as far as Noel was concerned. But it was simply one of the most wonderful days she had ever spent, and she told Nat this with tears glistening in her eyes as he kissed her gently and handed her a nicely wrapped box. She had opened it and gasped. "Oh, it's beautiful. But Nat . . . you shouldn't have been so extravagant." A bracelet of the purest diamonds, set in soft white gold. It must have cost him more than two months salary.

She gave him a fully loaded laptop computer with a large selection of additional software. He had held her close and said, "Thank you, honey. I'll treasure this. Always."

It had been a magical day. One for the record books. And

when it was finally over, Noel had snuggled in Nat's arms as they lay together before the fireplace. And she was besieged by feelings of joy and contentment. She had fallen into slumber until just before midnight, when Nat had shaken her gently awake to say, "Time to light the Kinara."

He turned the lights off so that the blinking Christmas tree cast a dappled pattern across the walls. Then together they lit the candles, repeating the seven principles of Kwanzaa as they did so: *Umoja. Kujichagulia. Ujima. Ujamaa. Nia. Kuumba. Imani.* Unity. Self-determination. Collective work. Cooperative economics. Creativity. Faith.

Later the next day, Noel stood in the middle of South Central Los Angeles, in the midst of the biggest block party the city had ever known. There were rows and rows of vendors, selling everything from African masks to software with Afro-centric themes. The food stands were loaded with barbequed ribs, fried Louisiana crawfish, and a variety of other delicacies. The pastries and cakes were warm, delicious, and plentiful. But nothing attracted the crowds like the carousel and donkey rides. And the constant rotation on three stages of some of the best jazz and R&B musicians in the region gave the proceedings the proper festive air. It was a spectacle like none other, and Noel was proud.

"Noel," someone called now. "You did it, girl."

She smiled and waved. She had no idea who the woman was, but she was slowly getting accustomed to having perfect strangers call her by name.

Nat appeared suddenly from out of the crowd and he caught her about the waist, spinning her around. Noel laughed heartily.

"Are you happy yet?" he asked, holding her away from him.

"Yes," she said without hesitation. *Yes. Yes. Yes.* She

didn't think it was possible to be happier than she was right then. Everything had come together so well. And it had been a community effort, not something she had orchestrated from the confines of her executive office. She was even more determined, now, that the Windsor project not happen. Not in her neighborhood. And whatever she had to do to make Inner Visions back off, she was willing to do.

Chapter Ten

A week later, those very words were echoing in Noel's head as she walked into the corporate offices of Inner Vision Management. The building was on Wilshire Boulevard, in the high-rent district.

She walked with purpose to the elevator, and pressed the button that said Penthouse 4. And all the way up, she silently rehearsed what she would say to the CEO. She couldn't appeal to him on the basis of right and wrong. He wouldn't understand or care if he disrupted the lives of hundreds of people. She had run the numbers again last night, and they still supported South Central Los Angeles as an ideal location for the condominium project. But she had come up with a way to twist things, a way to use the numbers. She had learned in her many years of negotiating deals that very wealthy people always became reasonable when she talked money and showed how they might lose it.

Noel took a deep breath and then stepped from the elevator. She smiled at the receptionist.

"I'm Noel Petersen," she said, coming forward with a brisk step.

The woman beamed at her and said, "Yes, Miss Petersen. The owner is waiting for you." Noel's brows lifted. "The owner?" Boy, was she in it now. Had they somehow gotten wind of the fact that she no longer wanted to be a part of the Windsor project? Was that the reason why the owner himself was here?

"Yes." The woman nodded. "A special treat for us all. He's hardly ever here, you know. But he came by today and heard you were coming. And since you've been doing such a great job for us, he wanted to thank you personally."

Noel swallowed. *Oh, God.* She hadn't counted on this at all. Now what was she going to do?

"You can go right in," the receptionist said. "Through that door. He's just wrapping up a meeting." She pointed to a pair of streaked mahogany double doors.

Noel adjusted the front of her pin-striped suit, thanked the woman, and walked toward the doors. Never in all of her business life had she ever been this nervous. She pushed the smooth wood and entered. And instantly the cold and analytical part of her brain began to work. Her gaze swept the suite. It was huge, much larger than hers. There was no desk, just a sunken area with a black leather sofa arranged around an intricately fashioned solid-glass table. At the opposite end of the massive suite was a bar and a bank of television sets. And curving around the entire suite were sweeping floor-to-ceiling windows that provided a panoramic view of Los Angeles. It was without question the suite of a tycoon. A truly wealthy man.

Noel walked down the short flight of carpeted stairs and made her way across to the leather sofa. This was probably going to be one of the most difficult things she would ever have to do. She sat and waited, her brain churning. She would begin by thanking him for the opportunity to work on Windsor. Then she would launch right into it. There was no other way.

The door behind her opened after only a brief period of waiting, and she turned, a smile of greeting on her face. But the polite expression of professionalism turned into a beam of genuine warmth.

"Nat," she said. "What're you doing here?" Had he somehow found out about her meeting and dropped by to lend her some moral support?

Her eyes darted over him. And where had he gotten the clothes? This was a power suit if she'd ever seen one. A navy blue Armani, no less. And it was molded to his frame in the most amazing way. She had never seen a man look more splendid in a suit.

He came slowly down the stairs, a smile on his face.

"So," he said. "Here we are. Finally."

Noel blinked at him. What did he mean, finally? "How'd you know I'd be here?"

They told me you'd be here."

Noel met his eyes. "They? They who?"

"I own this company, you know," he said slowly, letting his words sink in. Noel swallowed hard. "No, you don't. You can't. You're poor. You don't have any money at all." Her words were badly chosen, but she was in a state of shock, and her tongue was moving almost independently of her brain.

"I never once said that I didn't have any money. You just assumed I didn't, honey."

She turned away from him, and then spun back around to face him. "You hired me . . . my company to build luxury condominiums in . . . in South Central . . . how? Why? When you were never in support of the project in the first place? It doesn't make any sense."

"I hired you," he said gently, "so that you could find yourself again. I've kept an eye on you for many years. You were so driven, and so lonely. I couldn't stand aside any longer and watch you go it alone.''

Hot tears stung the backs of her eyes. ''You mean, you did this . . . all this for me?''

''Yes. My gift to you. I wanted to give you back all those things you'd lost.''

She blinked rapidly, and a tear slid over the edge of an eye. ''So . . . there's no Windsor project?''

''There's no Windsor project.'' He paused. ''Are you mad at me?''

Noel shook her head. Mad? No, she wasn't mad at him. She just couldn't believe it all. He was really rich? Richer than she was? What about his truck and his ragged clothes? All those horrible things she had thought about him in the beginning. What a superficial fool she had been.

''I . . . I . . .'' For the first time in her life, she was at a complete loss for words. ''I don't know what to say,'' she finally managed.

''Can I come over there?'' he asked. Noel nodded, and he folded her in his arms. ''You're shaking,'' he said against her ear.

''I just can't . . . can't believe you did all this for me. No one . . . no one before has ever cared . . . only my mom.'' She sniffed.

''I have so much more to show you,'' he said. ''Will you let me?''

Noel lifted eyes still wet with tears. ''Yes,'' she said. And she rested her head against his chest and uttered a silent prayer. *Thank you, God. Thank you for Nathaniel Hawkins. He is the gift I'd almost given up hope that I'd find.*

About the Author

Niqui Stanhope was born in Jamaica, West Indies, but grew up in Guyana, South America. In 1984, she immigrated to the United States, and has lived here ever since. She admits that novel writing never occurred to her until after she had graduated from the University of Southern California with a degree in Chemistry. She has been chosen as Author of the Month by Romance in Color magazine, and has been nominated for the 2001 EMMA award and the 2002 Golden Pen Award.

You can write to her at: PO Box 6105 Burbank, CA 91505 or email her at Niqui@aol.com. Her website address is: *www.niquistanhope.com.*

IMPROMPTU

Kim Louise

For Valencia and ReTonya

January

Not everyone marries for love.

Wanessa Taylor sat in the booth of La Hacienda restaurant repeating that sentiment in her mind while extending her left hand. Soon a diamond, just large enough to catch and hold the light, would twinkle on her ring finger. She imagined the white-gold band she and Gerald had seen once in a jewelry store wrapped around her finger. The ring was inexpensive by anyone's standards, but that was okay. It didn't look bad, really.

She tried not to stare at her finger, but she couldn't help herself. A wedding ring would certainly be a change. *I guess it will take some getting used to,* she thought, picking up a menu.

The menu matched the décor, cheery and festive. The light blue background covered with orange and yellow printing shimmered like a celebration on the page. Likewise, the walls of the restaurant sparkled with bright flecks of paint as if someone had taken a confetti gun and sprayed the place. A perfect compliment to the loud music playing, full of dancing trumpet sounds and laughing guitar rhythms. Wanessa tapped her feet and scanned the food selections. Tacos, enchiladas, tamales. Everything sounded so good, she wanted it all.

She couldn't wait to tell Olivia the news. Well . . . actually she *could* wait. She was so nervous about the whole thing. One minute she and Gerald were drinking hot apple cider at his parents' house, and the next, he was asking her to marry him.

Her cheeks warmed at the memory. They were seated at the dinner table. After a modest meal of lamb chops, sautéed rice, and salad, they had all settled into the low hum of after-dinner conversation. His mother had just finished commenting on how the military career he'd established suited him and that the next item on his agenda should be to settle down and have a family. Then slowly he'd turned to her, placed his hand firmly upon hers, and said, "Great idea, Mum. Wanessa, will you marry me?"

Wanessa had been dumbstruck, as though someone had appeared out of nowhere, stolen her breath and all her sensibilities, and socked her in the stomach. She stared up from where his hand rested on hers.

Her first thought was heartbreaking: that Gerald might be playing some cruel joke. Any minute, she expected the Greene family to break the silence with laughter. But after a few moments she realized that he was serious. And Wanessa, grateful for a chance she thought she would never have, smiled with a trembling heart and said, "Yes."

All her life she'd been a misfit. When she was young she'd longed to be one of the pretty and popular girls. They giggled a lot, had the attention of all the cute boys, and always got what they wanted. Her mother's selection of hand-me-down clothes and her strict rules disintegrated that fantasy. When she got older and entered college, she wanted to be one of the active girls. The ones who were involved in student government, sororities, and parties. But school didn't come easy for her, and she spent all her free time studying. Working at Federation Bank gave her more opportunities to shine. Being out front, she was proud of her customer contact. On the flip side, she sometimes compared herself to the personal bankers who had offices and worked with customers for extended periods, wishing she hadn't been passed up for that job.

Wanessa sighed. No matter how she tried, she would never measure up. As she lifted her gaze from the space on her finger where a ring would soon be, her only reassurance approached from the distance.

Olivia Moore was Wanessa's best friend. She also worked at the bank, and after attending a First Fridays meeting together had sort of latched on to her. Wanessa had felt she looked pitiful and out of place at the gathering, but Olivia made her feel like an equal.

In contrast to Wanessa's conservative appearance in basic blue and brown business suits, Olivia looked like a fashion model. The plum pantsuit she wore made her legs look a foot longer than they actually were. She always appeared as though she'd just stepped off the runway. And unlike the popular girls of Wanessa's high school years, who made her feel uncomfortable and inferior, Olivia never had that effect on her. Wanessa was grateful.

Her friend slid into the seat across from her. "Now, Wanessa," Olivia said, following the direction of her friend's stare. "The way you're looking at your hand you had me thinking there was a ring there."

"Not yet," Wanessa said, smiling. "But there's going to be. Gerald proposed last night."

The surprise and concern on her friend's face was not what Wanessa expected. She, in turn, could not hide her disappointment. "You're not happy for me?"

Olivia reached across the table and took her friend's hands in hers. "Now, you know I'm happy for you. You're like family. But . . ."

Wanessa swallowed a lump of nervousness. "Yes . . . ?"

"But I just want you to be one hundred percent sure. Honey, in all the times we've talked about Gerald, you just seemed so casual about him. Like he's just a good friend. The fact that he's your husband-to-be just took me by surprise."

Olivia wasn't the only one taken by surprise. It had only been her wish since high school to marry a handsome man who would cherish her, love her.

She gave it a long thought. Gerald was handsome enough. He certainly wasn't ugly. Compared to her, he was a prince. And although he had never ravished her with his affections, she knew she was darn lucky to have a man like him interested in her in the first place. And then to propose marriage . . . she dared not ask for anything more.

Self-consciously, she lowered her head.

"There you go again. Doubting yourself. What did I tell you about doing that?"

"A person in doubt loses out."

"Right. Now, if you doubt Gerald or anything about this marriage—"

"No! I don't."

"So you love him?" Olivia asked.

Wanessa looked her friend in the eye and held her gaze. "Love and I don't get along."

Olivia sat back against the booth. "Oh, that's right," she said, her voice thinned with sarcasm. "A man you once loved left you at the the altar, so this time—"

"This time there's no love involved. And if Gerald decides that he doesn't really want to be married to someone like me, then when he breaks it off, I won't be hurt."

"Someone like you. A smart, ambitious, pretty someone like you, huh?"

"You're only saying that because you're my friend."

"No, Wanessa. I'm saying it because if your man doesn't make you feel and believe those things, then you shouldn't be with him."

"Gerald is a wonderful man!"

"I'm sure he is. But is he the wonderful man *for you?*"

No, some people don't marry for love. Some people marry because they feel it's their only chance. Some people marry because they are lonely. For others, it's a combination of the two.

Wanessa nodded and then looked up. "I'm sure."

February

Gerald was being sent to Korea. His yearlong assignment would take him away from her until just before the wedding. He had tried to negotiate a way for her to come with him, but the army had strict regulations regarding single officers. Wanessa wouldn't be able to accompany him on long assignments until she was officially his wife.

The news had left her feeling like a twig twisting in a cold breeze.

Olivia checked her makeup in the rearview mirror. Flawless, as usual. She didn't use a lot, just jet-black eyeliner, bronze-glow foundation, and mauve lipstick. She grabbed her Coach bag and stepped out of her car.

The City Center outdoor mall brimmed with people. An unusually warm day in February brought shoppers out of the woodwork in packs. She squinted. The sun shone so brightly, her Ray-Bans offered little protection. She stepped lively from the parking lot and into Resplendence Bridal Boutique.

Once inside, she looked around for Wanessa. When she didn't see her she was grateful. It would give her more time to put her thoughts in order. During the entire drive to the mall, she had rehearsed all the different ways she could tell her friend she had just received the promotion of her dreams and was moving to Chicago.

She knew her relationship with Wanessa was more than what could simply be described by the word *friend*. It was a sisterhood and kinship. Like extended family. Over the years they had been friends, Olivia had seen a change in Wanessa. She was becoming more daring, more outgoing, and more accepting of herself. Olivia had tried in every way possible to help Wanessa become the strong, confident woman she knew she was capable of being. And Wanessa had come to depend on her more than her own family. But now . . .

"Hey."

She heard Wanessa's soft voice and spun around toward the entrance. "Hey, sweetie."

Wanessa glanced around the shop, a look of dread claiming her delicate facial features. "This place is so big."

Olivia took her by the arm. "Don't worry about that. Just think of how beautiful you're going to look walking down the aisle."

Together they marched into the bridal showroom. Mannequins decked in every variation of bridal dress imaginable stood like runway models frozen midpose. There were white-white gowns; cream-colored gowns; beaded gowns; sequined gowns; long, flowing gowns; short, tight gowns; angelic gowns; and one multicolored carnival-type gown.

Olivia watched as Wanessa's half smile dissolved. "Olivia, I don't know if I'm ready to pick out dresses yet."

"Why?" Olivia asked, stepping around the first dress they came to. The mannequin was posed as if she were accepting an invitation to dance from a prince. The elegant swoosh of her hand in midair, the turn of her neck just so.

"Because . . . isn't there an order to wedding planning? I mean, shouldn't we reserve the church, select a minister, call the—"

"Wanessa, you've got a year to plan. Why not do the fun stuff first? Picking out the wedding dress is the emotional first order of business. Everything else comes after that."

"I really want this wedding to be perfect, and I just thought—"

"Oh, look at this one," Olivia said, sauntering off toward a long, formfitting dress near the back of the room. It was low-bodiced with thin rows of pearls sewn into the skirt. "You would be lovely in this!"

The scowl turning up her friend's mouth convinced her that even a woman as timid as Wanessa had her limits. Maybe she should have invited her for dinner and then broken the news. But it was too late for that now. She had to tell her.

"Good morning, ladies." A tall, thin woman swept into the showroom from the back. With her pink satin skirt outfit and big hair, Olivia thought the woman just a little too perky for first thing in the morning.

"Good morning," they replied.

"Who's the bride to be?"

"I am," Wanessa answered.

The woman's face lit up like a sparkler on July Fourth. "I'm Kay Wheaton, bridal consultant." The woman stretched out a long arm. Her hand and fingers were also long, with tapered nails that had been filed to a point. Her pink polish caught the light and reflected it like tiny mirrors on each finger.

The three women shook hands and completed introductions.

"When is your special day?"

"Christmas," Wanessa said.

Kay clasped her hands to her chest. "A Christmas wedding! How wonderful for you!"

Olivia thought the woman was as phony as a million-dollar bill.

"We have a winter gown collection upstairs that you'll love! This way please."

Wanessa and Olivia followed the woman up a white-carpeted staircase and into the store's mezzanine. The room, smaller than the downstairs, was populated by more posing mannequins. As soon as the three women were surrounded by a sea of various shades of white, Kay proceeded to give the best sales song and dance imaginable. Inside of fifteen minutes, Olivia had learned more about wedding dresses than she ever wanted to know, and Wanessa looked as if she were in pain the entire time. And the worst part was that Olivia still hadn't broken the news of her move. Her plan of sharing that bit of information during a leisurely stroll around dress racks and lingerie tables had failed miserably.

Olivia inhaled. The floral bouquet permeating the boutique was almost overwhelming. Like the salesclerk, self-stlyed bridal consultant, it was trying too hard.

Wanessa's face clouded with uneasiness, and Olivia realized that maybe *she* was trying too hard. "You're really not ready for this, are you?"

"No, Olivia. I'm not."

"Okay. Let's get out of here."

"When do you leave?"

Considering Olivia's reservation regarding telling her friend about the transfer, things were going relatively well. Wanessa had merely stopped eating her salad and set her fork down next to her knife

"Some time in April."

Wanessa lowered her lashes and appeared to study her food.

The pit of Olivia's stomach sank heavily. Just as she had begun to help Wanessa out of her shell, she was abandoning ship.

"Wanessa . . ."

Wanessa looked up, a thin smile growing in intensity on her lips. "Gotcha!" She laughed and jumped up. "Now come here, so I can hug you!"

The two women embraced tightly, then sat down.

"Scared, weren't you?"

"Yeah, I mean, I wanted to tell you back at the bridal shop, but the vibe just wasn't right."

"Ooh, I know." Wanessa resumed eating. "What was up with the Stepford wife?"

Hmm, Olivia thought, sipping her tea. *Wanessa might be all right without me after all.*

"I've got this idea," Olivia replied after a few spoonfuls of French onion soup. "I think someone should help you with your wedding plans, since I won't be able to."

"Olivia, I'll be okay."

"With Gerald overseas, you're going to need as much assistance as you can get."

Wanessa waved her hand, but Olivia knew she was trying to be brave.

"I'm going to get my little brother to help you."

Now, instead of brave, she just looked worried.

"Don't trip. Byron is a great guy."

"No, Olivia. No!"

"Yes, girlfriend. Yes! He's coming home from Nebraska next week, and I know he'd just *love* to pitch in."

"That's not necessary."

"Oh, but it is, and it's a done deal. Now, finish your salad, so we can go shop for *my* dress, 'cause I'll definitely be back to stand with you on your day."

March

Byron Moore walked off the jetway into the Cleveland airport with a spring in his step. He was home.

He had been gone almost five years after receiving a scholarship to attend Barnett College in Omaha, Nebraska. He thought about his brief visits home during that time, mostly at Christmas and Thanksgiving. They had never seemed long enough. But now . . . now he could begin the task of putting his thirty-seven-year-old life in order.

The airport whirred with passengers rushing by and the occasional loud greeting of happiness from friends and families reuniting. His eyes searched for a familiar face as he made his way out of the terminal and into the flow of people headed toward baggage claim.

Maybe she forgot. He rooted through his jacket pocket for his cell phone. He dialed the numbers, then pushed the end button when he saw her striding toward him. Her smile was as bright as the sun, a trait they both shared with their mother. A quick rise of adrenaline coursed through him as the perfect welcome home approached him.

He enveloped his sister in a tight bear hug. He was more than happy to see her and more than grateful for all the things she had done for him in the past five years. He couldn't have made it through school without her.

"All right, all right. You're cutting off my circulation!"

"I love you, too, Oli," he said, stepping back. His older sister looked good for her age. Forty-five, but she didn't look a day over thirty-five. And when she smiled, not a day over thirty.

"Let me see it," she said, eyes wide and expectant.

"I don't have it yet."

"What!" Olivia said.

Byron laughed. "They only hand out the jacket during the graduation ceremony. I won't get the actual diploma for a few weeks yet."

"Oh," she said, walking beside him. "I thought you meant you needed *another* class."

Now it was his turn to smile broadly. He remembered last summer when he thought he was about to graduate. Then he found out at the last minute that somehow his counselor had miscalculated his requirements and he needed one more Humanities class to graduate. By then, he was out of patience and out of money. And the scholarship he'd received was for a specific number of semesters. So he had called on his sister once more. She had already come to his aid over recent years by helping him purchase textbooks and supplies. She had also helped him with lab fees that were not covered by the scholarship.

For his education, he owed his sister a lot. He'd kept a running total in his head and intended to repay her as soon as he found work.

He stopped, hiking his carry-on against his shoulder, and touched his sister's hand. "I won't forget what you did for me, Oli. You helped me prove something to myself, and I will make good on my debt soon."

"You know," she said, her bright eyes turning serious, "I need to talk to you about that."

They resumed their pace through the fast-moving throng. Finally they came to a luggage carousel marked with Byron's flight number. They milled around like lemmings waiting for his bags to come around.

"What do you want to talk about?" He hoped she didn't need the money right away. He didn't have it. Or anything close to it. The life of the everyday college student was often one of poverty.

Olivia looked up, hesitant. She searched his face for a moment, then let some of that famous Moore smile break through. "I need you to do me a favor."

"What kind of favor?"

"If you do this favor for me, you can consider your debt paid."

"Anything, you know that."

"Did I tell you my good news?"

She's beating around the bush. That ain't good. His sister rarely compromised her typical straightforward nature.

An assembly line of baggage rode past them on the conveyer belt, all shapes and sizes, and in various conditions. However, after a while, they all started to look alike. Twice Byron had bent down to retrieve a bag, only to discover that it wasn't his.

"What good news?" he asked, spying his large suitcase emerging from the back.

"I got a promotion."

He scooped up his luggage from the carousel and set it on the floor to give his sister another big hug. "Oli, that's great!" They resumed their walk, heading toward the exit. "Is it the division manager position?"

Her whole face lit up like a star bursting with light. "No. I made *regional* manager."

"You're joking!" he said as a rush of pride swelled his chest.

"I just found out a few weeks ago."

"When do you start?"

"End of next month."

"Awesome. I'm so proud of you."

"Thanks. I'm proud of myself, actually."

Byron was thoughtful. "Now, with a regional position, you don't have to relocate, do you?"

"Yes, I will."

His stomach sank. "That stinks. I just got back and here you are going away."

"I know. I'm sorry."

"Don't be. I'm being selfish. I just missed you when I was away."

Olivia looked over at him, her eyes shining with love. "Me, too."

They stepped outside. The early evening Cleveland sky was overcast. Gas fumes from taxis, courtesy vans, and shuttle buses grayed the winter air even more. Byron pulled up his collar.

"I'm over here in the parking garage," Olivia said, marching across the remnants of snow. As he walked beside her, Byron realized that she hadn't told him about the favor.

"So do you want me to house-sit while you're gone?"

"Actually," she said, approaching the parking structure, "I'm pretty sure I'm going to sell my house. But you're welcome to stay in it until I do."

"Well, what, then?"

He was eager to repay his sister's generosity. But this hesitation was starting to make him nervous.

"I have a friend. Her name is Wanessa Taylor. She and I met right before you left for Nebraska. Anyway, we hooked up during a First Fridays meeting and just clicked. Now she's one of my closest friends."

Once in the parking garage, they walked up the stairs to the third floor. Byron and Olivia proceeded to walk to her car amid the sea of automobiles.

"You have a friend, Wanessa. Yes. And . . . ?" he said, hoping to speed the conversation along.

"Well, Wanessa is a very special person. A person who's cautious and sensitive."

"Are you trying to fix me up? Because if you are, the last thing I need is—"

"No. Not at all. As a matter of fact, Wanessa is engaged, and I was helping to plan her wedding. Then I got promoted."

It was not difficult to find Olivia's car. Hers was the big, champagne-colored Lincoln. Owning a Towncar had been her dream since they were kids,

Byron placed his bags in the trunk and they got in. Olivia started the car and maneuvered the large vehicle toward the exit.

"So . . . what's the favor, Oli?"

"Well, since I'm being transferred to Chicago, I thought maybe you could pick up where I left off and help Wanessa with her wedding plans."

The quickness of his laughter surprised even Byron. He'd been gone so long, his sister had lost her mind.

"You must be crazy," he said after regaining his composure.

"I'm serious," she said, steering the car toward the exit.

"You can't be."

"By, I know it sounds like a lot, but—"

"No!"

"Please."

Byron turned his head from side to side like a washing machine agitator. "No. Nope. No way. Uh-uh. I can't hear you."

"Well," she said in a huff. "After all I've done for you."

Byron threw up his hands. "Here you go. Playing the education assistance card. Some kind of sister you are."

"Then you'll do it?"

"Heck, no! I'll tell you what I *will* do, though. I will pay you back what I owe—with interest. How's that?"

Olivia's mouth hardened into a thin line. "No deal. You help my friend out, or no matter how much you pay me, I won't accept it."

"Damn, sis."

"Don't you 'damn, sis' me! You will never be able to repay your debt to me—*ever.*"

He remained resolute.

"You will owe me for the rest of your life!"

Olivia stopped the car at the attendant booth. Byron retrieved his wallet and drew out a twenty.

"Don't even think about it," she said, handing the attendant the parking ticket and a twenty of her own. She took her change and receipt, then drove out of the parking structure and headed for her home. She stole one last sidelong glance at him.

"For the rest of your life," she repeated.

Why can't I have a normal sister like everyone else? Byron sighed. Olivia was stubborn and used to getting her way. But he didn't care. There was no way he was planning any wedding.

April

"What have you got on?" Olivia asked, stepping into the living room. "Wanessa will be here any minute."

Byron yawned and wiped the crusties from his eyes. He had gotten up, come out to watch television, and drifted off instead. Sleeping late was a rare luxury for a college student. For a few weeks, Byron was determined to take full advantage of his alumni status. He looked down at his dark gray sweats and thought nothing could be more comfortable.

"Did you hear me? I said Wanessa will be here any minute!"

Byron scratched an itch near his behind. "I heard you. I'm just trying to block that out."

"Byron Moore, you will get in the shower, get dressed, and be presentable for my friend. I can't have her thinking I'm leaving her in the hands of a scoundrel."

"You would lie to her, then?"

Byron's humor made them both laugh, but unfortunately

it didn't change the situation. His sister had cooked up a scheme this time. And he had too much respect for her and himself to allow a debt to be long-standing between them. He just couldn't figure out what help he could be to a woman needing assistance with a woman's affairs.

Maybe that was it, he thought. Maybe he could do so poorly at helping her that she would beg him to stay out of it.

"What, By?"

"Nothing," he replied, getting up from the warm spot he'd made on the couch and heading off toward the bathroom.

"You may have been gone five years, but I still know my brother. Now that look meant something sneaky. What is it?"

"Oli, I'm going to take a shower and get dressed like you suggested. Can I do that?"

She gave him a curious once-over. "Would you please?"

When Byron stepped out of the shower, he heard voices in the other room. *I guess she's here.* He entered his sister's guest bedroom and dressed quickly, knowing Olivia would want him to hurry. He started out of the room and then stopped, deciding to splash on some cologne and check himself in the mirror. He hoped a cardigan and corduroy pants would do. Otherwise, he would not hear the end of his sister's protests for the two weeks she had remaining in Cleveland.

He turned the corner into the living room. *Wow.* The woman was not at all what he expected. His sister was an outgoing, robust, take-charge kind of woman, much like the other women in his family. He had imagined someone like that. But the person seated next to Oli looked like if he said *boo,* she'd jump out of her skin. And she was almost homely in her pink plastic glasses and ponytail. The argyle sweater she wore looked two sizes too big, and her gray slacks were just that, gray. And he would have to straight-up ignore the shoes she wore. The brown cloglike monstrosities were simply hideous.

Well, there's someone for everyone. He stared, amazed she'd found a man to marry her.

"By," Olivia said, standing, "this is Wanessa."

The funny-looking woman stood and pushed her glasses up on the bridge of her nose. Byron extended his hand.

"Nice to meet you, Wanessa." He gave her hand a quick squeeze. Surprisingly, it was soft and warm.

"You also, Byron."

Her voice didn't match her appearance at all. It was low, almost sultry. He liked the sound.

They all sat, and Wanessa smoothed the fabric of her slacks back and forth with her hands. "I told Olivia that she didn't have to make you do this. I can manage on my own."

"Oh, no, you can't," Olivia responded. "This is the most important decision you've ever made in your life. You need the support of someone you can trust. Plus, planning a wedding is a big job. You'll need all the help you can get."

From what Byron could tell, his sister was right. Wanessa looked too timid to assert herself the way she'd need to in order to get a wedding planned by year's end. *Oh, man ...* Was he really going through with this? His boys would ride him hard for this one.

He smiled and hoped it looked sincere. "I don't mind, especially since I'm not working yet. This will give me something constructive to do besides job hunting."

Olivia's living room furniture was just like everything else in her life, big and expensive. The steel-blue leather chair engulfed him. Byron sank like a boulder thrown in a lake, then shifted himself up.

"I don't think this chair is soft enough, sis."

And then he saw it. Bright and spectacular. Just for an

instant, a glow in Wanessa's eyes that touched him, warmed him. Maybe there was some magic hidden beneath that dowdy exterior. He took one more look at the woman wearing the awful shoes. *Nah!*

"Excuse me for a moment while I brag on my little brother. He just graduated from Barnett University in Nebraska. He made the dean's list all four and a half years he was there, and his GPA was three point eight five."

"Three point seven five," he corrected.

"Close enough. And he even received a scholarship!"

"What's your degree in?" Wanessa asked.

"Leadership."

Her brows furrowed. "Leadership? I've never heard of a degree like that."

"They're a recent phenomena. It's a response to all the baby boomers who will retire in the next ten years and how there's not going to be enough leadership talent to replace them."

"Q got to intern with some major companies: Mutual of Omaha, Union Pacific, Campbell Soup."

"That's impressive, but who's Q?" Wanessa asked, brows wrinkled.

"My silly sister thinks I look like a young Quincy Jones, so she calls me Q sometimes."

"Hold on!" Olivia sprang from the corner of the desk she'd been sitting on and grabbed pictures from her sofa table. The pewter frame held two photos. Both were of young men, probably in their twenties, smiling widely.

"Okay," she said, handing the frame to Wanessa. "Which one is Byron?"

The soft and silky commotion in her belly warmed and spread outward. Both men looked delectable, like something that should be served on a plate and sopped up with a biscuit. Olivia was right. There was a strong resemblance. However, it was easy for her to tell the difference. A light came through Byron's smile like a shimmering sun. She felt its warmth even from the picture.

"This one," she said, distinguishing Byron from the picture of Quincy Jones.

Byron and Olivia exchanged curious looks.

"Wow. Most people don't know one from the other," Olivia said.

"Hmm," Byron said, flashing her some real-live warmth.

For the rest of their meeting, Olivia played the gracious hostess and Byron tried his best to play fly on the wall. He listened while the two women, mostly his sister, yapped on about wedding details. Still unsure of his role in all this, he offered the obligatory grunt from time to time to signal he was still listening. But his mind kept wandering to other things he'd much rather be doing, like having a drink with his old buddies, reading the want ads, or trying to talk his way into the bed of the neighbor next door. Now, *she* was a looker.

When Wanessa rose to leave, Byron was barely aware of it. He had been rehearsing a million different ways to tell his sister she would have to find some other way for him to repay his debt. And then Wanessa's eyes caught him again. But a well-deep sadness had replaced the light. His stomach twisted. He had been ignoring her, and the effect of his rudeness was staring him in the face.

He'd come back from college a different man than when he'd left, hadn't he? *Yes,* he thought. *And it's time I start proving it.*

But before he could offer encouragement to Wanessa, she was gone, and Olivia went out behind her, but the look on her face was not of anger, as he had expected. It was disappointment. He promised himself that was the last time he would ever disappoint his sister.

*   *   *

"Whoa! Okay! Dang! I mean, oh, my *Lord!*"

Wanessa shook her hands out. They had gone cold while she had been at Olivia's house.

She paced in her apartment, thinking that one look at Byron and all the blood had receded from her extremities and pooled in places she dared not think about.

"I just hope I didn't come across as a stupefied idiot," she said, rubbing her hands together as though they were two sticks and she were desperate to make a fire.

Her first instinct was to call someone and tell that person that she'd just seen the most handsome man on earth. But there was a problem: the only person she could think of to call was Olivia. No way was she going to dial up her best friend and say, "Thanks for getting your brother to help me with my wedding. Oh, by the way . . . is he single? Because I think I want to marry him instead of my fiancé."

"I'm talking to myself," she said, increasing her stride. "Like, having a conversation with myself." Then she stopped. "He wasn't that good-looking."

But warm memories of his cocoa butter–brown complexion, eyes like a sweet dream, and smile of spun gold took her over. Her heart beat like a Yamaha kick drum on fusion night.

Yes. He was *that* fine.

Okay. She swallowed, wrangling her composure. *I am engaged to a very nice man.* She forced images, smells, and touches away from her psyche, where they had taken up residence.

Slowly her good sense, as Olivia called it, returned. She hadn't even taken off her coat! Moments later Wanessa was out of her clothes and into a flannel robe. In her bathroom she ran hot water, then added liquid rose-scented soap for bubbles. She perched on the edge of the white claw-footed tub, letting the steam moisten her skin and relax her muscles. *Nothing like a hot bath to take your mind off . . . things.* She sighed.

Wanessa tied her shoulder-length hair up and took off her robe. After turning off the water, she dipped a toe into a tub overflowing with petal-scented bubbles. As she eased her right foot slowly down into the hot water, the phone rang and she nearly tumbled in.

She almost stepped out to answer, but decided to let the machine pick it up.

It didn't take her long to realize that the hot water she was soaking in didn't raise her temperature like the voice on the phone did. It was Byron. His tone held a degree of warmth and concern. She couldn't make out everything, only the words *forgive* and *promise.*

Delight surged within her as she dashed out of the bathroom and picked up the phone.

"Byron?" she said, only slightly winded from her sprint.

"Hey, there, Wanessa. I felt a little uncomfortable when you left the house today, and I just wanted to call and say that you shouldn't feel as if you're imposing. You're not. And if I came across as not wanting to help you, I didn't mean to."

And he's thoughtful, too. She would have melted where she stood if it hadn't been for the water drying coolly against her skin.

"No, Byron. I'm glad you're helping me. And I'll try not to be too much of a burden. There're a lot of things I can do on my own."

"And there are a lot of things we can do together. So when you're ready, call me. I'll be here."

Anticipation rippled through her. The sensation drenched her skin and prickled her flesh with goose bumps. "Good-bye, Byron."

"Good-bye, Wanessa."

May

After meeting the rather remote Wanessa Taylor, Byron found that her apartment was just what he had expected. Small and pristine almost to a fault, with every knickknack, picture frame, and candle in its place. Her living room looked like it belonged in an issue of *Better Homes and Gardens*. *She probably vacuums every day.* Good thing she hadn't seen Olivia's place since she had left. It definitely had that air of male disarray.

"Please have a seat," she said.

And he did—on the perfect, all-American couch. Not frilly or overly contemporary, but sturdy, with a navy background and large white flowers in the foreground, with splashes of red for accents. The only thing missing in the room was a stainless-steel tea service.

"Would you like something to drink?" she asked after taking his jacket and hanging it up.

"No. Thank you." He sat still, not really sure where to begin. They hadn't talked much since his sister had left.

Wanessa sat in a chair that seemed to be the one farthest away from him and fussed with her skirt. It was brown and full, like part of a cheerleader's uniform, only much longer. The arms to the tan wool sweater she wore hit her at about the second knuckle.

He hated long silences, so Byron decided to start at the beginning.

"Why don't you tell me what you and Olivia have done so far?"

"Well," she said, looking up and away from him, "We've picked the church, the reception hall, the photographer, the caterer, the florist, the baker, and the deejay."

Byron sat forward. "Wow! What could possibly be left?"

Wanessa went into the dining room and got a packet of paper from the table. "This," she said, handing him the stapled sheets.

The packet was labeled, *The Wedding Checklist*. A few items were crossed off on page one, but there were seven other pages full of things to do broken down by month. Byron's mind reeled with apprehension. It would have been better to owe his sister for life.

Wanessa lowered her lashes. "I know it's a lot to ask. Please don't feel obligated to—"

"It's all right," he said, trying to convince himself as much as his sister's friend. "I'll just look this over and familiarize myself with what it takes to plan a wedding." Even as he heard himself say it, he knew he would dread every moment.

For the next hour, Wanessa explained the details of the arrangements she and Olivia had already made. While she did so, she tried her best not look directly into Byron's eyes. His beautiful, dreamy eyes made her feel woozy, just a little drunk, and scared. Scared that if she stared for very long, she would actually fall into them and never return.

Just sitting across from him made her warm. She wished that he would let her get something for him. A drink. A snack. At least then she would get away to the kitchen for a break from the dizziness she felt. At least then she could do something constructive with her hands. And then she could move away from that hypnotic cologne that smelled like an irresistible combination of power and temptation.

"Are you sure you don't want anything?"

He smiled. One simple change of expression and she felt as though all the power of the Cleveland Public Power District had been turned on and beamed in her direction.

"No. I'm fine." Then a look of concern turned the wattage down. "But you look as though you could use some water or something. Are *you* okay?"

"I just . . ." she said, rising and resting her hand against the base of her throat. "All this planning can be overwhelming, and it's not easy with . . . with . . ." *Gerald. Say Gerald. His name is Gerald.* "With Gerald being gone."

"That must be hard," Byron said, rising as well. "Maybe we should call it a night."

"If you think so."

"I feel caught up now, but what I would like to do is take that checklist with me and make a copy. Get a feel for what's left to be done."

"All right." She walked him to the door, not sure of her legs.

As Wanessa approached the door, she bumped into her buffet table, disturbing an angel figurine. Byron pivoted and caught the ceramic object just inches before it hit the floor.

"Thank you," she said, taking the angel from him.

He nodded. "I'll give you a call when I figure this out. Actually, after a strategic planning workshop and an English class I had in college, this doesn't look too bad."

"Well, thanks again," Wanessa said as he stepped out the door.

"You're welcome, Wanessa." He flashed that sunshine smile at her once again and was gone.

She closed the door and sank against it. She was embarrassed and ashamed of herself. Her reaction to Byron was inexcusable. She was acting like a sixteen-year-old schoolgirl with a crush on the star basketball player. That had been her once. And the object of her admiration was as untouchable then as he was now. From now on, she vowed to keep her stray thoughts, palpitations, and tingling sensations reined in.

Byron Moore sat in his sister's living room nursing his concerns. He had no idea how he was going to help sell his sister's house, find a job, and assist with a wedding. He'd flipped through the wedding checklist Wanessa had given him several times and wondered how anyone ever managed to get married if they had to address every single item. Bridal portraits, centerpieces, personal attendants. And what the heck was a groom's cake? If this was what it took to get married, he would resign himself to bachelorhood forever.

There had to be someone else who could help the frumpy woman with her plans. Since he wasn't comfortable enough to ask Wanessa himself, he decided to call his sister to find out.

He dialed the numbers, thinking, *Olivia, you'd better be at home.*

After the fifth ring, he became doubtful. The receiver was almost back in the cradle when he heard his sister's loud voice.

"Praise the Lord. Hello," she said.

"Since when did you become so religious?"

"Since I got the promotion and everything I've ever wanted is coming true. I even have a date tonight."

"Man," Byron said, ruminating. "How can I be down?"

"What do you mean?"

He settled back into the couch and replayed recent events. He was still looking for a job, still looking for a place to stay, and hadn't had any real interest in a woman since freshman year in college. Back then he'd had his eye on a cutie pie named Sonji Stephens. But she was interested in only his friendship. Fortunately for him and his studies, she became a great friend, and he had thrown himself into his schoolwork. He had dated occasionally, but nothing except a much-appreciated sexual release had ever come of those dates.

When he explained as much to his sister, she tossed off his plight like a used tissue.

"I thought you had real complaints. Your life is falling into order slowly but surely. You've got your priorities right. Find a job and a nice place to stay. Then when you have something to offer someone, God will bring you a mate."

He didn't have the heart to tell his sister that not only was he thinking about asking out the next-door neighbor, but he had every intention of taking her to bed with or without a job or a place of his own. Then a sharp pain of remembrance jolted his heart. That was how he had wasted his adult life in the first place: chasing behind women and not taking any responsibility for himself.

For years, he never owned his own car. Never had his own place. He always managed to find some beautiful, upwardly mobile black woman to take him in and let him take over. Then one night, after arguing with his current woman about his future woman, he got kicked out. When he had pounded on Olivia's door at three-thirty A.M., she'd called the police on him and told him that he would never get any help from her until he straightened out his life.

The next day, after sleeping in an abandoned car, he vowed to get his life together. Family meant everything to him, and if his only sister could turn her back on him like that then he must have hit rock bottom. He knew there was no direction to go but up.

"Okay. I'm hanging up on you now."

"What? Oli, I'm sorry. I was just thinking how fortunate I am to have you as a sister. You turned my life around, you know."

"I'm not sure about all that."

"I am."

"Thanks, By. But you don't have to keep thanking me. Just don't break the chain. Keep it going, and take good care of my friend."

"Well, actually, that's really why I was calling."

"She's all right, isn't she? She hasn't gone back into her shell, has she?"

"Did she ever come out of it?"

"With me she did."

"Oh," *Now there's a segue,* Byron thought. "How is she around family or her friends?"

"Wanessa is painfully shy. She doesn't have many close friends. And as far as her family goes, that's almost a joke."

"Why do you say that?"

"Well, let's just say she had a less than wonderful childhood—you can probably tell from the way she carries herself. And if she wants to tell you more than that, then that's her choice."

"Honestly, Oli. What do you see in her?"

"She is the sweetest person I've ever met in my life."

"Well, that may be true, but you need to book her on *Jenny Jones.* The girl needs a fashion makeover, but soon!"

"Actually, that was on my list of things to do. I guess you'll just have to take on that responsibility."

"You are asking the impossible."

"Yeah, well, you graduating from college is like the impossible."

"You're sure she doesn't have any girlfriends or family who can help her?"

"Wanessa is shy and terribly unsure of herself. So no, not really."

His heart broke at that thought. "Oli, I'm glad you're her friend."

"I hope she has two friends now."

Byron closed his eyes. He'd never known what it was like to be without friends. He'd always been outgoing and popular. What a hard life that must be.

"She does," he said, opening his eyes. "Definitely."

The inside of JD's Lounge looked like the set of a seventies Blaxploitation film: frosted mirrors on the ceiling and walls, thick and heavy dark-wood furniture with red leather accents, orange shag carpet, and a strobe light blinking toward the dance floor. As Byron wiped down the bar, he thought it wouldn't surprise him if someone wearing platform shoes, a lime-green jumpsuit, and a twelve-inch Afro strutted through the door and shouted, "What it is!"

It was hard for him to believe that he'd spent almost ten years drinking and picking up women in this place. He'd practically grown up in the bar. Squinting through the low light and permanent cigarette haze, he thought it seemed like a lifetime ago.

"I need two Old E's, a Tanqueray and Seven, and a rum and Coke back." Nicolette slid her tray onto the bar and waited expectantly.

Byron went to work. First order of the night for the only people in the bar. A group of four had come in as soon as JD's opened at five. His brief stint as a bartender ten years ago told him that they looked like all-nighters, buoyant, celebratory. They were toasting something, and the festivities had just begun.

"Order up," he said, placing the drinks onto her tray.

"Thanks," she said, and swished away.

He liked Nicolette. She'd been at the bar a long time, a fixture, like one of the crushed-velvet paintings on the wall. She never let the bad moods, bad tips, or the bad breath of the customers get to her. She was what he imagined some guys might call a tough broad, feisty. Hot-spirited. When he'd first started working at the bar, he'd tried to take her home on many occasions. She'd refused, which made him want her all the more. At five-foot-five, slim in all the right places, full in all the others, she'd fought off his advances, as well as those from many other men. Then J.D., the owner, told him that she wasn't married, but she'd been living with a guy for fifteen years and was still head-over-heels in love with him. And that was when Byron's concept of love and relationships had changed. He stocked the cooler with Colt 45 and Schlitz thinking about how much he respected Nicolette's commitment and wondering if he would ever have a woman that committed to him.

The thought reminded him of Wanessa. He took a book from the counter and flipped through its pages. They were pink and shiny, not at all what you would expect in a juke joint like this, he thought. He turned to the table of contents and ran his index finger down the list printed there. Some of what he read caught his attention: "Always and Forever," "Ave Maria," "Endless Love," "Evergreen," "Here and Now," "I Have Nothing," "Love Is Here to Stay," "One Hand, One Heart," "So Amazing," "The Closer I Get to You," "Truly," "We've Only Just Begun." Before he realized it, he was humming the tune of one of his favorite songs.

"Well, if it ain't Joe College!"

Byron knew the voice even before he looked up.

"Danny!" he said, coming from behind the bar to embrace his old friend. The two hugged, then stepped back, all smiles.

"I heard you were back."

"Yeah," Byron said, resuming his place behind the bar. "I got back a few weeks ago."

"Dang, I guess you forgot how to call a brother. My number's still the same, man."

"I know, I'm just trying to get settled, man. You know."

Danny nodded. "So what's up with your sister, man? They say she moved to Chicago. Got some big-time job up there."

Byron was amazed at how quickly word got around, but then again, Danny had a way of knowing everything about all his running buddies.

Danny started laughing.

"What's so funny?"

"You, man. Every time I think about you walking around with papers, that shit just cracks me up. I mean, you really did that shit, yo. You legit now, man."

Now it was Byron's turn to laugh. Ever since high school, Danny Mason had been this beefy, wild guy. Nothing was too outrageous for him. Byron thought he'd missed his calling. He should have been in the entertainment business, like a rapper or something. The man lived to perform. Byron knew with certainty that before there was Busta Rhymes there was Danny Mason.

"So what you got there?" Danny asked, eyeing the book.

"Nothing," Byron said, closing the cover.

"Yes, it is. Let me see." Danny snatched the book from the counter. He read the title and looked up at his friend, curiosity dancing in his eyes. "Well, I'll be danged. Original Gangster Byron, gettin' married."

"Not me!" Byron replied, just a little too quickly and loudly.

"This here says, 'Love Songs for Your Wedding.' Why

are you looking at a wedding book if you ain't gettin' married?''

The nervousness in his stomach bubbled into laughter. ''I'm just helping a friend is all.''

Byron produced a shot of Hennessy V.S.O.P. and offered it to Danny. ''Here, man,'' he said, hoping to change the subject. ''Drink up, on me.''

One of the women from the group of four got up and plugged coins into the juke box. James Brown's ''Papa's Got a Brand-new Bag'' blared through ancient speakers. Nicolette came back for another round, and Danny's gaze never left Byron.

Finally, the hefty man spoke. ''It's somethin' to this. Ain't no road dog of mine taking up a wedding song book as light reading *or* as a favor for no friend. What you ain't tellin' me, man?''

Byron tensed. ''See, that's why I didn't want to hook up with you for a while. I knew you'd be all in my business.''

''Aw, man. You know I ain't mean nothin'—just want to make sure my boy is aw-ite. And besides,'' he began, then downed the shot in one gulp and slammed the glass on the counter, ''I just want to know if that book has anything to do with that little honey you been seen with. I hear homegirl's a little tardy on the fashion fair, dog. That ain't like you.''

Anger flashed like a strobe inside him, quick and hot. He leaned over the counter. ''Two things, Danny. First: you don't know Wanessa, so don't talk about her. And second: don't ever call me *dog* again.''

The bulky man raised an eyebrow and sat back a bit.

Same old Danny, Byron thought, *with his s-curl haircut, squeaky leather jacket, and knit pants*. He was always so busy meddling into other people's business that he couldn't take care of his own. In twenty-some years, he hadn't changed, hadn't grown, hadn't matured. Danny would always be Danny, Byron realized, pouring him another drink.

But Byron, on the other hand had changed and grown and matured. He had a plan for his life of being more than he had been. And now the old surroundings, sights, sounds, smells, and even friends didn't fit. Not anymore.

It was hard for him to believe there was a time when Danny was in his hip pocket, close and tight like his money. But now he was a dull memory, fading almost out of reach.

Danny took his second drink more slowly. For a moment he held up the glass and stared at Byron through the golden-brown liquid. "You ain't from around here no more, man," he said. "You ain't from around here at all."

June

She had the most beautiful eyes he'd ever seen. Five weeks, five days, heck even five minutes ago, he wouldn't have believed it.

He had taken his sister's advice and gotten Wanessa a makeover. He was tactful, though, and had not *called* it a makeover. What he'd done was suggest that they go to a salon where she could get some hair and makeup ideas, as the checklist suggested. Olivia had mentioned a place in the downtown area. So he picked Wanessa up that morning and took her to Nubian Nurture, where they did everything from hair, nails, makeup, facials, and pedicures to something called hot-waxing.

The walls of the salon were painted a brilliant, almost surgical white. Beauty consultants donned long white jackets and worked cosmetic feats of legerdemain on their customers. As Wanessa flipped through sample beauty books on a counter, a woman whose name tag read *Pamela* in big blue letters approached.

"What can I do for you today?" she asked.

Wanessa looked up in surprise. "Oh, no. I just want to look at a few things."

Byron frowned. "Yeah, but you can't get a good idea by just looking. You've got to try things out."

"I tell you what," Pamela said, "I'll throw in a free facial and makeup with a shampoo, cut, and style."

"See that? Now, you can't beat that, can you?"

"I don't think—"

Byron was insistent. "I'm certain I saw this on the wedding checklist."

"Yes, but this step is a few months away."

"Well, then. Why not be spontaneous? You don't plan out everything you do, do you?" But before he finished asking that question, he knew the answer. The woman standing next to him probably didn't blink off schedule. She would be too scared to do anything on impulse. Always following her head, never her heart. He imagined she hated surprise birthday parties.

He, on the other hand, couldn't imagine life without the occasional wild whim—although not as wild as he had been in the past. Just enough to keep life interesting.

"Congratulations! When's the big day?"

It took Byron a few minutes to realize that Pamela was speaking to them both, as if they were a couple.

"No," he clarified. "I'm her friend." When he said it, he realized that it was true. Wanessa was a sweet girl, and something about her made him feel protective of her. He smiled.

Wanessa's eyelashes fluttered. "My fiancé is overseas, so Byron is stepping in to help me."

The attendant perked up. "Well, then, let me make you beautiful for your fiancé. I'll do your hair and makeup and take your picture so you can send it to him."

Wanessa covered her mouth with her hands. Instinctively,

Byron took her wrists and gently lowered them. "Oh, no! Don't cover it up. Go on and smile. You know you want to."

And there it was. A smile to rival his own. But it was nothing compared to her eyes. The attendant reached across the counter and slid Wanessa's glasses from her face. For the first time he got a good look at her eyes. They were henna brown and beseeching. They made him feel both needed and needy.

She giggled. "Okay. But I can't see without my glasses."

"That's all right," Pamela said, taking her arm. "This way."

"How long?" Byron called over.

"Give me two hours," she said, helping Wanessa into the styling chair.

"I'll be back," he responded.

As he left the building, the image of Wanessa's smiling face haunted him. *She's actually kinda pretty. Who'da thought?*

He wouldn't have known it was her except that she was wearing the same clothes. When he walked into the salon, he stopped in his tracks. She hadn't seen him yet. She was talking as Pamela flourished a large makeup brush across her face—Wanessa's beautiful face.

It was as if a wizard had come, said magic words, and cast a spell. *But on me or her?*

Byron approached slowly, drawn by the transformation.

Pamela turned the chair so he could see her more clearly. "So, what do you think?"

Appreciation rippled through him. "I think you are very good at what you do." But there was something else. Yes, her hair was different—swept into a cascade of shiny brown ringlets. And yes, she was wearing makeup—frosty pink and white pastels that accentuated her innocence. But those things were just enhancements. Wanessa's beauty was there, had been there all along. It just needed a little help to shine through.

"I can't see a thing," Wanessa said. "Please hand me my glasses."

Byron was glad she couldn't see his reaction. She would have caught him checking her out and embarrassed them both.

"You're looking good, Miss Taylor," he said as she brought the plastic frames up to her eyes. Pamela handed her a mirror. Wanessa gasped just as he knew she would. He hadn't pictured her mouth hanging open, though. She looked like a six-year-old girl who had just been visited by Santa—a very generous Santa. She touched her face, then her hair, then her face again.

Goodhearted amusement drew Pamela's lips into a smile. "Be careful now. Don't ruin my work."

"I ... I ... Is it me?"

"We've got a full-length mirror over there if you want to get a better look."

Wanessa slid off the chair, dazed excitement on her face. She walked up to the mirror and stared.

"Pretty good, huh?"

"I'll say," Byron responded.

Pamela folded the cloth bib that she'd removed from Wanessa. "So how good of friends are you?"

Byron tore his gaze from the well-coifed woman wearing the frumpy clothes. "Huh?"

"You sure you two are just friends?"

Byron chuckled. He must have really been staring. "Yeah. I'm sure."

Wanessa bounced a few curls against her hand and headed back to where he and Pamela were standing.

"Well, could I call you sometime?"

A brush of warmth caught him. He'd given the hairstylist the once-over when they'd come in. She was a chocolate-brown-complexioned woman who looked like someone had squished a five-foot-ten body into a five-foot-five frame. Definitely compact. But he had nothing against a well-rounded woman, and since he hadn't had a date since he returned from college, he decided to say yes.

Give her the smile, he thought, and flashed his trademark woman weakener. Her reaction was immediate. She looked as though someone had just stroked her softly on her inner thigh. *Old habits.*

"Do you have a pen?"

She rifled through a drawer at the styling station and handed him a Sharpie permanent marker. When Wanessa returned, he was writing his phone number old-school style in the palm of Pamela's hand.

"She's right."

"Who?" Byron asked. "And about what?"

"Pamela, about the new dress."

Before they left the salon, Pamela told Wanessa that all she needed now was a new dress.

"If I'm going to look like this today, then I'll have to change my outfit."

Women, he thou..... He'd gone to the barbershop many times for a haircut and a shave. Never had he felt compelled to shop for a new shirt and pants afterward. Then another thought occurred: that Wanessa in a new dress was a sight he'd love to see.

She glanced at him, then glanced away. "Once, when I bought a new clock for my living area, I ended up changing the entire room. I was shopping at the Afternoon, and they were having a sale on clocks. The salesclerk showed me this one clock that was made from ink-stained tin. The gears and motor were exposed in a bizarre way. I mean, the whole thing was twisted and mangled. It looked like it had exploded from the inside out but refused to die.

"Well, I told the guy that my furniture and accessory tastes were moderate and conservative. After all, I'd just come to look for a garlic press. But he assured me that I couldn't live without it. So I bought it."

"How much did it cost?" He was intrigued that Wanessa was actually carrying on a conversation.

"I don't remember anymore. Probably about fifty dollars."

"Fifty dollars? For a clock you didn't want?"

"Yes. So when I got home, I took my pendulum clock down and put the mangled clock up. It looked real funny and out of place. But I thought that after a while, it would grow on me."

"And did it?"

"No. Not really. But in the meantime, I realized that the pictures of lighthouses that I had on each side of the clock were clashing big-time. So I went out and purchased something more abstract."

Byron could hear the domino effect coming. But he didn't mind. The sound of her voice was wonderful.

"Unfortunately, the abstract pictures didn't go with my furniture. I stood it for as long as I could, then I finally broke down and bought new furniture. Well, when the furniture arrived, it was obvious that I needed new carpet. It took a few months of saving, but I eventually put away enough money to have the living room recarpeted."

Byron couldn't believe what he was hearing. The woman seated next to him was clearly neurotic. "I don't remember seeing a clock like that on your wall. What happened to it?"

"One of the carpet installers hammered on the floor so

hard that it dislodged the clock and it fell to the floor and broke.''

Byron recoiled. "Aw, damn," he said. "That's awful. All that for nothing. That's aw—"

The sound of Wanessa's laughter stopped him. It sounded sweet and pure, like small golden bells ringing in the wind.

"Gotcha!" she said.

He frowned, realizing that he'd been duped. "You've been hanging around my sister too long."

She laughed even harder now, and he found it impossible not to join in. Soon they were both laughing uncontrollably.

"I can't believe I said all that." She giggled.

"*I* can't believe I fell for it."

"I don't understand why your fiancé wouldn't want to pick out his own tux." Byron strode uncomfortably around in the Gentleman's Choice rental shop with Wanessa at his side. They were there to pick out tuxedos for the groom and groomsmen.

"Gerald thought it would be best if I picked them out. He says I'm better at these things than he is."

"Sounds like he was just trying to get out of doing it himself," Byron said under his breath.

"I'm sorry?" she said, indicating that he should repeat his statement.

He shook his head. "Nothing." He was beginning to resent the position that Wanessa's fiancé was putting her in. She was shouldering all the responsibility for coordinating the wedding. That might have been all right for the average woman, but Wanessa was a special case. She was delicate and fragile. He hoped she wouldn't get too stressed out about all the details.

They were surrounded by plastic men who had been cut off at the knees. Three short rows of mannequins in suits, crisp, pressed, and ready for wear. Byron felt as if his shirt were suddenly two sizes too small. He loosened his collar.

"Find anything?"

The salesclerk was back. He'd greeted them with handshakes and a bow them when they walked in. When they told him they wanted to look around, he'd simply said, "Be my guest," and left them alone.

"We're still looking," Byron said.

"Just let me know if you want to try anything on."

This was going to be harder than he'd imagined. Maybe his first sentence to everyone for the next six months should begin, *I'm not the groom, but . . .*

"By the expression on your face, I take it you're not the groom."

"No, I'm not. My friend is looking for something for her fiancé."

"Splendid. Are you having a formal ceremony or something more casual?"

Wanessa touched her throat. "Formal, I suppose."

"Of course. Right over here."

The man reminded Byron of a butler with just a little too much authority.

"I'm Morris, by the way."

"Byron."

"Wanessa."

"Superb. Here we have a Ralph Lauren. Classic lines. Traditional. I assume this is for daywear?"

"Yes," Wanessa said, touching the sleeve. To Byron it looked as though it were made out of black cardboard: stiff, hard, and abrasive.

"How does it feel?" he asked.

"Hmm?"

"Comfort. Is it comfortable?"

"Well . . . humph. I don't . . . I would imagine that . . ."

Morris wrung his hands. "If you're really interested in

how our tuxedos feel, you could certainly try one on. Are you a member of the wedding party?"

"No."

"Well, it might help the bride-to-be decide on a style if she actually sees what they look like on." The man gave Byron a thorough once-over. "We've got a few tuxedoes in the back. Forty-two regular?

"Yes, but—"

"That's a great idea," Wanessa added. "I would like to see the real thing instead of these mannequins."

"This way," the salesclerk said.

Oli, I'm going to kill you, Byron thought, walking into the back.

When Byron emerged ten minutes later, Wanessa felt herself wilt inside. The clerk's runwaylike description faded away after the words Perry Ellis, and all she could do was stare at the man standing like a model before her.

Her mind fought over words like *dashing, debonair, suave,* and *magnificent* to describe him. All fell short. Satin shone from the collar of the coat-cut jacket and down the sides of the pleated pant legs. The silver microbrushed pattern in the vest provided an elegant contrast to the jet-black suit.

Now that's what a groom should look like, she thought. Byron glanced at her, a questioning look on his face.

"What do you think?" the clerk asked.

She put a hand to her throat. "I'll take it," she said, flushed and warm.

"Now that that's over, can we get out of here and get some coffee or something?"

"Sure," Wanessa said, starting to fill out the rental paperwork.

As soon as Byron changed clothes, they drove to Starbucks, and over a mochaccino, a caramelishous, and two biscottis, they shared light conversation.

"There weren't very many tuxedos to choose from."

"What do you mean?" he asked.

"I counted twenty different styles. When Olivia and I were in the bridal boutique, there must have been a thousand different dresses hanging on racks."

Byron sipped his mochaccino. "Well, there's only so much you can do with a suit. But with a dress, you women can find a million things to change on a dress to make it different."

"I'm not sure what you mean by 'you women,' but you might be right about us changing things."

"Let's face it. Women change one aspect of their wardrobe, and suddenly they've got something completely different. Take a normal dress. Cut it short, it's a mini. Lengthen it to your ankles, it's a gown. Split it and sew it, it's a skort. See, men don't need that many options."

Wanessa laughed.

"Give you another example. How many pairs of shoes do you own?"

"A few," she responded.

"The average man has three pairs of shoes: the real comfortable pair that are so raggedy our wives and girlfriends want us to throw them out, a pair of all-purpose tennis shoes, and a pair of dressier shoes for those times when we try to impress you."

"Me?" Wanessa blinked.

He gave a quick shrug. "Women, I mean."

He watched her nod and sip her coffee, wondering why he had implied that he was trying to impress her. Maybe he was. After taking a bite of biscotti he decided there was absolutely nothing wrong with that.

* * *

Wanessa couldn't believe her ears or her eyes. She sat up in her recliner and pushed the plus button on the remote control to turn up the volume.

"The investigation started after officials received reports from the Better Business Bureau regarding unsanitary practices of workers at several establishments. The Drake-Brown Company owns several restaurants, fast-food companies, and catering services in the area."

She felt as if she'd just fallen and gotten the wind knocked out of her. The phone, ringing in the background, was barely noticeable above the turmoil flying around in her head.

"Hello?" she said, picking up the receiver.

"Wanessa, it's Byron. What's the name of the catering service you're using for the wedding? Is it Drake-Brown?"

She sighed. "Yes."

"I just saw on the news that the Health Department just closed them down."

"I know. I'm watching it." It just figured that with her life and her luck, something like this would happen. She sighed fitfully.

"Do you still have the original bids from all the caterers you and Olivia contacted?"

"Yes."

"Okay, here's what we'll do. I'll come over tomorrow and help you call up those folks to make sure their original offers still stand. I might even call a few other places to get a good selection. Then we'll just go through them one by one to select the best deal. And if you need someone to haggle, I'm your man."

Relief washed over her. "Thank you, Byron. I feel much better now."

"No need to thank me. That's why I'm here."

July

Summer in Cleveland was in full swing. For weeks the temperature had been ramping up, and air conditioners were getting a workout as temperatures topped out at the highest of the year. However, if Wanessa was honest with herself, it wasn't the weather that was making her warm these days. Byron Moore came into her life like a magnificent beam of sunlight. Four months ago she'd felt hapless and over-whelmed. Now she felt confident and determined.

He'd stepped in and helped with so much—tuxedos, the invite list, meetings with the minister. He even ordered travel brochures for potential honeymoon locations. Byron was more than a help to her. He was a blessing.

As she changed from her work clothes into something more casual, she felt a twinge of guilt for taking advantage of Byron's generous nature. *Maybe he's helped me enough,* she thought. *Maybe it's time that I take over the details.* Byron had his own life to live and plan, especially since he still hadn't found the kind of job he was hoping for.

He told her over coffee he wanted a position in upper management, but he found when it came to top positions, most companies promoted from within. So he'd taken a part-time job as a bartender in a lounge just outside the downtown area. That way he could work at night and job-search in the daytime.

Wanessa checked herself in the mirror. She wore a sleeve-less tan shell and formfitting white skirt. The outfit was one of the many wardrobe presents Olivia had given her. Olivia's tastes were so far removed from Wanessa's that she rarely wore the clothes she'd received, but ever since her makeover, she'd felt compelled to take some risks with her attire and the new contact lenses she wore.

With considerable effort, she'd managed to re-create the hairstyle she'd received. Her makeup was not as successful, so she'd settled for lipstick and a light covering of foundation. Looking in the mirror, she couldn't believe what a difference it made.

Her only disappointment came from Gerald's reply to her E-mail. She'd sent him digital pictures of her makeover at Nubian Nurture, and he'd been far less excited than either she or Byron had been. He remarked that she shouldn't be spending so much money before the wedding. His comment almost spoiled her frame of mind.

But Byron kept her mood buoyant and optimistic. She was so grateful for his sincere efforts to ensure that her wedding was as perfect as she'd dreamed.

Even this evening, on his night off, he was coming over to provide her moral support while she attempted to make centerpieces for the guest tables at the reception. A few days ago they had been shopping for decorations and talking about the outrageous prices of everything they found. Then an equally outrageous thought occurred to her: she could probably make some of the decorations for less than half the cost of the ones they found in the stores. So they had gone to a hobby shop and picked up the materials. And now those materials were spread out all over dining room table.

She looked at the jumble—silk flowers in her wedding colors, violet and cream, golden gossamer bows, glass vases shaped like melting tulips, and a mosaic of marbleized ceramic fragments—and wondered what the heck had come over her. She'd never done anything like this before. In the past, she'd thought about trying her hand at something creative, but she'd never had the gumption to attempt it. But Byron's trust and assurance gave her the confidence to try.

When he knocked on the door, she knew it was him. He never used the doorbell. She wasn't sure why and had never bothered to ask. It was just part of all the things that were Byron. Maybe he did it because a knock on the door was more inquisitive, more old-fashioned—like asking permission to enter. A doorbell, on the other hand, was more intrusive and demanding, like saying, "Let me in." And maybe, she thought as she swung the door open, she was just being silly.

"Hey," he said, smiling.

"Hey," she said back.

He came in looking as good as always in a yellow T-shirt and gray Dockers. But it wasn't the clothes; it was the way his body moved inside them, the way her imagination took over, and the way she felt incredibly guilty in his presence at times. She liked him too much.

"Wow. You look great."

Wanessa lowered her eyes and stepped aside to let him enter. "Thank you."

"No, I mean it. You really look nice."

If he didn't stop complimenting her, she would pass out. She couldn't look at him, into his seductive eyes, so she gazed at his hands. From the way he fidgeted, she could tell that he was a little uncomfortable also.

"What you got to drink up in this camp?" he asked.

"Milk and ice water mostly."

"How about some coffee?"

"Sure."

It didn't take Wanessa long to make the coffee and join him in the living room with two steaming cups.

"Thanks." He took a sip and stared at the mass of materials scattered on the table in the adjacent room. "Looks like you're ready."

"I'm starting to wonder."

"Well, you shouldn't. With the way you've tackled that wedding checklist, I'm about ready to nickname you Superwoman."

Wanessa's face warmed at his words. No, that wasn't right. Her whole body warmed at his words. "Thank you, Byron. You know, even if I figure out something decent, they still have to pass the mother-in-law test."

He placed the coffee cup on the table in front of him. "Did you talk to her yet?"

Wanessa's stomach shrank. "No."

"Wanessa, I thought we discussed this. You can't continue to run everything past her like she's some kind of quality-control inspector."

"I know."

"Do you want me to talk to her?"

"No. That wouldn't be appropriate."

"All right then. Handle yours."

"Now you sound like Olivia."

"Sorry. We were raised by the same parents, and sometimes it shows."

They both laughed and finished drinking their coffee.

"Well, Ms. Taylor, I'm not the least bit creative. Like I told you, I can only offer you moral support. But if you need me to help you with the arrangements, I will try my darnedest."

Wanessa picked up their coffee cups and headed into the

kitchen. "Just having you here is a big help. But promise me something."

"Anything," he called from the other room.

"You won't laugh when I experiment?"

"Never."

"All right then. Would you like another cup?"

"Yes, I would."

She wondered if *courageous* was the word for what she was experiencing. *Courageous* and *daring*. She filled Byron's mug, feeling as though she could accomplish anything. Back in the living room, she handed him the white porcelain cup, realizing that the sensation was akin to invincibility. She approached her task with newfound determination.

Wanessa's first few attempts at centerpiece making were less than perfect. No matter what she did, she couldn't get the long-stemmed orchids and stargazer lilies to stay upright in the vases. She tried adding more tile pieces. That only made it hard to get the stems inserted. She tried fewer tiles and more flowers. Then it just looked like the flowers had been stuffed into the containers willy-nilly.

Frustration furrowed her brow and made it difficult for her to concentrate. It wasn't as easy as she thought. It wasn't easy at all. Now she knew why the arrangements they'd seen cost so much. People were paying for imagination, ingenuity, and labor. Buying centerpieces might not be such a bad idea after all.

"What if you cut off part of the stems?" Byron asked, rising from the couch.

"I don't think you're supposed to cut them."

"Well, they're your flowers now. You can do anything you want with them."

"But—"

"Nope. No protests. All I need is a pair of wire cutters."

Wanessa hoped she did the right thing by giving Byron

the cutters. He grabbed a few of the silk flowers. Working through the plastic stems, he took off about three inches.

"Now try it."

She picked up the amputated lilacs and placed them in a vase filled with multicolored pieces of ceramic. She could tell from the feel of the greenery in her hand that the placement was different. They were more maneuverable and stayed in place much better.

"Um-hmm," Byron mumbled. "Just what I thought."

For the next hour and a half, Byron cut the flower stems and handed them to Wanessa. Before long they had a table full of beautifully arranged centerpieces.

Wanessa stepped back, pride swelling in her chest. "Wow! We did it."

"You did it," Byron replied. "I just took off the excess."

"It was more than that." And it was. They had arranged the last three centerpieces together, selecting the flowers, pouring in the tile, moving the stems around until the petals were beautiful displays of color.

Then he smiled that heart-melting smile and said, "I guess we just work well together."

It was starting again, that familiar sensation Wanessa had whenever she and Byron were alone: a strong yearning to hold and be held. No, it was beyond that. She was drawn to him as if caught in the gravitational pull of a large galaxy. If she wasn't careful, she could easily combust into a million love-swept pieces in his atmosphere.

"I guess we do," she said.

"So can I get you something to drink?"

"No. Thank you."

"How about a snack? I know it's not quite dinnertime, but I can whip up some chips and dip."

"That's nice, Byron, but no."

"You know, every time you come over here, you refuse my hospitality. I'm starting to get a complex."

He hoped his humor would enliven the situation. It didn't. But the loud growl coming from Wanessa's stomach did.

Her eyes widened like saucers, and she placed a hand against her abdomen. "Oh, I'm so embarrassed."

"Don't be," he said, taking a box of spinach from the freezer. "Now, I don't cook a lot of things, but what I *do* make, I make very well. Like this spinach-and-artichoke dip I'm about to throw down on. I serve it warm, and I guarantee you'll love it!"

"All right," Wanessa said, barely above a whisper.

She resembled a porcelain doll sitting on the stool at the breakfast nook. So delicate and fragile, as though if she weren't treated with care and respect, she would break into a thousand pieces. Now he knew why Oli had acted like she was Wanessa's guardian. He felt the same way. Something about the innocence in her eyes, the meekness of her demeanor made him want to be a warrior for her.

When he finished preparing the snack, he placed the dip in a glass bowl and poured potato chips and crackers on a matching glass serving dish. "Would you like a separate plate?"

"No. This is fine. Thank you, Byron."

He watched her take a chip. Her fingernails were always cut short and covered with clear polish. She slid her chip into the dip, so proper and controlled. Slowly she lifted it to her lips and took a bite. Nothing like the women he was used to, which mostly added up to his sister, mother, and aunts. They attacked their food with the aggression and deliberateness of a man, often burping their approval of a good meal. He couldn't imagine Wanessa burping in public. He knew she was mortified that he'd heard her stomach growl. But she needn't be. He felt comfortable with her and hoped she would eventually feel just as comfortable with him.

"Aren't you having any?" she asked.

"Yes," he said, thinking he would much rather watch her. He took a chip and sat down on the stool next to hers.

"You were right. It is very good."

"Thank you," he said.

Her eyes darted everywhere but in his direction. He wished he knew how to put her at ease.

"So how's the apartment hunt coming?" she asked.

"Not good. I don't know if my standards are too high or what, but all I want is an apartment with some character. Everything I've looked at so far is ordinary and mass-produced."

He took a bite off a large potato chip. "I really like your apartment. It has its own personality—unique and homey." Wanessa lived in a huge house that had been turned into ten one-bedroom apartments. The house was at least eighty years old and had all of the original mahogany-wood paneling around the ceiling and baseboards. Because of the way the apartments were divided, the rooms were cut into unusual and surprising angles.

"Thank you," she said, sharing her smile with him. "You really can't beat an apartment-house for character. And the price fits my teller's salary."

She stopped chewing. "Have you ever thought of living in an apartment-house?"

"No, but I don't know why not. It would definitely be more along the lines of what I've been looking for."

"My landlord owns several houses that she's turned into apartments. I could ask her if she has any vacancies."

"That would be great, Wanessa. Thank you."

"With everything that you've done for me, it's the least I can do for you."

Byron didn't feel as though he'd done all that much. He'd

just run interference here and there, and tagged along with her sometimes for friendly support.

"And your job search," she said, picking up another chip, "how's that going?"

"About the same as my apartment search. Even with my management internships, no one wants to take a chance on someone with limited experience."

"Where've you been looking?"

"Sherwin Williams, the *Plain Dealer,* American Greetings. Places like that. I've applied to every major firm in the city."

Wanessa was thoughtful. "What about nonprofits?"

"What about them?"

"At a First Fridays meeting last year, one guy came and spoke to us about career development. He said that smaller companies are often overlooked when people are job hunting. And they shouldn't be."

"Go on," he said, intrigued.

"He gave us some statistics. I don't remember what they were now, but they showed that most of the employment opportunities are occurring in the smaller companies. And where larger firms are focused on promoting from within, a smaller company like a nonprofit is more willing to take a chance on someone from the outside."

"That makes a lot of sense."

"He listed some organizations in his handout. I've got it in a file if you'd like to see it."

"I would," he said.

"Okay, I'll have it ready for you the next time you come over."

"Thanks."

"And what kind of job is it that you're looking for?" she asked.

Byron smiled. "Something in management, upper management preferably. I realize that's a tall order, but that's what I'm looking for.''

Wanessa thought about the managers she'd had. Most were controlling, autocratic, and focused on the bottom line. ''You don't seem like the boss type.''

''Maybe because my style is more in tune with a new management philosophy called servant leadership.''

She frowned. ''What's that?''

Excitement surged through him. Since he had decided five years ago that he wanted to actually *do* something with his life, he had come to the conclusion that what he really enjoyed was helping people to be the best they could be. And he also wanted the ability to enjoy a comfortable lifestyle. When he combined these two desires, he came up with the idea of being a leader in a corporate setting.

''Servant leadership is when you're not just a dictator or controller of people and events; you're a visionary. It's your job to support people and make sure they have exactly what they need to get their jobs done. Servant leaders guide instead of direct and are more focused on serving those they work with than controlling them.''

''That sounds a lot like what you've been doing for me.'' She looked up at him, her eyes as soft as a doe's.

He hadn't considered that, but maybe she was right.

She blinked, and he realized how beautiful her eyes were even without makeup.

''Maybe it's just part of your nature,'' she said.

''A couple of years ago, I was enrolled in an English class. I'll never forget the instructor, Grayson Gilmore. Hard as nails. Gave more assignments than in any class I've had since. But I learned more in his class than in any leadership class I ever took, because he was a servant. He made sure we had exactly what we needed to become competent writers. He gave us every experience imaginable.''

Byron could see that Wanessa was listening intently, craning her neck to hear, staring into his eyes.

"Anyway, I overheard some students talking about how they were going to try to get rid of him, and I just couldn't sit back and do nothing. So I helped organize other students to speak to the dean on his behalf. And that's when it really hit me. I wanted to be a leader—someone people can count on, someone who will step in when people need help. And like Professor Gilmore, I wanted to challenge people to be the best they can be."

Byron sighed. "Every man wants to make a mark on this world. That's how I want to make mine."

The chips and dip were almost gone. Byron stepped off the stool and went into the kitchen. "Would you like some more?" he asked, taking the dishes.

"No. That was wonderful. I'm full now."

"Full of me talking, I'll bet." Byron hadn't meant to get so intimate with the details of his aspirations, but the earnest expression on Wanessa's face coaxed it out of him, made him want to share it with her.

"You are so helpful, not only to me, but to everyone."

"Thanks. I have the kind of past that makes me ashamed of the person I was. I am a much better man now than I have ever been, but it's not all of my own doing. I had help from all directions. And quite frankly, I owe. I owe my family. I owe Barnett University. I owe my friends. But what I owe them is to be the best person I can be, and if I can give someone the same kind of help that I've been given, then I'm doing my job as a human being."

He rinsed off the dishes and put them in the dishwasher. "So what about you?"

"What do you mean?"

You must have dreams, aspirations. What do you want to be when you grow up?"

Wanessa looked far away. "It's nothing as lofty or ambitious as what you want."

"It doesn't have to be," he said, ushering her into the living room. "It just has to be yours."

"Well, I would like to move up from my current position. Be a personal banker, maybe."

She looked up and smiled a little. "That's helping people, too."

He smiled back, marveling at her generous heart. "Yes, Wanessa. It sure is."

The inside of the Groove Bar & Grill was dark and brooding. Undertones of brown with burnished gold highlights in the ceiling and walls surrounded the small room of thirty or so customers talking and laughing at various tables throughout. The room buzzed with light conversation, and smelled as though it had been soaked in the aroma of searing meat and garlic.

Byron guided Wanessa to a table in front. She sat down, uncomfortable. She rarely went out, and when she did, she always sat in the rear, where she could fade into the background if necessary.

"This isn't too close, is it?" he asked.

"Well, no. I guess not." For some crazy reason, she suddenly felt like trying something new.

"Good. I want to be able to see the whole show without some tall person, with a hat they refuse to take off, blocking my view." He turned to her. "I can't believe that you and Olivia hadn't checked out the band before you hired them."

"We were going on a friend's recommendation that they were really good."

"Well, we'll see," he said, and winked.

The gesture sent a wave of warmth curling around Wanessats lower torso. She squirmed at the sensation.

Eight thirty-five. The band was scheduled to start at nine. What could she do between now and then to distract her from the tingling sensation she got from sitting close to Byron?

"Can I get you two something to drink?" a young woman asked. She looked barely old enough to be serving drinks, with her bangs and two braids.

Wanessa knew better than to have any alcohol. One drink and her words would slur and her vision would blur. "Ginger ale, please."

"I'll have a Coke."

"Great. I'll be right back."

Byron checked his watch. Except for a few wires, there were no instruments on the stage. "I wonder when they plan on setting up."

Wanessa didn't want to sound too concerned, but she wondered that same thing. "Me, too."

A few minutes later, the waitress came back with their drinks. Byron paid for them and gave the server a nice tip. He checked his watch again.

"Okay, I really don't want to jump to conclusions here, but I don't like them already."

Just a few minutes before nine, and the band still hadn't shown up. When the waitress came back to check on them, Byron asked, "Is the band still scheduled for tonight?"

"Yes, they always come late, though."

"All right. Thanks," Byron said. He turned to Wanessa. "Had enough?"

"What do you mean?" she asked, feeling alarmed.

"I don't think you should do business with a band that has a reputation for being late."

"Shouldn't we at least hear them play?" She welcomed the opportunity to hear a live band. She hadn't heard one in more years than she cared to count. But she also wanted to do just about anything to prolong the feeling of euphoria and quiet calm she felt just sitting next to Byron. It was like being gently massaged. All of the day's tension, both at work with customers and at home talking with Gerald's mother, was being eased out of her. What was left was beautiful and relaxing.

"I have no problem leaving right now. But if you want to stay, we will."

"Thanks," she said.

The band came in not five minutes afterward. Wanessa expected that they would probably be in a hurry and assemble their equipment with some sense of urgency. She was wrong. They took their time as if it were eight-ten instead of nine-ten.

She and Byron watched for another thirty minutes while they hauled in amplifiers, guitars, drums, and a keyboard. Then they plugged in what had to have been a couple miles' worth of thick black cables. After that, they spent another fifteen minutes tuning instruments and testing microphones.

This time Wanessa checked her watch. It was a few minutes before ten. The waitress had just dropped off a third round of drinks. Byron leaned over toward her neck, his lips just inches away from her ear.

"You'll have to tell these bozos the reception starts at three instead of five."

She covered her mouth, but a giggle escaped anyway. The sound of the band starting drowned out the rest of her laughter.

A tall, thin man in a black T-shirt and brown corduroy pants approached the mike. "Thank you for your patience this evening, ladies and gentlemen. We are the First Choice band, and for your auditory and eargasmic pleasure, we will be rockin' the house tonight. So sit back and relax, if you can. Better yet, get up and party!''

They sounded good. Professional even. Four young guys playing New Age funk. Byron was impressed. His head nodded to the rhythm of drums and a strong bass. He checked out Wanessa. She had her own nodding action going. First Choice definitely had his attention and his vote for proper wedding reception entertainment. The only thing he found distracting was the occasional feedback from the speakers, but other than that, he was almost ready to get his dance on.

Three songs later, the group still had his attention, but not for the music. Byron was focused on the feedback that occurred with greater and greater frequency and the exasperation on the lead singer's face. When an earsplitting noise blared out of the speakers, the lead singer kicked over the mike stand with his foot and left the stage.

"I don't know why you flunkies can't hook up a simple microphone.''

"Who are you calling a flunky?'' the bass player shouted, marching after the vocalist.

"You!'' the young man said. And that was when the keyboard player leaped from where he was sitting and knocked down the singer with a right cross. Before you could say DMX, they were engaged in an all-out melee. Concerned for Wanessa's safety, Byron stood up and ushered her to another part of the room. Then he returned to see if he could help separate the brawling musicians. For a few minutes all Byron could hear was curses, fists smacking into skin, animalistic growls, and furniture breaking. Finally he, a bartender, and the drummer pulled the men apart and stopped the fight.

"I made this band!'' the singer yelled. Though it sounded more like "I mace to spend'' on account of the split lip, bloody and swelling on his face.

"Every time," the bass player said, struggling against Byron. "Why you gotta mess up *every* time?"

Even with a ripped shirt, the singer remained smug. "Well, this is the last time, 'cause I'm out! O to the U to the T. Out!"

"You know what, I'm sick of all of you," the keyboard player said. "You can all go to hell!"

A tall woman in a red pantsuit hurried out of a back room and into the commotion. Byron assumed she was the owner.

"This is the last time you all will cause trouble here. Now you all can go quietly or I can call the cops. Which would you prefer?"

Byron let go of the bass player, who seemed much calmer. The band members exchanged venomous looks and headed toward their equipment.

"I'll make sure you get your equipment. But for now, you all need to leave," the tall woman said.

Another volley of growls and curses and they were out the door. The bartender followed behind them, probably to make sure the scuffle didn't continue outside.

Byron spied Wanessa looking on from a corner of the room, her eyes wide and frightened. He tried to put her at ease by making light of the situation.

"I can't wait to hear what people will say about your reception. 'Loved the fighting. Hated the music.' "

His humor failed. He didn't even get a smile. Byron touched her lightly on the elbow. "Come on. Let's get out of here."

Two days later, Byron surprised Wanessa by showing up at her apartment with information on six bands. They spent the evening listening to audio tapes, watching videotapes, and reviewing the Web sites of potential replacements. Before Byron left for home, they had narrowed down the choices, and to show her appreciation for his help, Wanessa cooked him dinner. She treated him like a king, and Byron knew he could get used to her special attention. Maybe he already had.

August

After a long workweek, Wanessa had taken Olivia's advice—plus the gift certificate she'd sent—and treated herself to an evening retreat at Oasis Spas. The national chain of pampering villas was famous for their after-work treatments of full-body massage with a body-warming lotion called Steam Cream, herbal-extract facials, and aromatherapy meditation sessions. To depressurize from some of the stresses of wedding plans gone wrong, Wanessa had gotten the works and had driven home at ten P.M. on a cloud of relaxation.

She climbed into her bed, anticipating one of the best night's sleeps she'd had since the beginning of the year. When the phone rang, she started not to answer it, then changed her mind, praying that whoever it was, was calling with good news.

"Hello?"

"Where have you been? I've been trying to reach you all evening."

"Umm," she moaned, turning over and relaxing. She liked the sound of Byron's voice. It always soothed her.

"Are you all right?"

"Perfect," she purred.

"Wanessa, I'm sorry. I'm about to spoil your mood."

She opened her eyes but refused to become alarmed. "What is it?"

"It's the reception hall. It caught fire today. There's not much left. The authorities think some fireworks left over from a Fourth of July celebration caught on fire and started the blaze."

"That's terrible," she said, closing her eyes.

"Now, don't be too upset."

"I'm not," she said. "I'll take care of it in the morning." On the other end of the line, Byron's mouth gaped open in shock. *"You'll* take care of it?"

After watching Byron fix mishap after mishap, she was beginning to let his self-confidence and his calm approach to things rub off. *Stuff happens and plans change.* "I'll call around in the morning and get another place."

She drifted. In her mind she'd already started to dream. She was walking down the aisle in a platinum gown. As she approached the altar, Byron was standing there patiently waiting to make her his wife. She smiled.

"Good night, Byron," she said.

"Good night, Wanessa."

When she awoke the next morning, two things were prominent in her mind: one, she needed to find a new reception hall, and two, her dream about marrying Byron was so real it made her nervous.

All morning she worked to put the dream out of her mind while calling around to various venues checking their Christmas-day availability. There weren't many openings, and those that were available wanted so much money that she would have felt guilty spending that much.

At eleven-thirty, Byron called to check on her.

"So, find a new place yet?"

"Not unless I want to spend a thousand dollars."

"Did you tell them it was for a wedding?"

"Yes," she said.

"Don't. Sometimes when they know it's for a special occasion like that, they'll jack up the price because they know people will pay it."

"Thanks for the tip. You're so good to me."

"Just let me know if you want me to make some calls. You'd be surprised what a male voice can do."

No, I wouldn't, she thought, realizing the delicious effect Byron's voice had on her. "I'll call you back once I've booked something."

"Cool," he said, and they hung up.

He was on a date. Wanessa busily wrote items for her gift registry, distracted by the fact that Byron was out with the woman who had now become her beautician. All Pamela could talk about during Wanessa's last appointment was how much she was looking forward to seeing Byron again.

Apparently they had gone out on a couple of dates, to a coffee shop and to a movie. Tonight they were going to a concert to see a singer called Allgood.

Dual alarm clock, Crock-Pot, ottoman, place mats, bath towels, casserole dish, don't think about Byron, don't think about Byron. She told herself that he was like a brother to her, and she was concerned because she didn't want him to be hurt. She wouldn't dare consider the fact that underneath that concern were feelings, the kind she should have for Gerald and didn't.

Eight o'clock on a Friday, she thought as she continued with her list. Any minute now her phone would ring. It would be Gerald calling for their weekly talk about Mum and the arrangements. Just once she wished they could carry on a conversation without bringing his mother into it. It was like the three of them were getting married instead of just her and Gerald. He wanted so much to include her in everything, and Wanessa just didn't see the need. But as a bride-to-be, she respected her future husband's wishes and included Maude Greene as much as possible, even if it made things more difficult or downright hard.

She really should take Byron's advice and speak with Mrs. Greene, if for nothing more than to assure her that she was perfectly capable of taking care of the details herself, and that when it came to her wedding, she would have the final say on everything. So far, nothing like that had the nerve to make its way out of her mouth. Only, "Yes, ma'am" and "I think so, too, ma'am." But Wanessa was growing tired of it.

Briefly, she contemplated adding "different mother-in-law" to the list of things she wanted for her wedding.

"All right. This has gone on long enough." Wanessa picked up the phone and dialed Maude Greene's number, determined to clear the air once and for all.

"Wanessa? Is that you?"

"Y-yes. It's m-me. I kn-know it's late, but . . ."

He could hear her sobs over the phone. The sound almost made him double over in pain.

"Wanessa, what's wrong!"

"I can't . . . there's no way I can . . ." Her voice dissolved into tears.

"Are you home?"

"Yes," she said, her voice paper-thin.

"I'm on my way."

Twenty minutes later, Byron was taking the stairs to

Wanessa's second-floor apartment two at a time. When he reached her door, he pounded on it hard.

She opened the door, her face wet with tears. Before he could stop himself, he pulled her into his embrace and held her so close he thought she could hear his heart beating like thunder in his chest. She held on tightly while he stroked her hair and whispered in her ear.

"Whatever it is, I'll fix it. I'll make it right. I promise."

All he wanted to do at that moment was change the world for her. Angle the sun so that it illuminated the sky just for her. Steal the moonlight so that it shone on her alone. Take away every sadness she had ever experienced and bring her a silver tray of happiness. He wanted above all to love her and protect her, and keep her safe.

He pulled away, but only slightly. "Can you tell me?"

Wanessa looked up at him, eyes spilling over with pain. "She won't pay."

Dread sat like a cold stone on his heart. He'd been afraid this would happen. "Maude?"

Wanessa nodded, her eyes brimming with fresh tears. Closed caterers he could fix. Burned rehearsal halls he could fix. Feuding bands he could fix. But some days he didn't know where his next meal was coming from. There was no way he could help pay for a wedding. There had to be a way to salvage the situation and make Wanessa happy.

He walked her into the living room and sat down next to her on the couch. "Tell me everything."

Byron listened as Wanessa recounted the story of how her future mother-in-law resented being cut out of the wedding planning and as a result threatened not to pay for any of the wedding arrangements, as she had previously agreed upon.

"She's trying to manipulate you. And if she's trying to do it now, chances are it will get worse once you're officially her daughter-in-law. Is that what you want?"

"No."

"Then you've got to tell Gerald."

Wanessa's face paled.

"What's the matter?" he asked.

"I just don't think he'll be much help. He . . . does pretty much what his mother tells him."

"Well, it's time for him to grow up and make some decisions on his own. And you should give him the chance to do that. Now, do you want to tell him or should I?"

A nervous laugh bubbled out of her lips, surprising him. "Why are you laughing?"

"You're always ready to jump in the middle of things. I'm always so afraid to. This wedding is the first thing in my life I've ever tried to really *do*. You know what I mean?"

"Yeah," he said, thinking about his decision to go to college and to find a decent job. "I know *exactly* what you mean."

A weak smile broke through the sadness on her face. "Thank you, Byron, for coming to my rescue again. I know you're probably tired. I'm sorry if I interrupted anything."

He frowned. "Anything like what?"

She looked away. "Your date with Pamela."

"My date with Pamela ended hours ago."

Wanessa stood and walked over to the end table, where she took a tissue from the drawer. "How was the concert?"

"It was good, I think."

"You think?"

"Yeah. Alicia Keys can really blow. But when Allgood came on, all the women lost their minds. Including Pamela. I could barely hear the brother sing for all the screaming."

Wanessa smiled. "Yeah, he's nice-looking."

Byron's heart flip-flopped. "Oh, no, not you too. I just spent all evening listening to Pamela and some girlfriends she ran into talk about how *fine* he is."

"Sorry."

"Not half as sorry as I am. I don't know what possessed me to go out with her again."

He rubbed his chin and thought quietly for a moment. "It's amazing what people do when they get a little lonely."

"Byron, you don't ever have to feel lonely. You've got me."

At that statement, their eyes locked. Wanessa felt fastened in place by the heat of his stare. And then it came, the smile she'd wanted to see, so full of warmth it made her tearful again.

"Thank you," he said, basking in the love he felt growing for her. "When are you going to call Gerald?"

"Tomorrow."

Relief washed over him in great sheets. "Good," he said, and gave her one last hug before leaving.

Byron liked the way Wanessa had incorporated techniques from her makeover. She had taken to wearing makeup, just a touch, and trying different styles with her hair instead of just pulling her hair into a ponytail, as she'd done when they first met. She'd even started wearing a different style of clothes. Certainly more modern and feminine. She was a flower blossoming right before his eyes, and he loved what he saw.

Today she looked especially nice. He reasoned that since she was having her dress fitted, she wanted to see what she would look like on her wedding day. They had picked up the dress from the boutique and were headed to the home of a seamstress who did alterations. But while they were in the mall, they would stop and pick up the rings that had come in the day before.

When the clerk opened the boxes, light from the fluorescents overhead caught in the white gold and made it shine like stars. He took a polishing cloth to give each ring a final once-over before handing them over.

Wanessa's face was a beam of light, just like the rings. She touched them reverently, as if they were sacred objects just unearthed for the first time. Byron watched as she turned one around to read the inscription. Then pain lanced through her expression and his heart. "What's wrong?"

"This is wrong," she said, holding the ring away from her as if it were rancid.

"What's wrong with it?" Byron and the clerk asked simultaneously.

"The inscription . . . it says, 'Michael and Julie forever.' "

The color in the clerk's face faded. "I'm sorry. I don't know how you got the wrong rings."

"No, no," Wanessa said, her voice low and unsteady. "These are the right rings, but the inscription is wrong."

"Oh, my God." Again, Byron and the clerk spoke in unison.

"Nothing like this has ever happened before. I-I don't know what to do."

"Well, you'd better think of something." Byron's words came out cold and hard.

The clerk shuddered nervously.

Byron remained calm. "Why don't you go get the manager?"

"Just one moment," he said, and dashed off into a back room.

Wanessa sighed. "I don't believe this."

"Don't worry. Everything will be fine."

A tall man in an expensive black suit came out of the back. He came to the counter wearing a look of grave concern. "I understand there's been a terrible mixup." The man's voice sounded sincere.

"Yes, there has, and we'd like to know what you're going to do to make it right."

"Well, of course we'll redo the inscription." He took a yellow slip of paper from inside the box and unfolded it. " 'Gerald and Wanessa, 12/25/02.'"

"Yes," Wanessa said.

"I'll approve a fifty-percent discount on the service."

Byron gave the man a don't-mess-with-me stare.

He cleared his throat and spoke again. "Actually, since it was such an atrocious mistake, we'll engrave the rings free of charge."

Wanessa's eyes widened and her mouth formed a cute little O. Byron smiled. "Thank you."

"That's quite all right. One of my staff will call you in a few days when they're ready."

Byron took Wanessa by the arm and led her toward the door. "We appreciate that," he said, and then they walked out.

When they were away from the jewelers, Wanessa said, "Wow, you're amazing."

"It's called insistence and self-confidence."

"I could sure use some of that sometimes."

"You've got it. We all do. It's just that some folks have to dig deeper to find theirs."

A warm sensation moved through her as she realized how much he made her want to dig deep into buried things, feelings she hadn't felt in a long time—or ever.

Weddingpages, Modern Bride, Town & Gown. Byron flipped through the pages of the magazines, wishing he'd brought some reading material. Wanessa was in the other room with the seamstress, and he was in the outer room bored out of his mind. A pin here and tuck there. What could possibly take so long? It seemed like they'd spent the entire afternoon at the woman's house.

He was about to call out to see if she had anything else

to read besides wedding magazines, when the seamstress came bounding around the corner.

"Thanks for waiting," she said. "Most men are not as patient as you've been."

Now Byron felt like a heel. "No problem," he said.

"We're almost finished, but we need a man's point of view. Come in the living room, will you?"

He did as she asked. The short, swarthy, Italian-looking woman seemed like she wasn't one to take no for an answer. He followed her around the corner and stepped right into a fairy tale. Wanessa stood in the center of the room, the most magnificent creature he'd ever seen.

She looked like she'd just materialized out of his dreams. No—out of his heart. Emotion stopped him in his tracks, and all he could do was stare.

"Well?" the dark-haired woman asked.

Wanessa smiled like the brightest star in the heavens. "What do you think?"

"I think . . ." He swallowed hard. "I think Gerald is the luckiest man on earth."

The seamstress touched his shoulder. "All right, that's enough drooling. You can go back now."

Byron walked back to the hallway, smiling at the tail end of the two women's conversation.

"That's not the groom?"

"No. He's my friend."

"Aw, too bad. I hope this Gerald person likes the dress as much as your friend does."

* * *

"As long as we're out, do you mind stopping at DK Entertainment? With all that's happened, I feel like I should double check everything."

"No problem," Byron said, and headed downtown to the heart of the city.

DK Entertainment was a large store downtown in Key Tower. The company provided everything from clowns and magicians to deejays and karaoke equipment. The preliminary entertainment for the reception was a deejay named MC Music, otherwise known as Carl Johnsen. After an hour, Carl was to be followed by a great band called Special Touch.

Carl greeted them as they came in and escorted them to a back room with all sorts of equipment and a small open area.

"So we're all set for December twenty-fifth?" Wanessa asked.

"Yes, ma'am," he said.

He looked as if he'd just graduated from high school, but Byron pegged him at about the twenty-five-to-twenty-eight age range.

"I've got a standard list of ballads and love songs, just like you asked."

Byron tensed. "Let me see it."

The young man opened a file cabinet and pulled out a sheet of paper. Every romantic slow song he could imagine was on it.

"This is terrible!"

"What?" Wanessa asked, not sure if she could take another disaster.

"These songs will put people to sleep. What you want at a reception is a celebration—a party. People want to get their groove on and congratulate your happiness."

"That's the kind of stuff I usually play," Carl responded.

"But there should be an atmosphere of love," Wanessa countered.

Byron shook his head. "I beg to differ. There should be an atmosphere of funk gettin' ready to roll," he said, snapping his fingers.

Carl pulled another playlist from the cabinet. "Last weekend I was playing at this reception out in Lakewood. They requested all old-school jams. Everybody loved it. People were leaving sweaty, like they'd just worked out at the gym or something.''

The young man walked over to the deejay equipment and started pushing buttons and turning dials. "We have a try-it-before-you-buy-it policy. That's why we have the performance area right there. I'll play a little something, and then you guys be the judge.''

Carl put on a headset and slid a CD into a player. The Carpenters' "For All We Know" came out of five small speakers. "It's beautiful," Wanessa said, swaying her head.

"It's tired," Byron retorted. "You'll start a yawn fast with this kinda stuff." He gave Carl the "cut" signal. "Carl, flip that old-school, man.''

This time the speakers roared to life with the up-tempo hit "You're the One for Me" by D Train. Byron bobbed his head. "Now *this* is what you *need*." He looked over at the performance area and then at Wanessa. "Try it before you buy it, huh?" He extended his hand. "Dance with me.''

Wanessa shrank back. "Oh, no, Byron. I can't dance.''

"Let me be the judge of that." He started moving his hips and snapping his fingers. He loved to dance, and the rhythm in the music was contagious. "Come on," he persisted.

"I don't have any experience dancing. I was the one who always got passed over." She looked down for a moment and then returned his gaze.

If it had been up to him, she would never have gotten passed over—for anything. Impulsively, he took her hands and led her to the open area. Then slowly he coaxed her to dance, twisting her, turning her, taunting her with his body movements. Pretty soon the music took them over and they were smiling, laughing, and spinning on the floor.

"Whew!" she said when the music stopped. "That was wonderful!"

"See how much fun your guests could have?" Byron said, catching his wind.

Wanessa's brows furrowed with concern. "I'll have to check with Maude." She turned to Carl. "Can I get back to you on the choice of music?"

"Sure," he said, removing the headset. "I'll need to know at least a week before the ceremony."

"I'm sure I'll be able to get back to you by then."

Byron left the store with Wanessa, deep concern gnawing at his psyche.

They got into his car and headed back toward Wanessa's apartment.

"What's wrong?" she asked.

"I'm just wondering," he said. "What kind of wedding do *you* want?"

"Isn't it obvious?"

"The only thing that's obvious is that you use words like 'there should be' instead of 'I want.' And every decision you make is not really your decision. It's your future mother-in-law's."

Wanessa turned away and watched the cars drive past. She'd never been good at expressing herself—at asking for what she wanted. At first, when Maude began making most of the wedding decisions, like the number of people, food selection, dress styles, and even the date and time, Wanessa had welcomed her help. But every day it seemed less like help and more like interference. But she wasn't sure what she could say or do to change the way things had become. A ribbon of unease trickled through her body. "I know," she said finally.

Byron changed direction, and instead of heading toward the interstate, he headed back downtown. He parked the car at the dock of Lake Erie near Brown's Stadium.

"This is a wedding, Wanessa. *Your* wedding. Now, is this what you want or not?"

"I don't know."

"Sure you do. I'd bet a million dollars that just about every woman in America has fantasized about the type of wedding she wants. That's the kind of stuff women do."

She turned to him then.

"Close your eyes, and picture your wedding the way you've thought of it all your life."

She did as he asked.

"Can you see it?"

"Yes," she whispered.

"Tell me."

She swallowed hard, trying to manage her answer. "It's evening. Maybe nighttime. Yes. It's night. I can see ... stars."

"Keep going."

Her mind filled with the pictures she'd painted of her wedding over the years. Pictures she'd shoved away like winning the lottery or having parents that actually cared about her. Things she'd never have.

She didn't know it then, but it was obvious to her now. Her parents didn't really want children. Wanessa had smoky gray young-girl memories of a mother who barely spoke to her when she was growing up. Magnolia Taylor became a hermit in her own family's house. Gunny Taylor, her father, was a quiet man who disappeared every night behind a newspaper. His idea of giving Wanessa attention was lowering the *Plain Dealer* while he continued to read it and saying, "That's nice," just as soon as she finished talking. She sucked in her bottom lip, realizing she was an only child for a reason. Sighing, she turned her mind to more pleasant thoughts.

"Music is playing. A flute or a harp. It sounds like angels singing. And a small gathering of people turn as I walk outside. I know and acknowledge each face. The man I love takes my hand and I join him to stand before God. I'm wearing a simple dress. Not a white bolt of fabric like most brides wear, but something unconstrained and the color of spun honey.

"The ceremony is simple. We light candles, exchange vows that we've written from our hearts, and the minister blesses our union. Then, without a lot of fanfare, our close friends and family wish us well, and we leave to begin our life together."

Byron listened. In place of the groom he knew vaguely as Gerald, he saw himself, and he knew that if Wanessa were marrying him, he would make sure her wedding was exactly as she'd dreamed it.

September

She was having the time of her life. Who knew wedding planning could be so much fun?

Since the tearful good-bye she had shared with Olivia, she and Byron had spent more time together than Siamese twins. Just the other day, Byron had shown up at Wanessa's doorstep with two large coffees from Starbucks and an armful of bride magazines. They spent the better part of the morning and part of the afternoon looking through them, laughing at some of the ridiculous dresses, and picking out some of the things they liked. It was as if Olivia had never left.

Wanessa was curious. Not only was Byron helping her, but he seemed to be enjoying their conversations about photographs versus video, three tiers versus four, and whether something old could also be something blue. Recently she asked him about his surprising disposition.

"I never thought I would be having these kinds of talks

with a man. I mean, you really have good ideas about the flowers and other stuff.''

Byron's smile came on full force. ''Well, to tell the truth, I thought this was going to be boring. Then I thought it was going to be quick and easy. But I found out it's neither.''

He thumbed through the pages of *Bride to Be* magazine, but seemed to be staring through them. ''Don't get me wrong. I will never, ever volunteer to do anything like this ever again. But what I really like is you. You're very different from anyone I've ever known. I just . . .''

He set the magazine on Wanessa's kitchen table and stared up at her. ''Well, I enjoy your company.''

Sometimes she found it hard not to react to his handsome face, his smooth voice, or his suave gestures. Like then, when his comment sent tiny sparks of awareness igniting in her body.

She was leery of that feeling. She had had it when she was engaged to be married six years before. All she had wanted was for that feeling to continue. She would have done anything to keep it. And she had paid for her foolhardiness with the pain and anguish and embarrassment of a horrible breakup. Of being left at the altar. Of being deserted. Of being abandoned. Love would never make her vulnerable again.

She glanced at the clock. It was four-forty-five P.M. Byron said he'd call her at five if he was available to join her for First Fridays. She'd invited him so that he could do some networking. He had gone on several interviews but was still looking for a job. She thought that maybe she could help him for a change. It would be good for him to make contacts in the business world.

Wanessa turned over on her bed. She had been lounging and reading wedding pamphlets and brochures since she got home. Groaning, she realized she was getting tired of all the sales pitches and decisions yet to make. What she wanted was a rest from all the planning. She hoped she'd get one tonight.

When the phone rang she sprang up, full of optimism.

"Hey, Q-man! You'd better not be calling to say you're running late. Dinner is almost ready." She couldn't believe what she'd just said. It was so bold and forward. She was never like that in the past. But something about Byron made her feel comfortable enough to be a little daring. When she heard the voice on the other end of the line, her reserved nature took over again.

"Wanessa, my dear. How are you? And who is this Q-man you're seeing tonight?"

Wanessa's enthusiasm deflated. "Oh, it's you, Gerald." The absurdity of her previous remark made her giggle. "I'm sorry. I was expecting someone else."

"Really?"

"Yes, but that's okay. How are you?"

"I'm fine. This assignment is wearing on me a little, but I just keep thinking it will be over soon."

"Just in time to get married."

"Yes," he responded. "Just in time."

Since they'd started dating, she and Gerald had never spent much time on the phone. Usually he called to find out how she was doing and to invite her to dinner. She would accept and they would hang up. Now that he was gone, he called her weekly. After she would say she was fine, they would stammer and fret a bit and then he would find an excuse to hang up, saying he would call her next week.

This time the silence lasted for quite a while. As always, Gerald finally spoke up.

"How are the arrangements going? I wish I could do more from here, but I'm sure Mum's been helpful."

Wanessa's stomach tightened. Just the thought of Gerald's mother, with her expensive tastes and strong opinions, filled her with dread. "Things are working out," she said.

"That friend of yours ... Baron? He's assisting you still?"

"Yes, *Byron* is a big help. And he's ..."

The knock at the door startled her. She walked to the entryway and took a look out of the peephole. It was Byron with a bouquet of flowers.

Byron's bright smile lit up her living room when she opened the door. He came in damp from the rain. It had been falling all day, and the inside of her apartment was thick with humidity.

She smiled and took the bouquet. He took off his jacket, hung it on the coatrack, and headed into the kitchen.

"You want something?" he called out.

"No, thanks."

"I'm sorry, I didn't know you had company." Gerald's voice sounded tight and dry. "I won't keep you if there's someone there."

"That's all right, Gerald. It's just Byron."

At that remark, Byron frowned. She waved off her comment, knowing he had taken it the wrong way.

"Well, then I won't keep you."

"Okay. Talk to you next week?"

"Yes. Next week."

She hung up, wishing she were just a little bit more excited about receiving his phone call next Friday.

"*Just* Byron?"

She turned. Byron was standing in the middle of her dining room, arms folded across his chest.

Something fluttered in her stomach. Butterflies? Hummingbirds? She couldn't tell. "See, I knew you were going to take it the wrong way."

"What other way is there to take it? But I'll have you know that *just* Byron has spent the last two hours in, of all

places, Sherri's Flower Shoppe. I spoke to a woman there—
Hazel, I think her name was. She must be new to the business,
because she seemed kinda confused about what I wanted.
But I have an order detail with the instructions.''

He took a pink slip of paper out of his pants pocket.

"That's great," she said, taking the bid from him. Since
Olivia had left, Byron had stepped in like Superman with a
big S on his chest. A voice in the back of her mind said,
Like Prince Charming on a smoky gray stallion.

"How was your interview?" she asked, shifting gears
away from errant thoughts.

"Terrible. Obviously I looked good on paper, but when
I got there, the interviewer's face fell."

"Oh," she said. He didn't have to say any more. Wanessa
had had her own experience with people who were still
prejudiced and not willing to give people of color a chance.
She wished she could help.

"Have you ever thought about the bank?"

"Key Bank? No, thanks. I want to create my own path,
not follow in my sister's footsteps. I've got a second interview with the Red Cross next week."

"Byron, that's great."

"I feel good about this one. Thanks for suggesting I try
out the nonprofits."

"I'm glad to help. Good luck on your interview."

"Thanks."

Wanessa glanced down at the flowers in her hand: calla
lilies, delphinium, and daisies. "I'm going to put these in
some water."

While she headed into the kitchen, Byron set the dining
room table. When he finished with place mats, plates, silver-
ware, and glasses, Wanessa brought out the bouquet and
placed it as a centerpiece.

"That looks nice," he said.

With Byron's help, she filled serving bowls full of piping-hot food and brought them to the table.

"These are all my favorites," he said, smiling.

She tried her best to return the sunshine she felt from his face. "I called Olivia. I wanted tonight to be special."

They sat down and bowed their heads. "When Olivia and I were growing up, our family always held hands when we said the dinner prayer. Do you mind?" he asked, reaching out.

"No," she responded, and clasped his hands.

"Heavenly Father," Byron began, "we come before you to give you thanks and praise for this day and our lives. Watch over us, Father, as we go forth and do your will. We ask for your blessings upon this food, that it sustain us as we follow your Word. Thank you for bringing us together tonight, Father. We ask that you guide us always in the right path, give us the strength to do what must be done, and the words to say what must be said. In Jesus' name, Amen."

Byron dug into the meal as if it were a feast. And he felt comfortable and at home, as though he had done this a million times, as though this were the ways things were supposed to be.

He looked across the table at Wanessa. She was exactly where she was supposed to be, with him. Not the frumpy and timid woman he'd met months ago, but a self-assured woman who was caring and giving and deserved the very best in life. And he wanted to make sure she got it.

"You know," she said, buttering a roll, "I still haven't found the right vows for Gerald and me. None of the ones I've seen really fit our relationship. Do you think we should write our own?"

"They would be more special that way."

"I'm not a writer or anything, but I believe I could come up with something. But Gerald . . . I'm not sure if he could."

Byron swallowed a sip of water. "Why not?"

"I think it's a guy thing. It's hard for men to tap into their emotions."

Funny, Byron felt his emotions keenly right then—all of them at attention, on alert, as if they were just waiting for a signal. "Not me," he said.

Wanessa's eyebrow lifted in disbelief. "Oh, really?"

He stared into her lovely face. "I'd just speak from the heart and say, 'Dear God, thank you for blessing me with a love supreme. This woman, this wonder, this blessing of all blessings has transformed a lowly man into a mighty king. With every cell of my body, I pledge a love undying, and vow to defend, honor, and protect her until my last breath. And every day I promise to rededicate myself to the love we'll share and the life we'll build together.' "

The room grew uncomfortably warm. Byron's unblinking stare radiated a heat in Wanessa's body she never imagined possible. His words were exactly what she would love to hear a man say to her. She was overcome with emotion.

"That was beautiful."

He nodded and turned his attention back to the food. He ate a few bites, then stared off into the other room.

"What's wrong, Byron? Don't you like it?"

"I more than like it, Wanessa. I love it," he said, holding her gaze again. Her features softened, and he realized that everything he had ever wanted was sitting right in front of him. *Dear Lord.* When had she captured his heart? He could have easily believed that it was when she had gotten the makeover, but it was well before that. He had seen the most important beauty, the beauty she had inside, and it made him believe in real love. Real love that he wanted right now.

"I love *you*," Wanessa, he said, putting his fork on the table.

His breathing quickened and his heart thudded against his chest. "I'm in love with you."

She swallowed hard and blinked. "No, you can't be."

"I can and I most definitely am."

And as if Wanessa had never seen the sun before, it rose in him like a bright new morning, and she knew he was telling the truth. Why did he have to love her? Why, when she'd resigned herself so wholeheartedly to marrying Gerald? She couldn't just break it off now. She'd been through the devastation of that situation. How could she wreak that kind of havoc on someone else?

"I know, I know," Byron said, rising. "It's not in your plans. But I feel something wonderful when I'm with you. And it's way too powerful for you not to feel it too."

He was coming her way. She got up and walked to the other side of the room. She couldn't bear to be close to him, not when her feelings were in such a state of flux.

"Byron, you have to go."

"Why? Because you know I'm telling the truth?"

Oh, God, why couldn't she have met him before Gerald? Why was her life always so complicated? Old fears and feelings of inadequacy rose from where they lay buried inside her. She turned away from Byron so he wouldn't see them on her face.

"Please, Wanessa. Don't shut me out. And don't retreat like you're afraid of me."

He came up behind her and held her in his arms. The sensation stole all her remaining strength, and she sagged against him.

"Don't be afraid. Don't be afraid," he murmured.

He turned her around, and she faced him with tears in her eyes. Byron kissed each lid, then slowly descended upon her mouth.

They kissed for all the weeks and days and moments when they had wanted to so badly they could taste it. They kissed for all the joy they'd experienced over the last few months. They kissed just as deliberately for all of the frustration and anguish they had been through. But above all, they kissed for the love they felt for each other, no longer a secret, no longer hidden.

After the longest, sweetest kiss either of them had ever had, they pulled away.

"I love you," Byron said again, this time needing to hear her say it, too. But she remained silent with her eyes closed, her breathing heavy.

"If you want, I'll explain it to everyone," he continued.

Wanessa's eyes flicked open. "Explain what?"

"That the wedding is off."

Her blood ran cold and she backed away from him. "I can't cancel the wedding."

Byron's body jerked as if he'd been punched in the gut. "You have to cancel the wedding."

"You don't know what it's like being in love with someone and having them back away from you."

"I have a feeling I'm about to find out."

She moved toward him.

He shrugged away. "Don't come over here with your soothing tones if all you're going to do is break my heart."

"And what about Gerald's heart?"

"What about yours?" he shot back.

"I can't betray him, Byron."

"So you don't love me?"

She lowered her lashes and he had his answer. He always fell for the ones who had already fallen for someone else. His heart hurt and he'd had enough. He left Wanessa's apartment without another word.

Taking his time to find a place to stay finally paid off. Byron signed a one-year lease for an apartment in the South Euclid area. He was twenty minutes away from everything, but more important, he was living in a place that had character. Wanessa's referral panned out, and her landlord showed him several large homes that had been turned into apartments. The first few he'd seen were disappointing. Although they had great character, they were too small for his tastes. Then she'd shown him a house that was split into two apartments. Each one was eighteen hundred square feet, and had large, heavy doors, high ceilings, and lots of wood. He'd fallen in love at once. Fifteen minutes later he was signing his name on the bottom line and contemplating a move date.

His discovery couldn't have come at a better time. A young couple had taken a liking to Olivia's house and were ready to close. Until he found his apartment, he thought he might have to camp out at Wanessa's. He'd liked the idea of that—seeing her before he went to bed and being there when she woke up in the morning. He knew if that happened, his attraction to her would deepen, and the last thing he wanted was to fall even more deeply in love with some other man's woman. Then he closed his eyes and realized that somehow, he already had.

October

The longest Wanessa and Byron had gone without seeing each other was a week. So after a week passed since his declaration of love, she assumed he was back to patch things up between them. When she opened the door, it wasn't for whom she expected.

She stood ready, but the faces staring back at her from the hallway did not belong to Byron. Gerald and Maude stood shoulder-to-shoulder, solemn looks riding their narrow faces. "Good evening, Wanessa," the oldest Greene said. "We'd like to talk to you."

Wanessa stepped aside to let the two enter. The conversation she'd had with Gerald about his mother's interference must have prompted this visit. Her heart pounded against her rib cage. "Gerald, when did you get back?"

"This afternoon."

She was anxious and hurt. "I didn't even know you were coming."

His expression was set. "I wanted to surprise you."

"My manners," Wanessa said, suddenly self-conscious about . . . everything. "Please sit down."

She swept a glance around the room. She hadn't dusted in over a week. A corner of her dining room table was still piled high with leftovers from the night she and Byron had made centerpieces, and wedding books and magazines cluttered her living room table until the top was barely visible. She was utterly and overwhelmingly embarrassed.

Maude lifted her chin. "Your apartment is, uh, quaint."

"Thank you," she said, unsure whether that was the proper response.

Wanessa had a terrible urge to vacuum, make her bed, and spray Lysol. Not because her home was untidy, but because something about Maude's demeanor made her want to make sure everything about her home was in its place. As if, heaven forbid, she was under the hard examination of her own mother. And for some strange reason, she now felt uncomfortable in her own apartment.

"I don't want to belabor the point, so I'll be brief. Gerald tells me you don't like the way I've been handling things."

"Well, I . . . I mean, it's just . . ." Wanessa could feel herself shrinking right before their eyes. It was two against one. How could she hold her own when they both were against her? She stiffened. Then a familiar knock both startled and bolstered her. "One moment, please," she said, almost running to the door. She swung it open, and Byron was propped against the doorjamb.

"Can we talk?" he asked.

Wanessa signed with relief and hoped against hope he would follow her lead.

"Byron! I was wondering if you'd get here. Dinner will be ready in a minute."

He walked inside thinking that all the wedding planning must have finally gotten to her. "Wanessa, we didn't—"

"Set a specific time," she interrupted, "I know."

When he saw the two people sitting in Wanessa's living room, he wondered if they could be the cause of her strange behavior.

"Maude, Gerald, this is my good friend Byron. Byron, this is my fiancé and his wife, uh, mother!"

He shook hands with the two, all the while pushing back the jealousy threatening to take him over. *So this is Gerald. He doesn't look like much, but there's no accounting for taste.*

"Byron and I are having dinner together. Right, Byron?"

She's gone crazy. But then he saw the look of desperation in her eyes and understood. "Yes, we are. I'm not late, am I?" he asked, taking off his jacket.

"No. As a matter of fact, you are right on time."

"Wanessa, Mum and I would like to talk with you privately."

"Oh, no, no, no, no, no. Byron is a *good* friend. I don't mind discussing anything in front of him."

Maude eyed him suspiciously. He tried his best to put on an I-wouldn't-harm-a-fly look.

He wasn't sure how she did it, but in short order Wanessa managed to whip up a meal for four. All the while, Byron kept an evaluative eye on Gerald. He didn't act like a man in love. He paid more attention to his mother—seating her at the table, passing serving dishes to her first, and hanging on her every word—than he did to his fiancée. Invariably Byron's attention would divert to Wanessa, who seemed filled with apprehension at Gerald's presence rather than with adoration.

A few bites into the meal, Maude took charge of the conversation.

"Well, Wanessa. You leave me no choice but to air your dirty laundry in public. So here goes. I want the best for my son. I always have. Since you seem like the type of woman who would serve him well, I've taken it upon myself to spare no expense for this wedding. In exchange for my generosity, I expect only the courtesy of having some input on the wedding details. After all, neither of you has been married before, and I, on the other hand, have been married for almost forty years. I think I know a thing or two about the way to start a successful marriage.''

The older woman swept a piercing glance in Byron's direction. ''And if you've decided that you don't need my help, then . . . well, you've decided that you don't *need* my help. If you get my meaning.''

Gerald's vague expression had not changed one blink since he'd arrived. ''Wanessa, dear. Certainly you can see Mum's point. I just want what's best for both of us.''

Although Halloween was two weeks away, the monsters were out early and seated right across from him. What he heard sounded like blackmail, and Byron didn't like it.

''So what you're saying is, if you can't control all of the arrangements, you won't pay for the wedding,'' Byron said, anger simmering just below the surface of his demeanor.

Maude tossed her head in Byron's direction. ''I wouldn't put it exactly that way, but yes. I believe I know what's best.''

His thoughts raced dangerously. He would not allow the plans he and Wanessa had made to be second-guessed and circumvented by some woman on a power trip.

''Since this isn't *your* wedding, I don't see why your opinion matters. And as for your money—''

''Byron!'' Wanessa said, cutting him off. She had a feeling that what was coming next would not have been pleasant. And she could not afford to alienate her future mother-in-law any more than she already had.

''Look . . . Byron, is it? My mother's concerns are my concerns. And being that Wanessa and I are the ones engaged, they are her concerns as well.''

"Is that true, Wanessa?" Byron asked.

She looked like a child caught in a rainstorm and afraid of the thunder.

"Is it?" he demanded, wanting her to speak up for herself once and for all.

Within the space of dinnertime, Wanessa's entire adult life had been rolled back to her childhood. She could hear her mother's voice telling her over and over that nothing she did was any good and that she would never be loved by anyone besides her parents. Now she had the chance to prove her mother wrong. She couldn't let the opportunity pass her by.

"I think she's right," she responded to Byron, only half-aware of what she was saying.

"Wanessa, you're not serious."

She looked up at him. Her eyes were tired, her expression strained.

"I don't think this is what you really want."

"Well, since this is not *your* wedding," Maude parroted back, "I don't see where your opinion matters."

Byron rose to leave, knowing that if he stayed he would start to break things.

"I'll walk with you."

When he and Wanessa got to the doorway, they paused. He saw the uncertainty in her eyes and believed with all his soul that if she would only let him, he could make it better. "I just want you to be happy," he said.

"I know," she replied, and closed the door behind him.

November

The first snow of the season had taken everyone by surprise. Byron drove cautiously but steadily to Wanessa's house with reconciliation on his mind.

For the past few days, he hadn't been able to sleep. Not since the spectacle at Wanessa's house with her fiancé. What a farce! *They weren't in love.* Gerald didn't deserve a woman like Wanessa—a warm, sensitive, and caring woman who wouldn't hurt a fly. A woman who needed protecting, not reprimanding or ordering around.

Since he'd discovered his feelings for Wanessa some time ago, Byron had shared them with a college friend of his, Andromeda Simmons. Andi, who had been trying to fix him up with various women throughout their entire friendship, was delighted that he'd finally fallen for someone. When he told her about the snafu at Wanessa's house, she'd sent him an E-mail with just three words: *Go get her!*

* * *

Wanessa stepped out of the shower, amazed that the phone was silent. It had been silent for a few weeks now. She reasoned that after the dinner fiasco, everyone needed some time off. Everyone, that was, except Gerald. She thought that surely at least he would have called. But she'd heard from no one.

It was just as well, she thought. She had used the quiet time to try to put recent events into some kind of order. Being with Gerald again was not a comforting or a familiar experience. It was cold and unsettling, as if he were a stranger intruding in her life. She had always felt a sort of distance between the two of them. But what she felt now was a long span of unease and incongruence. Whoever said absence made the heart grow fonder wasn't engaged to Gerald, she thought.

Then her soul melted like ice cream topped with hot fudge. Could she really be so attracted to Byron that she no longer wanted to marry Gerald? Had she allowed that to happen?

But *allowed* wasn't the right word. He'd eased into her heart silently. Crept in when she wasn't looking and, when she'd least expected it, laid claim to everything that made her a woman. It was fire she was playing with now—real fire—and she couldn't allow Gerald to get burned as she once had. She would do everything possible to cool her raging feelings before they got any more out of hand than they already were.

And then, as if her thoughts had summoned him, she heard a knock. Byron's knock. With a trembling hand, she opened the door.

Byron's expression was intense. "You don't love him."

"What?" she asked as he brushed past her.

"You don't love him. And from what I can tell, he doesn't love you. So why are you getting married?"

"Because he asked me. I mean, who am I kidding? Look at me. I'm not exactly fashion-model material. And I'm about as interesting as a postage stamp. I can't carry on a decent conversation. My wardrobe is atrocious, and I'm a lowly teller. What man in his right mind would want me? Gerald is as close as I'm going to come to Mr. Right."

"Oh, really?" Byron said, stepping in front of her. "Tell me you don't see me standing here."

"What?" She blinked.

"Here. *Right here.* Under your nose. Under your feet. Hanging on to your every word. Fascinated by what you might do next."

He shook his head. "You've got my nose so wide, I don't know what day it is."

"Oh, God, Byron," she said, slumping onto the couch.

He knelt in front of her and took her hands in his. "After the months we've spent together. Everything we've been through." He stared into her eyes. "After what happened between us, you can't tell me you don't feel something. Admit it. You love me, too."

"Love! Byron, no," she protested, twisting away from him. Wanessa retreated to the other side of the room and wrapped her arms around herself.

Byron frowned. "Look at me and tell me you don't love me." He cupped her face in his hands. She closed her eyes.

"Wanessa, do you love me?"

Her eyes opened and she looked up. He was so beautiful. More beautiful than anything she had ever seen. And he was saying the words she most wanted to hear, like the answer to her most ardent prayer. Yes, she loved him. Had loved him for some time.

His face was inches from hers. Before his lips could touch her again, the phone rang, and she jerked away from his hypnotic stare.

"Hello?" She lowered her lashes. "Hello, Gerald."

Byron's hopes burst into a million pieces. He watched as she smiled and nodded as if the man were right in the room with them.

"I know," she said. "I'm sorry, too. Yes, yes. Me, too." She glanced over at Byron, who was already headed out the door.

Wanessa obviously had no intention of altering her plans. Love or no love, she was marrying Gerald Greene, and there was nothing he could do.

Byron knocked on Wanessa's door, nervous and tense. He had no idea why he couldn't seem to stay away from the woman. Right now, he was hoping that she was at home and had not gone off on some errand. The past few weeks for them had been strained, and that wasn't good. He'd come to see if he could patch the rift.

When she opened the door, he sighed with relief. "I came to finish what I started."

"Byron—"

"Please hear me out," he said. After a few seconds, she let him in.

"It almost seems like a lifetime ago when we first met. Back then I wasn't sure if I could help you, or if I even wanted to. But now, despite my feelings for you, I still want to help. You've told me that I can't be your lover. All right. I'll accept that. But I still want to be your friend. And as your friend, if there's anything left to do to help you prepare for"—he swallowed—"your wedding day, I would like to help you do it."

"Thank you, Byron," Wanessa said. Her body deflated as the tension visibly left her frame. "As a matter of fact, I was in the middle of the invitations. I could sure use an extra pair of hands."

"You got it!" he said. He hung up his coat, and the two of them sat down in the living room and went to work.

"I don't know how I got so far behind," Wanessa said, stuffing what she felt like was her one thousandth envelope. In reality, it was probably only the fiftieth, but she'd stopped counting long ago.

"I know *exactly* how you got so far behind," Byron replied, stuffing his own envelope. "Every time I mentioned invitations, you put them off to do something else. First it was the announcement in the paper. Then it was the flower-girl basket. After that it was disposable cameras and bubbles."

"Those things are important," Wanessa protested.

"Not if no one shows up. And they won't show up if they're not invited."

Vlanessa knew he was right, but felt a twinge of playfulness as their relationship seemed to be back to normal. "Just shut up and stuff!"

Byron looked up, eyes wide with surprise. "You've been talking to my sister again."

"It's actually been a while since I talked to Olivia. She's really busy these days with a merger and layoffs pending."

He smiled and lit a fire around her. "So you're getting smart with me of your own accord."

She giggled. "As a matter of fact, I am."

He lowered an envelope to his lap. "Well, you know what?"

"What?" she asked, eager to know his response.

"I like it."

Their eyes locked, and Wanessa felt as though she'd been levitated three feet off the ground. Neither spoke for a few seconds. Each seemed stunned into silence by the pleasure of a mere glance. Then Byron looked away and resumed his work.

Against her usual instinct, which would be to turn away

also, she kept her gaze on him. Studying him. Committing his beauty to memory. A man like that would never really want her, never really need her, never marry her. On top of all his good looks, he was smart, ambitious, and from what she could tell, destined for greatness. A plain Jane like herself had no chance against the Pamelas and Olivias of the world.

She continued to watch him as he stared down and folded each part of the invitation, then carefully placed the packets into each envelope.

She'd gotten a good deal on the invitations: forty percent off at an offset printer. The company had done both the invitations and the addressing. And she had almost waited too late. At three weeks before the wedding, she'd waited until the last possible minute to send them. Once they were mailed and on their way, that would be a tremendous load off of her mind. She might even celebrate by—"

"Oh, damn."

"What is it?" she asked, not liking the sound of deep dread in Byron's voice.

"Wanessa, what's the address of the church?"

"1173 Decatur Street." She felt a lump as big as a golf ball in her throat. "Why?"

He closed his eyes, then opened them slowly. "Take a good look at the address on the invitation."

As if she were moving in slow motion, her eyes traveled down to the invitation in her hand. She brought it closer and blinked as she saw it. The address on the invitation read 11173 Decatur Street.

She dropped the invitation to her lap and her head to her chest. "Oh, my God."

"I'm ... I'm sorry," he said, stammering. "I checked over these myself."

"So did I, and we still missed it."

"Well, we'll just have to get them reprinted. I'll help you pay for rush delivery if it costs extra."

"Gosh, I don't know. I mean how much could it cost? I guess they will have to be reprinted, won't they?" Panic surged through her veins. All she could do was get up and pace the worry away. "Do you think they're open on Saturday?"

"They should be," Byron said, and handed her the phone from a small table.

Wanessa used the number from a packing slip and called the printing company, her fingers pressing unsteadily on the buttons on the phone.

She explained the situation to the printer, hoping against hope that they would be able to reprint the invitations so that she could at least get them out within a couple of days.

"I'm sorry, Miss Taylor. The best turnaround time we can give you is a week, and that's pushing it."

"But that's not fast enough. I'm getting married in three weeks. Isn't there a way you can squeeze me in?"

"Sorry."

Wanessa was frantic. "Well, what about another printer? Do you know of anyplace else I could try?"

"Any printer that wants to do a good job will tell you the same thing."

The tears she'd been fighting spilled onto her cheeks. She couldn't talk. She could only stare straight ahead into Byron's concerned face. Before she knew what was happening, he took the phone from her.

"Look, man. We're desperate here. We really need these invitations. I'll pay extra to get them done."

"Even if you had a million dollars, I couldn't help you— not without losing all the customers whose jobs came before yours."

Byron sighed. "I see."

"If you need something that bad, type it up on a computer and take it to Kinko's."

Byron pulled the phone away from his ear and stared at it. "No, thanks," he said, and hung up.

Wanessa cried into her hands. "What am I going to do?" she asked, sobbing.

December

After he'd spent a few days on the phone, she could tell by the look on his face that the news was not good. She felt as if someone had just handed her an elephant and she was struggling to hold it together. Slumping into her chair, she covered her face with her hands. "Why is everything going wrong? My wedding is going to be a disaster."

Byron knelt at her side. "No, it won't. I won't let it." He pulled her hands away from her face. "If we have to call every printer in the city, we'll find one that will do the job."

Half an hour later, Wanessa was more disheartened than ever. Byron was right: they had found three printers willing to do the job. But the prices they were charging made their offers out of the question. She had very little room left in Maude's budget, and considering recent events, she dared not ask for any wiggle room.

"This is the worst nightmare I've ever had," she said, feeling a tightening in her chest. "I can't postpone it. Too many arrangements have been made. Maybe I'll just call everyone and invite them to the wedding,'' she said, exasperation taking over.

"Not an option. I mean, what's a wedding without invitations? Besides, if that happened, Olivia would kill me." Byron paced back and forth, rubbing his hands across his hair. After a few minutes of vigorous walking, his face lit up as if a flashlight were shining on it. "We'll just have to make them ourselves."

"Byron, I've seen computer-generated invitations; they look so, so . . ."

"Not by computer," he said, sitting down next to her. "By hand."

He's lost his mind. "What?"

"I've seen your handwriting, Wanessa; it's beautiful."

"Not beautiful enough to write out invitations."

"Sure it is. Do you still have that wedding-crafts book we looked at a while back?"

"Yes."

"Go get it."

Wanessa hurried into her bedroom and shuffled through the pile of wedding books stacked up at her bedside. She found the one he asked for and brought it back with her. He took the book and flipped through the pages until he found the section on wedding invitations.

Byron pointed to the photographs of handcrafted invitations. "Remember, we talked about these."

Her stomach tightened. "I remember saying how much I wished I could do something like this." She thought the handmade cards were wonderful. The information for the wedding ceremony was handwritten on rice paper. The lettering looped and swirled on the page like a work of art. There were other examples of invitations with hand-printed letters so precise they looked as though they had been typed on the page.

"We can't—"

"You know, I'm about tired of hearing you use that word *can't*. You can do anything you want to do. Now, do you want to get married or not?"

"Of course, but to just—"

He stepped closer and placed a hand on her shoulder. She shuddered beneath his touch. "I know how you like to plan everything down to the last detail. But sometimes you have to improvise, be spontaneous, or like my friend Danny says, 'Work some impromptu.' Now, we can *do* this, Wanessa."

She sighed. He made her want to believe. Maybe if she went to an office-supply company or even an art store . . .

His smile returned. "I see the wheels turning. What are you thinking?"

"I'm thinking I could go shopping for paper and some envelopes."

"I'll do that. You just clear some space at your dining room table and round up the best pens you have in the house. We're gonna make us some invitations!"

"Oh, Byron!" she said, and flung her arms around him. He returned her embrace and time stopped. The press of his body against hers made her giddy and a little scared of the potency of his impression on her. They stared into each other's eyes and let go slowly. Then Byron cleared his throat.

"Well, I had better go get that paper."

Yes, you'd better, Wanessa thought.

After three hours, they both discovered just how tedious creating handmade invitations really was. After settling on a design, they had started in. The result was grunts, groans, puffs of hot air, a few expletives, and several failed attempts piling up in crumpled clumps on the floor. After a while they got into a rhythm, and the creative process flowed more smoothly.

Wanessa had taken the more dramatic approach and attempted to re-create the more artful lettering. Byron settled on the more practical approach and was diligently working on the block-style architectural lettering that more closely resembled his own printing. No one would ever have to know that there were two styles of invitations.

A couple of times she'd seen Byron stop writing to shake out his right hand. What they were doing was the stuff carpal tunnel was made of. But yet he persisted without complaint, and she was grateful.

It was two A.M. when they finished the last invitation. Wanessa yawned, stretched, and then offered him a sleepy smile. "That's all two hundred," she said. "You are marvelous, you know that?"

"Aw, shucks, ma'am. 'Tain't nothin'."

"If I weren't so tired, I'd laugh."

"Me too," Bryon said, then yawned. "See what you started?" He got up and stretched. "I'd better be heading home. Will you be all right with those in the morning?"

"Yes. I'll take them to the post office. But I can't let you drive home at this hour."

"I'm a grown, sober man. I'm sure I can find my way. Besides, I drive home at this time of night every time I work at the bar."

"Well, this isn't the bar, and I can see how tired you are. You're more than welcome to sleep on the couch."

Bryon yawned again. "Are you sure it's OK?"

"Yes," she said, and headed off to get some blankets and a pillow. When she returned he was already lying on the couch, shoes off, with his coat covering the upper part of his body. His eyes were closed as if he'd just fallen asleep.

Wanessa hung up his coat and covered him with the blankets. For a moment she just watched him sleep. Then he reached out and touched her hand. "Impromptu," he said, then drifted off.

Wanessa whispered "Impromptu," turned off the lights, and went to bed.

"Byron!"

"Andi?"

"Yes, it's me. How are you?"

For a moment, he considered letting her in on the misery his life had suffered of late. Instead he said, "Fine, and you?"

"Sebastian and I are great. But I had a weird dream about you last night. Are you, like, sure you're okay?"

That was just like Andi. She was probably the most perceptive person he'd ever met. "Wanessa's getting married tomorrow."

"Oh, that's terrible, Byron. I'm so sorry."

"Don't dwell on it. I'm trying not to." He closed his eyes. "So what's going on in good old Nebraska?"

"Sebastian is running for state senator."

"You don't say?" Byron wasn't surprised. He knew that that brother was destined for big things.

Then he heard a familiar voice in the background. "Put it on speakerphone, baby."

A few clicks and the voice came across loud and clear. "Mr. Moore!"

"What's up, Sebastian?"

"Everything, man. Sure wish you were here. I need a campaign manager real bad."

Byron laughed. If he had stayed in Omaha, he would have jumped at the chance to help with Sebastian's campaign. The future politician would just have to find someone else. "Why don't you ask P.G.?" He still remembered professor Gilmore's nickname.

"Man, you just don't know. He and Sonji have their hands *full* with Frederick Douglass." *Ah, Sonji.* Years ago Byron thought she was the sun. But now, a brighter star was shining in his universe, and she was all he could think about.

Frederick Douglass Gilmore. He still couldn't believe they had named their son that.

Sebastian continued. "That little boy has more energy than ten people."

They all laughed. Then Andi said, "And they're trying to have another baby."

"Baby! Stop spreading grown folks' business." At Sebastian's remark, their laughter increased.

"But speaking of grown folks' business," he continued, "we've got an announcement to make."

Byron knew what it was before either of them said anything.

"We're getting married," Andi blurted. Then Byron heard a smacking sound and knew the happy couple was on the other end of the line kissing.

"When?" he asked.

"Fourth of July, man. You have to come back for it."

"You got it," he said, smiling for the first time in days. He knew in his heart that Andi and Sebastian were made for each other. Their union seemed ordained. Like a line from a movie his sister made him watch, they fit together.

Sebastian broke Byron's reverie. "You don't have any interest in helping to plan a wedding, do you?"

Byron almost choked. "No way!" he protested, then proceeded to give them the long-story-short of how he'd spent the last nine months.

"It's a sign!" Andi said, excitement traveling across time and space.

"What's a sign?" the two men asked.

"All those wedding boo-boos. They're all signs. Vanessa is not supposed to marry that other man."

"It's Wanessa," Byron corrected.

"Well, whatever her name is, the universe is working

against that marriage. Maybe that's what my dream meant. You've got to stop her, Byron. Before she makes a terrible mistake.''

The urgency in her voice made him almost believe. It was too late, though. The wedding was less than twenty-four hours away. If confessing his love for Wanessa couldn't dissuade her, he didn't know what would.

''Thanks, Andi. I'll think about it.''

''You should do more than think about it, man. When it comes to stuff like this, my baby is never wrong.''

He heard more smacks on the other end of the line and decided that he'd had enough of the two lovebirds.

''I gotta go,'' he said, feeling suddenly tired.

''Okay,'' they said. ''Merry Christmas!''

''Merry Christmas.''

Wanessa examined her reflection in the mirror. Sheer long-sleeved bodice. Vee neckline setting off the shoulders, showing a hint of her cleavage. Full skirt draped with layers tapering to a four-foot train in the back. Satin-laced designed front topped off with a sheer veil trimmed with matching satin lace.

She sighed. ''I look like a cake topper.''

''No, you don't. You look beautiful,'' Olivia said, arranging the shiny tendrils of her hair.

Wanessa gathered up the dirndl feeling as though someone had weighted her down with ten tons of material. ''I can't *move* in this thing,'' she protested. The dress made a *swish-swish* sound as she maneuvered herself across the room. ''I mean, what if I want to sit down?''

''You'll have to wait until after the ceremony or your train will be ruined.''

So it had come to this. After all the arrangements had been made, the food, the song, the invitations, the decorations. On her wedding day, instead of being excited, she was tired from all the plans she'd made, and what she really wanted to do was go someplace quiet, sit down, and have her feet massaged.

And as if there hadn't been enough wedding disasters, she and Gerald had been dealt one final blow. Instead of the beautiful arrangement of pink roses, fern leaves, and baby's breath she and Olivia had ordered, the florist had delivered a broken-heart funeral spray made of white carnations and yellow roses. A couple of Gerald's groomsmen carried the thing down to the basement. The florist never returned.

What else can go wrong? she wondered.

Then her stomach lurched at the thought that this whole thing was wrong. This marriage. She didn't love Gerald. She wasn't even sure if she liked him anymore. And more important, she was absolutely sure she was in love with Byron Moore.

So why am I going through with this? she asked herself.

And the woman her parents had created—until a few months ago—answered: *Because you don't deserve a man like Byron. He's goodhearted, and smart, and ambitious, and handsome. What could he possibly want with a woman like you? You're not attractive, intelligent, or professional. You have absolutely nothing to offer him. Besides, a man like that is probably stringing you along anyway. But Gerald, on the other hand—plain, unassuming Gerald, who does whatever his mother tells him—is standing in the next room ready to marry you. So what if his mother is a little controlling? She's the only person on the planet willing to be your mother-in-law. So forget all that marrying-for-love crap! Life's unfair, and you can't always get what you want.*

"Wanessa, honey?"

She looked up, determined to keep the tears from falling.

"Are you ready?"

"Yes," she whispered, and walked out of the dressing room with Olivia.

Byron had been watching the clock on the wall all morning. He couldn't believe how fleeting time could sometimes be. The hours moved like seconds, and now at two-forty P.M. he knew his sister was helping the woman he loved get ready to walk down the aisle.

He paced the living room, cursing himself over and over. "I actually helped her marry another man. I can't believe what an idiot I've been."

But when he was in Wanessa's presence, he felt compelled to do anything he thought would make her happy. So he'd gone on appointments, made phone calls, argued with some salesclerks and threatened others, just so his Wanessa could be happy.

"Ow," he moaned, as the pain in his head grew worse. Not even thoughts of his new job at the Red Cross quelled his suffering. Overwhelmed by the pain in his heart, Byron had never known such anguish in his entire life.

His Wanessa, he thought again, as his own words came back to haunt him. *Sometimes you have to improvise, be spontaneous, or, like my friend Danny says, "work some impromptu."*

Two-forty-five the clock face read, and Byron started calculating. *If I take the interstate, it will take me only ten minutes to get there.* He grabbed his coat and dashed out the door.

Fifteen minutes later he was caught behind a line of traffic on the exit ramp that was backed up for at least three blocks. "Please, God," he prayed, pulling his car over to the shoulder. He turned off the ignition, jumped out of the car, and ran.

* * *

They probably think I'm crying because I'm so happy, Wanessa thought. Behind her satin-laced veil she cried desperately for the love she would never have. *I wish I could do it all again,* she mused, barely aware of the minister's words.

"And now we will hear the couple exchange their own vows. First, Gerald."

"Wanessa, I love you!"

All two hundred guests turned at the declaration of love coming not from the front of the church, but the back.

"Byron?" Wanessa said.

"You don't love him," he said, walking toward her. "I know you don't. You love *me.*"

Wanessa closed her eyes when she realized that the last straw had come from the very person who had helped her to plan and overcome so much. Despair threatened to break what little resolve she had left. "Byron, why are you ruining my wedding?"

He moved closer as the guests gasped and whispered among themselves.

"This isn't your wedding."

"Now, look, young man," Maude Greene protested, but Byron ignored her. His sister stared at him, her open mouth rivaling the Grand Canyon. He ignored her, too.

"If this were your wedding, it would be evening and there would be stars in the sky. If this were your wedding, all of these people wouldn't be here, just those you know and trust. If this were your wedding, a soft harp would be playing and you'd be dressed in a simple golden dress, not some bulky gown you can barely move in."

He closed the distance between them. "If this were your wedding, you'd be marrying *me,* not him."

Byron was trembling. She could see it. And so was she.

She turned to Gerald, who was standing next to her wearing a look of utter shock, and she knew she couldn't go through with the ceremony. "Gerald . . ." she began.

He shook his head. "I wasn't really sure how I could marry someone who couldn't get along with my mother."

Relieved, Wanessa almost laughed, but instead she ran into the arms of the man she loved and whispered in his ear, "I love you, I love you, I love you."

Epilogue

On January 1, 2003, Wanessa Taylor and Byron Moore married for love. They stood together under a cool evening sky, with a small number of friends and family, exchanging vows that would last them a lifetime. Poised before God and his majesty, they sealed their vows with a kiss and went off to begin a new year and a new life together.

And that night, Mr. Byron Moore made slow, passion-consumed love to Mrs. Byron Moore until she screamed out his name and all her fears of inadequacy were gone.

Dear Reader,

I'm so happy to be able to bring you Byron's story. I heard from so many of you who wanted to know what happened to him after A Touch Away. Thanks for your letters and E-mails of appreciation and encouragement. You are why I do what I do.

God Bless!
Kim

About the Author

Kim Louise was born and raised in Omaha, NE. She's been writing since grade school and has always dreamed of penning the great American novel. She has an undergraduate degree in journalism and a graduate degree in adult learning. She has one son, Steve, whom she is immensely proud of and in her spare time enjoys reading, card making, and watching the sun set.